I0599571

ROSE D. BENTLEY

Leo - Retail Edition

Second Edition: Expanded from the original novella

Copyright © 2026 by Rose D. Bentley

All rights reserved.

No part of this book may be reproduced in any form or by any electronic or mechanical means, including information storage and retrieval systems, without written permission from the author, except for the use of brief quotations in a book review. Any use of this publication to train generative artificial intelligence (AI) technologies is expressly prohibited.

This is a work of fiction. Names, characters, businesses, places, events, and incidents are either the products of the author's imagination or used in a fictitious manner. Any resemblance to actual persons, living or dead, or actual events is purely coincidental.

Cover design by BooksNMoods

Author: Rose D. Bentley

Edited by Mystic Books Marketing and Ash Tree Editing

ISBN: 979-8-9931545-1-0

For more information, visit www.rosedbentley.com

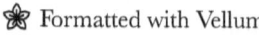 Formatted with Vellum

Grandma, your wild, adventurous, and free spirit has always inspired me to chase the moon and reach for the stars. Rest peacefully.

And for Amber, whose unconditional support has truly meant the world to me.

Note to Reader:

First of all, thank you so much for being here. Readers truly
make an author's world go round. Before you dive in, I want
to share that this story explores sensitive themes, including the
loss of a parent, the grief of a loved one lost at sea, discussions
of drug use and sales, sexual content, and mild violence.
Your care and comfort matter to me, so please take what you
need as you read.
With love,

Rose D. Bentley

Playlist

My Home by *Myles Smith*

Love of Mine by *Benson Boone*

The Night We Met by *Lord Huron*

Pink Skies by *Zach Bryan*

Belong Together by *Mark Amber*

Breezeblocks by *alt-J*

Stronger by *Thunderstorm Artis*

$\mathcal{L}\varepsilon o$

PROLOGUE

MY DAD WAS MY BEST FRIEND.

He was my compass, my safe place.

People talk about soulmates like they're always lovers. But sometimes, it's not about romance at all. Sometimes, if you're lucky, your soulmate is the person who knows you better than anyone else.

For me, I was blessed enough to have my father as my kindred spirit.

Tied to me in ways I can't explain.

Unfortunately, that tie was severed, taken by the sea.

In all of my twenty-six years of life, the last two have been the hardest.

The sun may shine, but I don't see it.

I don't *feel* it.

Not deeper than the surface level. Not beyond the rays touching my skin.

I have an emptiness. A hollowed vessel, the size of a soul inside my chest.

Well, that was the case… up until I met *her*.

1

Layla

I HAVE THIS NIGHTMARE THAT I'M DROWNING.

A dark, vast ocean surrounds me. My skin prickles with goosebumps, my lungs fill with salt water until not even the faintest scream can escape me. I don't feel alone though. In fact, I feel like I belong here and someone is in the abyss with me.

The seaweed wraps around my ankles like shackles and pulls me deeper, and I think I can hear the sound of a siren's song. It's hard to tell if it really is a creature of the sea, or if it's something inside of me.

Either way, it calls.

So, deeper the kelp pulls and louder the siren sings, the world around me starts to fade into a dark oblivion—

I wake up before I am completely lost. Before I can run out of air.

It's odd for me to have nightmares. I'm a happy person, and I had a great childhood. Maybe I'm just feeling a little overwhelmed about moving to a new town on my own. It's the first big thing that I've done in my life besides dropping out of college.

Maybe the nightmare is just my body's way of telling me to relax and that it's all going to work out here. I hope that's the truth, because I really like Morro Bay.

The sun's not out yet, and it's earlier than I'd intended to wake up.

I like to sleep with my windows open every night so I can hear the ocean. The first few nights, the heaviness of the air took some getting used to, and everything always feels a little damp. But now, I welcome it. I enjoy the calmness that the sounds from the outside bring, it feels like a weighted blanket gifted by Mother Nature.

I could try to go back to sleep, shake off the nightmare and curl up underneath my soft blanket. But my neighbor is blasting music next door. He works graveyard shifts, and must have just gotten home, deciding to unwind with some heavy metal.

My apartment building is pretty old. The kind of old that creaks anytime the wind blows too hard and sometimes— more often than not—it smells like mildew.

But, it adds to the charm. Plus, it drops the value of the place, making it more affordable for people like me. People who decide to leave the comfort of their childhood home on a whim and think everything will be just fine.

And it *will* be just fine.

However, no one really warns you about the kinds of places you'll live when you first move out on your own.

It all seems so glamorous when you play the movies in your head. You imagine having your own place, your own rules. You picture yourself doing whatever you want, *whenever* you want. Plastering the wall with whatever decoration speaks to you. No parents around to warn you it'll damage the paint or declare it *too tacky*.

The reality is this: when you are young and living on your own, on a budgeted income, you will likely be living in a small place with paper-thin walls. They'll remain bare, because a painting of a Greek goddess surrounded by flying cherubs isn't exactly a *necessity*.

This is unless you have some crazy high-paying job already, you're a trust fund baby, or you have parents that have extra money and just want to support you.

No shame on any of that. It actually sounds kind of nice.

It's just not *my* reality.

I'm okay with it though. I find happiness in the unknown. It's almost like a mystery book, but one that you have a say in. What's going to happen next? Is it something that I get to create, or will the universe surprise me instead?

For now, the universe has given me this cute little apartment, and a neighbor who worships heavy metal. I don't hate it and it could be much worse.

Besides, the beach is just a couple of blocks away. It's the perfect escape.

And an even *more* perfect morning routine.

I peek out of the open window that sits above my frameless bed. The sky is still decorated with that pre-sunrise gray. I slip out of the comfort of my giant, fluffy, sage-colored down comforter, and pull on some leggings, a sports bra, and a crewneck sweatshirt.

I tie my shoes, listening to the far-off buzz of motorboats and vehicles putting around the harbor. It's not the first time I've heard it before sunrise; fishing crews, delivery trucks and mechanics, I assume, are heading out while the rest of the town sleeps.

Whoever's in that harbor is already knee-deep in work while I'm only just starting my day.

I drink a tall glass of water, then head for the door. The cool air taps my face as I step outside, and the gray of the sky starts to grow pink as the sun rises.

The streets are quiet, except for an old man, sweeping in

front of the bait shop. He smiles and nods when I pass by. I wonder what his life has been like—if he's been here for the entirety of it, or if he chose this place like I did. I wonder if he has a big family with grandkids that visit him on the weekends or if he's content in his own little world.

There's a kind of beauty in those simple consistencies.

Some people wake up to coffee and birdsong. I wake up to crashing waves and morning jogs near the ocean.

Life is good, but I'm sure it can get even better.

2

Leo

My day started later than normal today.

I'm usually up and out on the boat by three in the morning, but I was so tired last night after one too many beers with the guys. I passed out the minute I laid down and forgot to set my alarm.

I'm two hours late, and the crew already has most of the morning work done. The gear's prepped, and the bait jars are set. It's just time to get out there.

Early mornings are the best time for *any* catch.

The harbor carries its usual business, other crews already heading out and beating us to the good spots. If Dad were here, he'd give me hell for sleeping in.

We're finishing up crab season, and soon it'll be time to gear up for rockfish and tuna. The change always feels overwhelming. Different bait, different gear, different weather, and different rhythms entirely.

I welcome it, sometimes even look forward to it. It means longer days, busier hours, and shorter nights.

Less time to *think*.

I make my way into the cabin, grab the logbook, and start

my rounds, first ensuring the sorting tables are clean and sanitized.

"Morning," Hank, one of the senior crew members, mumbles as he rinses out an old ice bin. "We need to remind the newbie to clean out the fuckin' bins."

"I'm on it," I say, moving on toward the main deck.

He calls after me, "You're late, by the way!"

"Yeah, thanks for noticing!"

Hank Houser *should* have his own boat with his own crew. He knows this harbor and ocean better than God himself, but he's never shown the interest. He's content in his routine, and I respect him for that.

He was a good friend to my dad, too. So whatever Hank wants, Hank gets. If that's making sure the new guy is thorough, then so be it.

Austin's leaning over one of the bait jars when I step onto the deck, already bouncing on his toes. He's our youngest and newest crewmate—the one Hank is *so* giddy about. Rowdy, a more seasoned crew member, leans against the rail with a thermos in hand, probably drinking the hair of the dog.

"Kid's gonna burn out before we even leave the dock," Rowdy mutters.

"Or maybe he'll outfish *all* of you," Austin shoots back, passing us by.

The morning banter is welcoming. This crew isn't perfect, but it's a good one. We work hard, keep each other in check, and, for the most part, know when to shut up and get the job done.

"Guys!" I yell from the deck. "We've got just a few more crab hauls left. Let's make them count!"

"Let's get it!" Austin shouts, pumping his fist in the air.

Hank just grumbles and starts untying rope. I hang up the logbook and help the crew get ready to take off... but not before something—*someone*—catches my eye.

LEO

The new girl in town is jogging down the road.

Layla Dumont.

In a small town like Morro Bay, you notice new residents fast and learn their names quickly, too.

She's been here a couple of weeks, maybe a little more. Word travels, and it's not hard to piece together that she got a job at the local coffee shop. Which seems more fitting than the fishing docks, or one of the tourist-season gigs.

Her honey-blonde hair is pulled back into a ponytail. She's not in a hurry, but she's not dragging her feet, either, keeping up a steady pace until she nears the seawall.

The guys notice her, and Austin waves when she glances toward us. She waves back, with a polite smile on her face. She stops by the seawall, and looks out over the fog that curls above the harbor.

I tell myself to look away, to focus on the lines and the deck and the day ahead. But my eyes drift back to her.

She's gorgeous. *Too* gorgeous for this place.

I'm not sure why a young woman would choose to live here. There's not much for building a career unless you're into fishing or opening a business for tourist season. Most who come here from somewhere else end up leaving before long to chase bigger cities and more opportunities.

Newbies never really stay.

I tear my eyes away from her and turn back to my crew and start giving orders. We've got work to do, and the tide waits for no one.

3

Layla

AN EARLY MORNING JOG ON THE BEACH IS JUST WHAT I NEEDED to wake me up. The streets are still sleepy. It's just me, the morning waves, and the seagulls.

Calling Morro Bay home is new. Like, three-weeks new.

California is no stranger to me, but I did leave the cluttered, chaotic, and supposedly *glamorous* city of Los Angeles. Which really... isn't glamorous at all. Over the years, the streets have become littered with trash, littered with people, and don't even get me started on the traffic.

My heart feels more at peace here.

I used to visit this area growing up with my family. My dad would pile my mom, sister, and me into a camping van and drive us up and down the coast. This place was always my favorite spot.

It's been quite some time since we were here last. Family trips faded when my sister—five years older than me—moved to New York for college, then decided to stay there. That's when our relationship faded a bit, too.

I recently turned twenty-two and decided it was my time

to venture out on my own. The first place I thought of going to was here.

So here I am, a few weeks in and loving every second of it. Mildew and all.

Being that it's a smaller town, I was able to get a job pretty quickly at one of the local coffee shops—The Busy Bean. I saw the HELP WANTED sign, walked in, had an immediate interview, and walked out with a job.

That's how I met my only friend here, Sara Rourke.

Sara also happens to be my coworker *and* the daughter of the owner, Dan. They share the apartment right behind the coffee shop.

She's a year younger than me; she's shy and mostly quiet unless she's talking about something she really loves, like baking or sitcoms. She's promised to take me out to explore the town a little more, but she also says there's not much to do outside of Embarcadero.

I think she's just a homebody.

I haven't been bothered about the lack of entertainment much until the last couple of days. It took the first week to move in, the second week to get comfortable with my new job, and now I'm starting to get a little itch to get out. Something more than just a morning run.

Typically, I'm out here later than this. During that soft spot between the harbor's morning rush dying down, and the shops opening for the day.

But today is different. The fishermen and I are in sync, both out here at the same time. They look like they're getting ready to head out onto the water. I don't know much about fishing, but I do know the earlier, the better.

The early bird gets the worm—or in this case, *the early boat gets the fish.*

There's something I really like about the vibe down here.

The weathered boats with chipped, painted names fading under the sea salt, the dim lights on the dock, the sounds of the creaking wood. Even the shouts from the men in sailor lingo I only half understand feel like part of the charm, their voices rough, probably from years of smoking.

One boat seems to be in a rush, running behind the others. A couple of the guys are in sweatshirts and hats, a couple in heavier jackets.

As I get closer, their heads turn, one of them waves, so I smile and wave back. They return to their work—all except for one.

And I don't think I have ever seen a man like *him* before. Tall and broad, with dark, wavy hair and a beard to match. I can't see his eyes from here, but I'm sure they are just as beautiful as the rest of him.

He doesn't wave. He just stares at me for a moment before looking away.

I get a flutter in my belly as I watch him move across the deck, guiding the other men. I catch myself smiling, wondering who they are.

Do they have girlfriends or wives to go home to? Are they ever scared, out on the open ocean like that?

My thoughts start to fade just as their boat disappears into the haze, a distant sea shanty trailing after them in whistles.

There's something beautiful about the whole scene. Strong men, sturdy boats, salty air, and a misty breeze. I know fishing is a tough sport and a lot of work, but the ocean makes it look almost peaceful.

I've always loved the tranquility of the sea... and the uncertainty of it.

So much of it is still unexplored.

My jog has crept into a fast walk, my lungs deciding that they need to catch up with the rest of my body.

By the time I round the corner back onto Main Street, the usual morning mix of fish and wood is overtaken by the aroma of fresh, warm bread drifting from somewhere nearby.

I'm tempted to hunt down the bakery behind the delicious smell, but a black Labrador trotting toward me steals my attention instead, ears bouncing and tail wagging. The woman on the other end of the leash looks to be in her late sixties, with a faded ball cap and a sweatshirt that reads *San Jose*.

"Morning," she greets me with a smile. "You're new in town."

I laugh, a little breathless. "That obvious?"

"Only because Captain here"—she gives the leash a light tug—"makes it his mission to meet everybody."

Captain leans into me, so I crouch down to scratch behind his ears.

He reminds me so much of my old dog, Rookie, from when I was ten. He was an awkward rescue mutt who always smelled like slobber and grass.

"Well, mission accomplished," I say, grinning up at the woman. "I'm Layla."

"Barbara," she replies. "And welcome to the neighborhood."

We stand there for a few minutes, trading small talk about the weather, the coffee shop that I now work at, and Captain's obsession with seagulls. She warns me that the dog will probably recognize me from now on and insist on stopping for pets every time.

"I can live with that," I tell her.

When I finally start jogging my way home again, I can't help but notice how different this feels from the city. Back in L.A., no one stopped you on the street unless they wanted something. Here, people—*and dogs*—just want to say hello and wish you well.

Which makes me kind of feel like I could really call this place home.

4

Leo

We're back by eleven, just in time for lunch.

The ocean was pretty quiet today. Barely any wind as well, which made for a smooth haul. But the crew was still dragging by the time we docked.

Hank complained about Austin not coiling the lines right the whole time. I was going to step in to correct him, but Hank beat me to it. Sometimes it's better when he does the teaching anyway. I think it sticks more that way. Seniority and all.

By the time the last crab pot is unloaded, the ache in my shoulders is heavy. I'm used to it. I even like it most of the time. It's hard, honest work. You do your part, and the ocean gives you what it gives you.

No pretending. No bullshit.

Now that the fog layer has cleared up, the sun is out, but there's always a dampness to the air here. It's best to keep your body moving, otherwise it sets into your bones, and it's hard to get rid of.

I help the crew clean up, double checking that the crab bins are cleaned to Hank's standards.

They are.

"Let's grab another beer tonight," Hank suggests, lighting up a cigarette.

"I'm in!" Austin says, popping up right behind us.

"Shit, boy," Hank grumbles, flinching. "You trying to give me a heart attack?"

"Sorry, sir!" Austin says, way too chipper for someone who's just been cursed at. "A beer sounds great!"

Hank squints at him through the smoke. "How old are you anyway? You even old enough to drink?"

Austin just laughs. "I'm old enough."

He's lying. I checked his ID when I hired him; he's only nineteen. But no one here is going to give a shit.

Hank rolls his eyes and turns back to me. "How about you, son?"

"I'll think about it."

"Well, you know where we'll be." He drops the cigarette, crushes it under his boot, and heads for his truck.

Austin follows him, tossing out rapid-fire questions about tonight. Hank just ignores him. I wonder how long it'll take for Hank to lose his shit; he has the patience of a toddler.

I climb into my truck, driving toward the outskirts of town, and I'm about halfway down the street when I spot Margie Walker outside her shop, Walker's Antiques. She's standing in the doorway, arms crossed, appearing frustrated.

She catches my eye and waves me over. "Leo, you busy?"

"Not really," I say out of my window as I cut the engine and step out.

She points a finger toward a solid oak display case inside. "Damn thing weighs a ton, and I need it moved before the delivery comes in. Thought I'd get it myself, but my back's been giving me hell."

I glance at the case. It's huge and probably older than both of us put together. "Where to?"

"Back wall. Just watch the floor, and please don't scuff the planks."

The display case doesn't look too heavy until I get my hands under it and realize it's much heavier than it should be.

"You need to stop buying furniture you can't move," I say, shifting my grip.

She chuckles, revealing the missing tooth in the front. "If I did that, when would I ever see you?"

I grunt in response and muscle the thing across the room, setting it where she points.

"Perfect. Thank you, sweetheart." She dusts her hands off. "You still playing that guitar of yours?"

"Sometimes," I lie.

"You should play down on Embarcadero again. People really liked that."

I don't answer, just give her a small nod and head back toward the door.

"Don't be a stranger, Leo. We miss seeing you around," she calls after me.

Once I'm back in my truck, I'm already thinking about getting home and putting food in my stomach. The beef jerky and protein bar I had for breakfast on the boat aren't cutting it.

My place waits just outside of town, tucked behind a line of Monterey pines. It's nothing fancy, just a quiet spot with good air flow and a solid roof.

I leave my boots by the door and drop my keys into the chipped ceramic bowl my mom made years ago. The air's a little musty. I forgot to crack a window in my rush out this morning. So I set a pot of coffee to brew to cut the smell and give me some much needed energy.

My guitar leans against the wall by the fireplace, the same place it's been for over two years, collecting dust. I really should clean it up and restring it. I've been meaning to get to it, but this season's been busy. Plus, I haven't really found the motivation to get to it.

I finish my coffee, eat, and shower. I think about Hank's invitation and decide that maybe it's not a bad idea to blow off some more steam before the season switches again.

I could go for a beer... or maybe three.

5

Layla

THE LATE MORNING SUN IS FINALLY STARTING TO WARM THE street as I make my way to work.

The Busy Bean, painted a bright blue, sits right in the heart of town. I've heard it gets packed during tourist season, and that's when high school kids come on for the summer to help keep things running smoothly. Until then, it's just Sara, Dan and I.

We have the brunch crowd today. And when I say "crowd," I mean the five or six locals who stop in for their mid-morning coffee fix.

I'm wearing my favorite jeans. The ones that fit just right, with worn holes in the knees. The kind of jeans that once they're gone, are impossible to replace. I paired them with a cropped white tee that has a faded sun on the front.

The bell on the door jingles as I step inside.

"Layla! You're here, thank God. I think the ice machine's broken, and my dad's out running errands," Sara blurts, a little panicked. "Can you figure out what's wrong with it? Mrs. Walker is going to be *pissed* if we can't make her afternoon iced chai."

I can't help but feel bad. She looks completely over-whelmed, which I've learned happens to her pretty easily.

"Sure, I'll take a look." I smile and head over to the machine.

Now, Sara's a dedicated barista who can make a mean cup of coffee, but attention to detail isn't exactly one of her strengths. I say that with love and also because, when I peek behind the ice machine, I see it's only partway plugged in.

I push the plug in all the way, and the low vibration kicks on instantly.

Problem solved.

"Wow, I feel so dumb," Sara says, her cheeks flushing pink.

"Don't. Everyone does stuff like that," I reassure her. "Did Dan say if it was busy this morning?"

"Nope. Just the regulars. You know, the fishing crews and their cowboy coffees."

Fishing crews.

My mind flashes back to the docks. Back to the men on that boat, and that one man who didn't wave, but *definitely* looked. Tall, broad-shouldered, dark hair.

I pull myself back to the conversation. "Fishing crews?" I ask.

"Yeah, they come in super early."

"How do we get our hands on an early shift?" I tease.

"Oh, girlie, you're way too pretty for any of those grungy men," she snickers. "I mean, there are some cute ones, sure, and the newbies that end up leaving town for bigger jobs. But most of them are old, married, and really need to eat some donuts or pasta or something."

I chuckle and start stocking the glass case with the cookies Sara just made. By the time I'm done, it's clear this day is going to drag. It's slow, which seems to make sense for the season. The tourists haven't hit their school breaks yet, so until then, I think we can expect more days like this.

I lean over the counter, resting my face in my palm and tapping my unmanicured nails against the surface.

Movement outside catches my eye. Walker's Antiques across the street has the door propped open and—of all people—the man from the boat is wrestling with some kind of large piece of wooden furniture. He's closer than he was at the dock, taller and barrel-chested.

He definitely *has* to be one of the "cute ones" Sara mentioned. I tell myself to stop staring, but my eyes don't listen, so I force my focus back to Sara.

"Do you have plans tonight?" I ask.

"Nope."

"Let's go out."

"Okay, where?"

"Is there a bar in this town that people like? Or maybe a club or something?"

Sara lets out a dry laugh. "No clubs, but there's a bar called Taboo. It's pretty popular, I guess."

"Let's go there."

"Okay, but don't judge me on my lack of alcohol tolerance."

"No judgment. We'll just stick to the fun kind of tipsy."

I'm not a huge drinker myself, though I can appreciate a good beer or mixed drink. Usually, I'd go for the mimosa, or a trendy beer at a new brewery. But I have a feeling it'll be an entirely different vibe here.

I wonder what kind of crowd a bar called Taboo brings. Locals? Tourists?

Fishermen?

I don't rush on my walk home. The sun has that sleepy kind of glow that makes you feel warm and fuzzy inside.

The local shop windows are dressed in shades of blue, teal, and sandy beige, filled with ocean-themed trinkets hanging within. A seafood place is setting up for dinner; the smell of garlic butter and grilled fish drifts onto the street. I make a mental note to check it out sometime.

It's nothing like Los Angeles.

The air here feels clean. There's no constant noise of cars, sirens, or people zipping through life too quickly, always rushing toward something. In L.A., even if you escape to the beach, you can still hear the madness buzzing all around you.

Here, the ocean gets to be the loudest thing, and there's something very soothing about that.

When I finally make my way home, I immediately grab my favorite snack—pickles and popcorn. People usually think it's weird, but the secret is simple: take a bite of popcorn, take a bite of pickle, chew at the same time, swallow, repeat. It's perfection.

I'm savoring my last perfect combo bite when my phone buzzes. A text from Sara:

> What are you going to wear tonight? I'm overthinking it.

> I'm not changing. I have a feeling Taboo doesn't have a dress code LOL.

> I think you're right about that! Let's meet in an hour.

I set my empty bowl into the sink and check the clock. *An hour.* A tinge of excitement hits me being that it's my first night going out here. I'm not expecting anything life-changing, but I'm looking forward to getting a little buzz, loosening up, and seeing more of what this town is like when the sun goes down.

I head into the bathroom and swipe on some foundation,

just enough to even things out and tone down the freckles across my nose. I've always been on the fence about them. Sometimes I love them, sometimes I hate them.

I spend a little more time on my eyes, brushing on lightly sparkled beige shadow and coating my lashes with mascara until the blue in them stands out. A touch of lip gloss, and I'm done.

I grab my small shoulder bag and hit the road.

Taboo is walking distance from my apartment, like most places in Morro Bay. That's something I immediately fell in love with. No hour-long drives to get anywhere, no fighting for parking spots. Just short walks, always paired with a light breeze.

Halfway down the block, I glance toward where my old Toyota Camry is still parked from last week. The faded red paint was already losing its battle with the sun back in L.A., and I know the ocean air here will eventually add rust. But that'll probably just make it fit in.

The streets are quieter than I'd expected for a Friday evening. A couple of shop owners flip their signs to CLOSED and chat with their neighbors as they lock up. A family passes by with ice cream cones. A father, a mother, and two little girls, reminding me of my own sweet family.

I turn the corner, and Taboo's neon sign comes into view, glowing brightly even though the sun hasn't fully set. The name and the dark-painted exterior stand out against the pastel-colored storefronts around it. A couple of smokers linger near the door, their voices loud, contrasting with the quiet of the street. Music plays from inside and the bass vibrates through the sidewalk.

I adjust the strap of my bag and keep walking.

Time to see what this place is all about.

6

Leo

"FIRST ONE'S ON ME!" AUSTIN ANNOUNCES AS HE DROPS ONTO a barstool next to Hank, who's already halfway through a beer. "Or... second one, I guess."

Hank grunts, barely acknowledging him.

I like Austin, but he's trying a little too hard to be on the *in,* and I think it's working against him in the old timer's eyes.

I'm in the seat on Hank's other side, nursing my own beer. Taboo is the local favorite. Dim lights, sticky floors, a jukebox that only half works. Not to mention the smell of beer-soaked wood and clothes seeping with cigarette smoke.

Yet we keep coming back, probably more often than we should.

Beer and liquor *do* keep a man sane in this town. Especially in the winter months, when the gloom and fog don't lift for weeks. People take sunshine for granted. But when you've been pulling twelve-hour days and the only thing you've "caught" lately is a bad cold, you'll take a beer over vitamin D every time.

And sometimes, it's the only thing that makes the silence at home feel less like a... void.

"It's getting too crowded at the bar. Let's find a table," Izzy, Rowdy's girlfriend, says as she pops up behind us, hand in hand with Rowdy.

I glance at Hank and Austin, then jerk my chin toward an open table.

"How was the haul today?" she asks once we're seated.

"Not bad, not great," I say. "What you'd expect at the end of the season."

"It'll get better. It has to—Izzy's bleeding me dry," Rowdy mumbles, chugging half his beer.

"Excuse me?" she shoots back. "I told you I had an expensive taste the second we met. You said it wasn't a problem, so don't complain now, asshole. Remember, I *choose* you. I do not *need* you."

"Yeah, yeah," Rowdy waves her off. "I didn't know expensive taste meant new clothes every damn weekend."

"You buy me those clothes because *you* want to see me in them, sweetie. Don't act like you're not whipped just because your boys are here."

"Enough, you two," Hank grumbles. "You're fuckin' annoying."

Izzy giggles and plants a kiss on Rowdy's cheek. "You love me and I love you. We put up with each other, that's what we do."

He grabs her face and kisses her back. "Damn right, we do."

Toxic. That's what those two are. Either bickering or screwing, there's no in-between.

"Another round?" one of the waitresses asks as she passes.

"Just keep 'em coming," Hank says, tipping his empty bottle toward her.

The waitress nods, collects our empties and shuffles off to refill our habit.

"Did you just look at her ass?" Izzy snaps at Rowdy.

"Oh God, here we go again," Rowdy groans, dropping his face into his hands. He tries to defend himself, Izzy interrupts, and they spiral into their usual routine.

I stop listening when the door swings open though, because there *she* is... for the second time today.

The new girl.

Tight bootcut jeans, cropped T-shirt, blonde hair loose around her shoulders. Every man in here notices her the second she steps inside.

I feel the shift in the room, all of the energy pulled into her direction. Even the jukebox seems to fade out once she makes her entrance. A table of regulars slouched over their drinks goes quiet, a dart clatters to the floor, and all eyes are on her.

Mine included.

We don't get women like her here. Not often, anyway. She's fresh, clean, untouched by this place.

I feel heat rush to my cheeks. I know exactly what most of the men here are thinking right now. Hell, I'm thinking it, too. But I like to believe I'm not a scumbag like eighty-five percent of them.

She walks right past me without so much as a glance my way or anyone else's for that matter, focused solely on where she's going.

She moves lightly, a faint floral scent trailing behind her. Either she doesn't notice the stares, or she's damn good at pretending she doesn't.

It's hard to look away; my grip tightens around the neck of my beer bottle. Then a voice cuts through from behind me, pulling me from my trance.

"Leo!"

I turn around and see Joey Finn. Immediately, I feel my stomach twist and my body tense.

Are you kidding me?

I turn back to the table, suddenly not in the mood for another beer. Rowdy and Hank exchange a look. Izzy's eyes cut away, and Austin just looks confused.

"Oh boy," Rowdy mutters.

I take a slow drink before standing. If Joey's back... that must mean Sam Murphy is, too, and absolutely *nothing* good can come from that.

7

TABOO IS A MEDIUM-SIZED BAR, AND EVERYTHING IS WOODEN and dressed in a nautical theme. Ship wheels, netting, mermaids, shells, and sea glass cover the walls and windows. It feels like I'm stepping inside a boat. A very grungy boat, smelling strongly of beer and... *burp?*

It's not overly crowded, just enough to feel full, which doesn't surprise me. The place is scattered with people of all ages, but I make a point not to stare. My focus stays fixed on the bar where Sara is sitting, waiting for me.

She's changed out of her usual sweatpants and oversized sweatshirt combo into baby-pink overalls and a jean jacket. The outfit hugs her curves, and the color is a perfect contrast to her mid-length brown hair and hazel eyes. When she smiles, she flashes her slightly crowded teeth which only makes her smile more genuine.

It's cute. It's very *her*—quirky and sweet.

"Hey!" I greet her.

"Hey, Layla." She stands and hugs me. "I like to get to places early, you know... Scope them out."

"I get that." I return her hug and sit on the barstool next

to her.

It feels good to be out of my tiny apartment, and it feels even better to have Sara as company. I glance at her; she seems to be out of her element and looks a little stiff.

"What do you want to drink? My treat," I say as I wave down a bartender.

"Oh, I don't know…" she says, fidgeting with her jacket buttons.

"Don't worry. I know something yummy."

The bartender walks up. He's tall, blond, handsome, buzz cut, in shape. My guess: mid-twenties.

His eyes skim up and down my body only bothering to meet my eyes once he's finished. He turns to Sara. "Hey, Sara," he says, then turns back to me. "And… friend? Haven't seen you around here before."

"I'm Layla, new to town." I offer my hand for a shake.

"That's apparent," he smirks, shaking my hand. "What can I get you ladies?"

"Two Mexican Mules, please."

"You really *aren't* from here, are you?" he teases. "I'll do my best."

Sara's eyes widen. "Tequila?"

"Don't worry, it's good. I won't let you get too wild."

She glances around, still carrying the wary look. Luckily, the drinks arrive quickly. Two copper cups with a heavy scent of tequila rising from them.

"Thanks," I say, taking mine.

Beer and straight liquor seem more Taboo's style, but it's hard to mess up a Mexican Mule.

"Name's Kyle. Holler if you need anything," he says, moving on.

"Cheers." I hold up my cup. Sara clinks hers against mine, and we both take a sip.

The place has the small town charm. Los Angeles has

oceanside restaurants with similar themes, but this is much different. Like I'm actually *inside* the ship. Or maybe it's because there are no windows… probably to keep day drinkers from noticing the time.

I'd bet my money some of the locals spend more time here than they do at home.

Sara downs her drink quickly, scrunching her face at the bite, but chasing it with a laugh. By the time I've worked through half of mine, her cheeks are flushed, and her words start tumbling out faster. Something about Will, her crush at a local diner, and the way she freezes up every time he stops by work for a coffee. She gestures with her half-empty cup, her laugh louder now.

The tequila's definitely working.

"Let's go dance," I interrupt, tugging her toward the middle of what *could* be a dance floor.

It isn't much, just a cleared patch near the jukebox, where the floorboards are scuffed and sticky. Colored lights are strung haphazardly across the ceiling above it, and a couple of older women sway with beers in hand.

"Okay! Let's do it!" Sara squeals, definitely riding the tequila wave now.

I grab her hand and pull her toward the empty patch. Her hips start to move, her confidence growing with each beat, like she's the most self-assured girl in the room. A couple of guys cheer her on from the bar as she shimmies.

It's amazing what one drink can do.

The rock music thumps, and we move in sync. Hips side to side, arms lifting above our heads as we laugh toward the ceiling. I'm starting to think we're not looking too bad.

Until Sara trips over her own foot and takes me down with her.

Her laughter makes me laugh harder. Half of her body is on top of mine, the other half sprawled on the floor. I'm less lucky; my entire backside lands in something wet. *Hopefully* a spilled drink and not anything else.

"I'm so sorry," she says between giggles, pulling me up.

"Don't be, that was fun!"

We brush ourselves off, except for the wet spot on my right ass cheek. If anyone saw us fall, it's probably nothing new here.

"Let's get another drink," I suggest, steering her toward the bar.

Sara stops short, eyes widening as she clutches my arm. "Wait, wait, wait. *Layla*." Her grin spreads, cheeks still flushed from tequila and laughter. "He's literally staring at you right now."

Who? I look behind me.

Oh.

Him.

The guy from the boat. The guy helping Mrs. Walker. The guy with the dark, well-trimmed beard and the beautiful jawline. He's talking to another man, voice quiet but animated, irritation evident on his face. Even so, he keeps looking in my direction.

I think his eyes are green; it's kind of hard to tell from here. But I *do* catch sight of the mermaid tattoo on his forearm. The forearm attached to the kind of bicep you can't hide under a black fitted T-shirt.

Shit. I've been looking too long.

Not cute.

"I saw him this morning at the loading docks," I whisper to Sara.

"That's Leo Anderson," she says, a little too loudly. "Local guy, a few years older than us. Everyone knows him, but *nobody* can have him. He's one of the handsome ones."

Handsome is an understatement.

Leo.

Hot name.

Hot body.

"Having fun?" Kyle asks, pulling my attention.

"*Soo* much fun," Sara says with a slight slur, attempting to take another sip out of her empty cup.

"We'll take some water," I say, changing my mind about another drink. She launches back into Will-talk, and I start to imagine finding him, kidnapping him, and then delivering him to her doorstep just to get it over with.

But before I can commit to that idea, a loud shout echoes through the bar, followed by a loud clunk.

It's Leo. He looks pissed, upper body flexed, his knuckles red.

The other guy is out cold on the floor, surrounded by a pile of glass from a shattered beer bottle.

Kyle rushes over to them. "Leo! Really, dude?"

No one else at Leo's table even flinches. They just keep talking, keep drinking, like this is none of their business.

Another bartender jogs over and crouches beside the unconscious man. "I got him," he says, hooking an arm under the guy's shoulder and lifting.

Kyle nods, then turns back to Leo. "You're cleaning this up, man."

"Did you know?" Leo snaps. "That he's back in town?"

Kyle freezes, looking caught off guard. "Just... clean it up, please."

A waitress appears with a broom, dustpan, and small trash bin. Leo takes them without another word, Kyle just walks away shaking his head.

Before I can fully process what just happened, the bar starts buzzing again, and a woman close to my age with long, straight black hair and full pink lips appears in front of Sara and me.

"Sara, when did you get here? Since when do you go out?"

Sara's glossy eyes lazily find hers. "Oh, hey, Izzy. I'm just here with a friend." She nods toward me. "Layla, this is my cousin, Izzy."

"Hi there," Izzy says with a smile before turning back to Sara. "If I'd known you were willing to leave the house, I would've invited you out ages ago."

As they talk, I hover on the edge of their conversation, nodding when I think it's appropriate, but too distracted to pay much attention. My eyes keep darting back to the table where Leo crouches, sweeping shards into the dustpan.

Before I can second-guess myself, I slip away toward him.

"Can I help?" My voice comes out soft.

He glances up at me, looking surprised for just a moment. His emerald-green eyes meet mine before dropping back to the floor.

Damn. He's even more attractive up close.

"I got this. Thank you, though," he says, polite but reserved.

Ignoring him, I squat down and start gathering the larger pieces. His shoulder lightly brushes mine, and I catch the faint scent of his masculine scented body soap. "Did he say the wrong thing or something?"

"Or something," he murmurs.

I should probably leave it there, but curiosity wins. "Friend? Or frenemy?"

"More like a brother," he says after a pause. "He'll be fine."

He drops the last shard into the bin and stands. I rise with him, realizing he's got to be at least a foot taller than me. For what feels like an entire minute, he just looks at me—real, genuine eye contact that sends a shiver down my spine.

My palms start to sweat. I need to do something with my hands, so I quickly wipe them on my jeans and hold one out. "I'm Layla."

His hand meets mine slowly. "Leo."

God. His voice is deep, smooth and rough all at the same time.

"I just moved to town, so maybe I'll be seeing you around," I press my lips together and try to smile.

He keeps my gaze, the corners of his eyes creasing like he's thinking hard. "Why?" he asks.

"Why... what?"

"Why did you move *here*?"

I think about my answer for a moment. "Oh, you know. A fresh start and all that."

The corner of his mouth curves briefly before it vanishes. "Interesting choice of town for a new start."

"Why do you say that?" I ask, curiosity piqued.

"It's not the place I'd imagine a young woman would choose for a reset." He tilts his head from side to side. "I'd say it's missing the scene most ladies are looking for."

"Well..." I pause, then smile. "Maybe I'm just the thing it needs."

He chuckles. "Right."

I glance back toward Sara; she's still deep in conversation with Izzy, and before I can think of what to say next, one of the older men from Leo's table comes over and says something about leaving.

Leo nods, then turns back to me. "Thanks for the help," he says, monotone.

He doesn't say goodbye. Just grabs the broom, dustpan, and bin, returns them behind the bar, and walks out without looking back.

He's already hot enough. God didn't have to add mysterious and broody into the mix.

I make my way back to Sara just as she's saying goodbye to Izzy. "Yikes, I think I'm drunk," she mumbles. "My cousin says she likes this look on me."

I giggle. "You can stay at my place tonight."

She nods and loops her arm around my neck. "I think you might need to help me a little."

"You got it."

We head home, my mind already turning over all kinds of questions. About Leo, mostly, and whatever the hell Morro Bay has done to him.

8

JOEY WAS SUPPOSED TO STAY AWAY.

Dry out, get stronger, stay clean. But I know what brought him back, and I know *who* invited him.

Sam Murphy is a name I thought I'd never have to bring up again. A man I never thought I'd cross paths with again, not after the kind of bullshit he started here. He was supposed to keep his distance after his prison time. For his sake, and for everyone else he dragged down with him.

Guys like Joey. Guys like me, if I'm not careful.

I've never danced with the devil that closely, not like these guys do. I enjoy my beer, the occasional shot of whiskey or rum, but nothing in my veins. Nothing in my lungs.

I grew up with Joey. We started as neighbors, became fast friends, and eventually more like brothers. From elementary school through high school we were inseparable, working on my dad's boat together, fishing, eating, partying, and even fighting over the same girls. You name it, we did it.

But Sam got to him and when he did, the downfall was fast… and ugly.

Last year, Joey was fighting for his life. He was one hospital visit away from meeting the guy upstairs. He came to me for help, begged me, *promised* he wouldn't touch that shit again.

Of course, I helped. That's what family does.

In a way, he was helping me grieve the loss of my father. So, his company was good for me, too.

He had lost everything in the downfall. So, he stayed with me for a while, crashed on my couch, drove my truck, wore my clothes. I gave him work, a roof over his head, real food. I held space for him… under one condition—stay sober.

And he did. Sam was arrested for selling drugs and was sent to prison. It was all coming together until Joey almost relapsed. Found some old stuff in his car while cleaning it out after he finally saved up enough to get it from the impound.

He didn't give in, but I saw how badly he wanted to. How he *craved* it. How his entire body literally shook for one hit. I could feel how desperate he was for just a tiny taste.

Heroin is the devil, and Joey had to get away. He had to separate himself from everything here in order to do that.

Including me.

So, I set him up in Northern Oregon. He was working with the lumbermen, cutting trees, and staying busy. I checked in on him here and there, but lost touch maybe four months ago.

I just thought he was busy. Thought he'd finally found that sweet slice of life of sobriety and honest work.

Until I saw him tonight, high as a *fucking* kite. The rage in me was unreal.

The heartbreak… much worse.

He tried to reason with me, told me he could handle it now. That it was just a social thing. Tried to lie straight to my fucking face about all of it.

So, I decked him.

Knocked him flat out, because I didn't know what else to do. Everything he worked for, everything I helped him with…

Gone, just like that. And who knows how long he's been drowning again.

I'd heard Sam was released a while ago, but word around town was that he was slinking around more inland, with no interest in coming back.

That must have changed, because the second I saw Joey, I *knew*.

Sam Murphy hates me. Hates that I intervened with him and Joey and anyone else for that matter. Hates that I was always there, always in the way. Hates that he couldn't pull in more people when I was around.

Misery loves company.

He must have known that bringing Joey back would get my attention, and it worked. He's got it. Now I just need to figure out what the hell he wants.

I called Joey's mom after I left Taboo. She immediately booked a flight for her and Joey to Connecticut. She said she was getting him far away from here to stay with family. I hope it works—for her sake and for his.

I wish I could have apologized for resorting to violence and told him that I still love him, but it's better if he just disappears.

Nothing's changed here as far as Sam goes. People aren't interested as far as I'm concerned. Hopefully, he'll get bored and go back inland, or wherever.

As long as it's not *here*.

And for his sake… He better pray we don't cross paths face to face.

———

I've been standing on the dock for a while, gulls crying overhead, drinking coffee that's gone lukewarm, trying to shake off last night. The water's calm again, the breeze chilly but light, both good signs for a full day of work.

"Yo," Austin calls, boots thudding against the boards. He's got a paper bag in one hand, an energy drink in the other.

"Morning."

He drops the bag onto a piling beside me and pulls out two breakfast burritos, handing me one. "Figured you'd need this. You were wound pretty tight last night."

"I'm fine." I take the burrito anyway.

Austin takes a sip of his drink. "*Or,* you could say thank you."

"Thank you," I mumble.

He smirks. "You're welcome. So… Why'd you punch some rando last night?"

I stop mid-bite. "He's not a rando."

Sometimes I forget how young Austin is, and that he wasn't around when the Sam and Joey shit went down.

He gives me a look, waiting for more, but when I don't take the bait, he lifts one hand in surrender. "Okay, okay. None of my business." He takes a mouthful of his burrito. "Then what about the girl?"

"The girl?"

"Yeah, the new girl." He gestures with his burrito like it's an obvious question. "The one who helped you clean up after you lost your shit. You know, the cute blonde that jogs around town."

I shake my head, ignoring what the words "cute blonde" do to my stomach. "She was just helping."

Austin snorts. "Helping? Come on, man. I've seen women look at you before. They're either intimidated or trying too hard. She was neither."

I don't answer, which is enough of an answer for him.

His grin grows. "Alright, alright. Haven't had enough coffee yet, I get it. I'll let you eat your burrito in peace."

I take another bite as he climbs onto the boat and disappears. I chew slowly, thinking about how close she'd been, how she so comfortably ignored me when I told her I had it handled.

Violence isn't usually something that draws in women like her... so I doubt she'll be looking for me again.

She can keep on believing this town's all sunshine and rainbows. Sooner or later, the routine will wear her down, and she'll be gone faster than she showed up.

9

Layla

COFFEE IS ABSOLUTELY CRUCIAL THE MORNING AFTER A STRONG drink.

Actually, coffee is crucial *every* morning.

Sara is still asleep, snoring softly on my paisley patterned couch. We have nowhere to rush off to, so I let her rest, moving around as quietly as possible. I perch on one of the barstools at my countertop, drinking coffee and eating a plate of eggs while doomscrolling on my phone.

My apartment is small—one bedroom, one bathroom, two barstools. No table. But from the living room window, you can see the ocean in the distance, a faint strip of blue that absolutely makes up for the lack of space on the inside.

I find myself staring out that window.

I've been thinking about a certain man, at a certain bar and how he knocked out a guy in front of an entire room and no one batted an eye. It *should* bother me. Violence isn't something I condone, but if I'm being totally honest with myself, there *is* something appealing to a large, strong man that can hold his own.

I don't know the situation. I don't know Leo or the guy

who was out cold on the floor. I really don't know much about anyone in this town.

What I do know is that my coffee is nearly gone, and the restlessness is starting to set in.

I need to go for a run.

I pull on some leggings, my favorite hoodie, and scribble a note for Sara telling her I'll be back soon and to make herself at home.

The morning air is refreshing as I jog toward the beach, passing the same dock as yesterday. The sun is climbing, burning away the fog that stubbornly clings to the shore. I slow to a walk, drawn in by the sunrise. The sand, the sea, the bursts of light prickling through that dense layer.

It's all so breathtaking.

When my family used to camp nearby, my dad and I would wake before anyone else to watch the sunrise. He always had a canister of hot coffee, and I loved how the sunlight would catch the rising steam, creating a picture-perfect moment. He'd let me have one sip—even at ten years old—and tell me the bitterness goes away once you acquire the taste.

But it never tasted bitter to me. I think I loved the moment more than the coffee, and somewhere along the way, my brain just mushed them together.

My parents aren't far from me. Maybe four or five hours, depending on traffic, and they're begging to visit the second I give them the green light. I do want to see them; I love them so much. But I want this new life to feel like mine before I bring them into it.

They'll try to fix things, lovingly of course.

Mom will immediately start rearranging my apartment and absolutely judge the amount of junk food in my cupboards. Dad will walk through, tightening every faucet and replacing every lightbulb. And while I know that's their way of loving me, there's something about this imperfect little place that feels perfect right now.

Leaky faucets and all.

———

"Good morning!" I call when I get home.

Sara's at the counter, eating a bowl of cereal. "Hey. I hope you don't mind that I helped myself. I woke up literally starving."

"Not at all. How'd you sleep?"

"I was out." She drops her spoon and rubs her temples. "I don't drink often, so I think my body's a little confused."

I giggle, feeling sympathetic for her hangover. "Did you have fun, at least?"

"Yeah, I did. Thanks for pushing me to get out of the house."

"Of course. It was nice for me, too."

I grab a banana from the fruit bowl and slide onto the stool next to her. I peel it back and take a bite before I notice her eyes glued to me.

"So…" she says slowly.

"So… what?"

"What did Leo have to say last night? I definitely noticed you sneaking away to talk to him." Now she's grinning.

"Uh, actually… He really didn't have anything to say." I laugh.

"Sounds about right."

"Does he have a girlfriend or something?"

"Nope. Don't think so," she says, taking her last spoonful of Cheerios. "He works a lot," she continues, "he's also always helping out in the community. Really close with his friends, too, my cousin Izzy actually knows him pretty well."

"Well, he's definitely mysterious."

Sara's expression softens into a frown. "He's been through some stuff that he's really taken to heart. He used to be more talkative and happier, and played guitar at a lot of the local events. Hasn't done that in years."

Now I'm even more interested.

"What happened?" I ask, filling myself a glass of water.

"I don't know all the details really, but... he lost his dad about two years ago. They were really close. Everyone in town loved his dad, Dean." She carries her empty bowl to the sink. "Then about a year after that, he almost lost his best friend to a drug overdose."

I think of my own dad, and the ache that would tear through me if I lost him. I think of my close friends back home, and how it would crush me to watch them go down a dark path.

"That's so sad..." I whisper.

"Yeah. The whole thing was heartbreaking. The town lost Dean... and in a way, it lost Leo, too. He's here physically, but emotionally not so much. Hence the no-girlfriend thing, I think."

That's understandable. *Maybe it's better if I just keep my distance and let him be.*

"Well," Sara says, slipping on her jean jacket, "I think I'm gonna head home, binge some TV, maybe take a nap. Self-care, you know?"

"Need a ride?"

"Nah, the walk'll be good."

I hug her goodbye and hop in the shower. Actually, self-care sounds like a great idea. For me, that means a clean space and some sketching.

When I'm done with my shower, I clean the apartment and tackle some laundry, grateful for my little stackable washer and dryer. Waiting for the dryer to finish, I pull out my sketch-book and start on a scene from the loading docks.

Something about the peacefulness there keeps tugging at me, asking to be brought to life. Sketching always helps me relax and helps me from thinking too much.

Especially about ridiculously handsome, emotionally unavailable men.

10

 Leo

It smells like diesel and live bait out here in the harbor today.

The sun's barely over the horizon, but the back of my neck's already wet with sweat. My shirt is sticking to my skin, and my hand is still healing from the nick I got yesterday when I was helping Mr. Harris gut some of his fish. I ignore it and try to focus on the to-do list in front of me. There's no use babying a wound when there is another one waiting.

The engine housing groans as I lean over it, wrench in my grip. She's old, but with a few turns and a firm tap with the heel of my hand, the bolt finally settles in. Metal can bite back when you work with it, but if you show it who's boss, it'll return the respect.

I drop the wrench into the toolbox and straighten out my body, stretching my spine until something in my back pops. The harbor's waking up slow today—waters are too rough to go out—so everyone gets the day off.

Except me, because I don't like to take days off.

A busy mind and a busy body keep the ache at arm's length.

Across the slip, Mr. Harris coils rope; no more fish to gut, so he's out prepping for the next. Guess he doesn't take days off, either, despite him being nearly eighty years old.

"Boat's looking good," he calls, his scruffy voice carrying over the water.

"Trying to keep her that way," I say, wiping my hands on the dirty rag I have tucked in my back pocket.

"Heard some talk at the bait shop this morning."

"Yeah?"

"Name came up I haven't heard in a while." His tone is still casual. "Sam Murphy."

My muscles tense, hands involuntarily curling into fists.

God, I hate that name.

"What about him?" I ask, trying to keep my voice steady.

"Not much. Just some guys saying he was sniffing around Cayucos and here. Asking about work, about people." He shrugs and goes back to his rope. "Could be nothing."

Could be nothing, *or* it could be Sam, trying to slip back into a place he's not welcome. The thought irritates me to the core, but I force it away. There's work to be done.

"Appreciate the heads up," I say.

Harris just waves it off, but the tension's already riddled through my shoulders. I try to ignore it and get back into the rhythm, checking the nets and ropes, stocking up the galley with the must needs for overnight trips.

By the time the deck's hosed clean, the sun's higher, and the weather is starting to warm. My stomach reminds me I'm hungry, so I lock up and head to the Harbor Café for a quick bite.

It smells like brine, rubber boots, and fresh shrimp inside. Beck, behind the counter, hands me my sandwich and coffee without a word.

It's routine. Out here, you learn to appreciate the quiet ways people look after you, like memorizing your lunch order.

I take my usual seat on the bench outside, already feeling the sun burn on my cheeks. Halfway through my sandwich, my phone buzzes.

Nate. One of the greatest guys I know.

"What's up?" I answer.

"Hey, buddy! The annual beach clean up is in a couple of days," he says. "Dockfront is organizing a little food stand, was hoping you would swing by early and help me get it hooked up."

He already knows I will. The annual beach clean up is something that everyone gets involved in.

"Yeah, I can do that," I say.

"Thanks, man, appreciate you."

We hang up, keeping it short and sweet. I toss my trash in the bin, shove my hands in my pockets, and head back toward the docks. There's plenty more work to be done, and I'd rather keep my mind there than on old names.

Or new ones for that matter.

11

Layla

"Mom, I promise we'll pick a date soon," I say into the phone, juggling my purse in one hand and a light jacket in the other. "I'm just still getting adjusted, you know?"

"I know, honey. We just miss you so much! When your sister moved, it felt like only half the nest was empty," she sighs. "Now, it's *completely* empty."

My mom's a Pisces, which means her emotions pretty much run the show.

"Ugh, that's tough. I'm sorry, Momma. But I promise it'll happen soon, okay?"

"Okay, love," she says, though I know the next time we talk she will absolutely be bringing it up again.

"I'm heading out for brunch with a friend. I'll give you a call later this week. Give Dad my love!"

We say our goodbyes, and I realize I'm running late.

Ten minutes later, I make it up the block and Sara's waiting for me outside Flynn's, the diner where Will works.

It took some persuading to get her here. She wasn't entirely sold on the idea, worried that I'd make a scene about her and Will. But once I told her my "goal" was to simply observe, she agreed.

I might've fibbed a little. I may or may not have some minor, very harmless matchmaking plans up my sleeve.

Sara's standing by the door when I walk up, looking... *different*. She's got a full face of makeup. Dark eyeshadow, red lipstick, the works. The skinny jeans I said would look good on her hug her curves just right, and the sweater she's wearing shows the tiniest hint of cleavage.

"They have the best clam chowder here," she says as we head inside.

"Mhm. And the best *Will*, too?" I tease.

She rolls her eyes.

From the outside, Flynn's looks like an old building with coral-colored, weathered wood. But the inside is the complete opposite. The walls are bright blue, and the floor is a black-and-white checkered pattern. Oldies music plays on a speaker as the hostess seats us at a booth by the window with a perfect view of Morro Rock.

A shorter, stocky guy with red hair and freckles walks over, and Sara's posture instantly shifts. She straightens her back and sweeps her hair away from her neck.

Must be Will.

He blushes the second he sees her, and she blushes right back.

"Hey, Sara," he says.

"Hi, Will." Her voice squeaks when she says his name, and her cheeks turn even pinker. She grips the edge of the menu and starts to study it.

"Will, hi," I chime in quickly, bailing her out. "I'm Layla."

"Nice to meet you." He smiles politely. "What can I get you gals?"

We order a couple of lemonades, and he heads off. I lean across the table the second he's out of earshot.

"So… He's cute," I whisper.

Sara ducks her head, twirling her straw wrapping around her index finger. She tries to fight back a smile. "Look, I know he's not the hottest guy in town, but he's really sweet. He was so nice in high school too."

She's still talking when Will reappears with our drinks, his timing almost too quick. "Ready to order?"

"I hear the clam chowder's great," I say, handing him our menus. "Let's do that."

He nods and disappears again.

"Ugh, why am I so scared?" Sara sighs once he's back in the kitchen. "What if I shoot my shot and he rejects me?"

I glance over my shoulder. Will's leaning against the doorframe, chatting with the cooks while sneaking looks at Sara. When he notices me, he snaps his head away.

"I'm not sure rejection's your biggest concern." I pull the paper wrapper off my straw, smooth it flat, and slide it across the table with a pen I found in my purse. "Life's too short, friend."

She doesn't need me to explain. She sighs, scribbles her number as neatly as she can, then slides it back.

"Okay, I did it."

"Great." I nod. "Now you just have to give it to him."

"I don't think I can do that."

"You can, and you should."

She rolls her eyes, and stuffs the straw wrapper in between the salt and pepper shakers.

Will brings our chowder less than ten minutes later, served in sourdough bread bowls that smell heavenly.

"Ohhh, this looks good," I say. And it really does.

Sara looks from me to the straw wrapper and back again before shaking her head. As soon as Will disappears into the kitchen, she groans.

"I couldn't do it."

"You could have, but I get it. It's scary." I take a spoonful of chowder.

"Maybe next time." She sighs.

Yeah, or maybe just when she isn't looking.

———

While Sara's in the bathroom, I slip Will the straw wrapper with her number scribbled across it, telling him she asked me to pass it along. I wouldn't call it a lie… More like a little *push*. He raises his brows, blushes, then tucks the wrapper into his front pocket with a quick mutter of thanks.

A moment later, Sara is stepping out of the bathroom just as Will is walking away, my heart racing at how close the timing was. I play it off, meeting Sara at the front door just as her phone buzzes.

"Oh, it's Izzy," she says, answering.

"Hey! …Yeah, I'll be there. Oh, really? Uh-huh. I'll be bringing a friend… Okay, see you then." She hangs up, shaking her head with a little laugh. "Apparently, my cousin seeing me at Taboo the other night sparked a reconnection. She's called me like four times since then."

"Reconnection is always nice," I say, thinking of my own sister in New York. "Am I the friend you'll be bringing to whatever that call was about?"

"Yes." She smiles, unlocking her car. "I *totally* forgot to tell you. Tomorrow we'll be closed for the annual beach and harbor clean-up. The whole town gets involved, and we're in charge of delivering cookies first thing, then helping with the sweep."

I tilt my head, remembering a sign about a beach clean-up taped to one of The Busy Bean's windows. "That actually sounds kind of nice."

She nods, sliding into the driver's seat of her car. "It's been around forever. Old fishermen's tradition; respect the sea, and it respects you. Supposed to bring good luck, too. Apparently, in 1953, the town skipped it, and a month later a tidal wave wiped out part of the harbor. So yeah, we don't miss it anymore. Izzy's boyfriend's a fisherman, and they go all out. They're there before sunrise and stay until after sunset."

"Fisherman? As in… Leo kind of fisherman?" My cheeks flush.

"Leo will *definitely* be there." She chuckles, pulling the door shut and rolling down the window. "See you at work. Come early, we've got a mountain of cookies to bake!"

I linger on the sidewalk, my gaze drifting toward the water. Somewhere out there, Leo's probably working. Fixing something, loading something, doing whatever it is he does when he's not punching guys in bars.

12

Leo

THE ANNUAL BEACH AND HARBOR CLEAN-UP IS ONE OF THE oldest traditions in town, and it's actually one of my favorite memories from childhood.

The whole town would gather, and I'd see all my friends from school. Sometimes we'd have matching shirts or hats, and we always got an ice cream cone afterward.

Dad always got there early and stayed late.

I always wanted to stay with him, but he said it was the fishermen's job to see it through and make sure it was done right. I hated when I had to leave, and he got to stay.

But now, I understand.

We are the ones who take from the sea, who reap the benefits of its life. It's our duty to uphold that responsibility. That's why the crew and I are already here. Helping set up tables, gathering bins, trash bags, and gloves that were donated by local organizations.

The townspeople will arrive soon, and the air will be filled with the sound of their energy and excitement.

Dockfront—Nate's restaurant—is passing out free lemonade and fresh fried fish sticks. They needed some help

moving their propane tanks to their stand down on Embarcadero, where the tables and other refreshments are set up.

"Morning, Leo," Mr. Harris says as he passes by me.
"Nice day for a clean-up, huh?"

"Yes, sir," I reply, glancing at the sky.

It's forecasted to be a decent day. The fog is minimal in
comparison to most days, and it should burn off in no time
once the sun comes out.

Nate already has his station halfway set up. Two folding
tables, a canopy, propane fryers warming up, and an open
cooler packed with cut-up fish.

"Fish fries, huh? Being stingy?" I tease as I help him
secure the canopy.

"We have a *plethora* of fish at the moment, and I need to
cook it up," he says, sweat forming on his upper lip as he
unfolds a table. "Besides, it fits the theme."

"Just teasing. Your fish fries are pretty good."

"*Everything* I make is good, Leo. You know this."

I nod. It's true. He's the best in town.

I look around and spot my crew making their way over to
me and Nate. Rowdy and Hank with cigarettes in hand,
smoke trailing behind them. Austin's in a faded band sweatshirt with the sleeves hacked off. Other business owners are
arriving too, hauling coolers onto tables, taping up handmade
signs battling against the early breeze.

The whole place is coming alive, bit by bit.

I plan to keep my eyes open today. This isn't the kind of
event Sam would show his face at, but he's been slithering
back into town, and I don't know what angle he's playing yet.

My gaze stops on Kyle, standing with the street clean-up
crowd. He glances over at me, gives a subtle nod, then turns
away. The crowd around me thickens fast, voices and footsteps
merging together. I'm used to this. I do it every damn year, but
large groups drain me quickly.

Overstimulation, noise, too many eyes.

"Excuse me," a feminine voice drawls behind me, pulling my attention.

I step aside to give her room to pass, but I choose the wrong direction and bump into her instead.

My arm grazes her shoulder, causing the tray to tip in her hands. I reach out and steady it before the whole thing goes down. My fingers brush lightly over hers for a split second, causing an electric current to run through the tips.

"Oh my gosh, I'm so sorry!" Layla says, gripping the tray tighter.

Thankfully, not a single cookie slides off.

She giggles, then looks up at me, her big blue eyes catching me off guard. "You just saved the people from a very tragic loss."

I can't help but let a small grin creep in. "It was more my fault than yours."

"Well, thank you anyways." She smiles, her eyes lingering on mine for a long moment before she continues on her way.

"You're welcome," I murmur, though she's probably out of earshot.

That's when I notice how well her leggings fit her and how they catch the curve of her stride as she walks off. I don't know *why* I notice that… or *why* I keep looking.

But I do know I have a sudden burst of unexpected energy.

13

Layla

It's definitely warmer today.

I ditched my sweatshirt an hour ago, and now I'm wearing a black tank with *Good Vibes Only* splashed across the front. The sneakers didn't last long, either; walking in sand is way easier barefoot.

Sara's with me, and together we've been tag-teaming the shoreline beside the harbor. Plastic bags and water bottles seem endless, carried in from the tide and scattered along the beach.

Her cousin Izzy was supposed to join us at the start, but, according to Sara, a fight with her boyfriend delayed her. She promised to catch up once things had smoothed over. But still, the vibe here is good.

Everywhere I look, people are combing the sand and even the sidewalks. A few boats glide across the water, nets dragging behind them in search of floating debris.

Someone calls out that a "weirdest trash find" contest has started and everyone starts to pick up their pace.

Outside of our trash bags full of… bags, Sara has found a lone combat boot, and I have found a faded garden gnome in a very compromised position. With one piece in particular broken off.

We're heading to turn in our findings when a man runs past us carrying a traffic cone covered in mussels. "Can't beat this one!" he calls, heading toward what looks to be a makeshift judges' table.

I turn to Sara. "We can't let him win!"

She nods and starts scanning the beach. Five minutes later, she points at something dark sticking out of the sand. "What's that?"

We jog over to the item and to our unfortunate surprise, it's dentures. A full set of upper teeth, halfway buried in the sand, looking like they've seen better days. Sara grabs them, and we run to the judges' table.

Out of breath, she slams them down amongst the other findings. The judges—a couple of locals I haven't met before —scan each piece laid out.

"I'm really not sure who can beat dentures..." the older man says. "This may just be the winner."

Sara and I high-five, earning nothing but bragging rights, but still feel accomplished.

I glance around the crowd that has slowly started to form around the table and spot Leo behind them. He's shirtless, skin tanned, and his lengthy hair is damp with sweat.

Everyone else is laughing, competing, showing off, but Leo isn't here for that. He's locked in on the sand, answering the unspoken order from the sea.

He looks toward us, offers a very small smile while shaking his head, and then sets his focus back on his tool.

I try not to watch him for too long, but I find it difficult to look away.

"I'm tired," Sara says, pulling my attention to her. "Let's go get some lemonade."

"That sounds great." I smile.

I'm parched, and a fresh lemonade sounds perfect. Plus, I need to get out of this spot before I'm declared the new town weirdo for staring at gorgeous men.

We tie up our trash bags, dispose of them, and head over to one of the food stands parked up on Embarcadero.

Izzy had spotted us at the food stands shortly after we arrived, and now she's sharing a bench with us, cookie in hand.

"Let's hang out tonight," she says, biting into her chocolate chip cookie. "I'm starting to love seeing my girl cousin so much! Why haven't we done this sooner?"

Sara shrugs, taking a mouthful of her own cookie. "I enjoy my TV shows. This whole going out thing is new to me."

"I guess I have you to thank for that then, Layla," Izzy says, grinning in my direction.

"Maybe so, just trying to get Sara out of her shell a bit." I pause. "Next mission is getting her to talk to that Will guy."

Izzy snorts. "Sara, you do *not* still have a crush on Will!"

Sara blushes.

"Okay, that is way too precious. We have to make that happen," Izzy says, finishing the rest of her cookie.

"I absolutely agree." I wink.

"*So* mean," Sara says, rolling her eyes with a smile.

"Not mean! Just wanting the best for our girl." Izzy nudges her and then pulls her into a side hug.

"Exactly, and I might have…" I pause, flashing a big grin. "I might have given him your number."

Sara's head snaps toward me. "You *what?*"

"If it's any comfort, he seemed really happy to have it."

Izzy claps her hands giddily. "Oh, this is golden."

"Oh my God, Layla! I should be mad at you right now, but I'm also kind of… excited." She giggles.

Izzy pulls her in for another hug, and Sara squeezes my hand. A silent thank you for giving the situation a little push. She's laughing, her shoulders relaxed, her eyes bright and this feels easy. Like the three of us have been friends for years, choosing to pass the time together.

It reminds me a little of my friends back home, the girls I grew up with, but now only keep in touch through texts and social media.

This is nice. This is natural.

The sun had begun to set twenty minutes ago, now carrying that afternoon glow. The purple and orange hues decorate the water's surface, just like they do during most sunsets here.

"The night's young, hunnies," Izzy says, standing up and brushing her lap from crumbs. "Let's go find the boys and see what kind of trouble we can get into."

She starts walking toward the end of the street, where I spot Leo and his friends hanging out around a truck.

My stomach does a little flip.

14

Leo

THE DAY WENT BY QUICKLY WITH MINIMAL MISHAPS, AND THE beach is looking pretty damn clean.

We packed up the tables and hauled the trash bags to the dump, the bed of my truck reeking of old plastic by the time we got there. We helped Nate break everything down and stow it all away, and in return, we got to finish off the rest of the fish fries.

Zero complaints from any of us.

Nate headed home not long after, feeling the hours he'd spent cooking under the sun. Can't blame him. I think we're all a little burnt out from the day. All of us except for Austin, of course.

"I'm thinking... bonfire?" Austin suggests, swinging his feet over the open tailgate of my truck.

"Nah, no way with your shenanigans. I'm heading home to bed," Hank says, already turning to leave. "Night, boys."

"You're missing out!" Austin calls after him, hopping off the tailgate. "Perfect night for a bonfire. Ooh, and s'mores! I can run down and grab some marshmallows from the bait shop."

"Bait shop's closed, buddy. Everything's closed," Rowdy says, his fifteenth cigarette of the day dangling from his mouth.

"Oh, right... Still, a beach bonfire sounds good after a day like today," Austin insists.

I half agree, but I'm leaning more toward sleep.

"I'll have to ask Izzy if she's up for it. I promised I wouldn't stay too busy before the next season starts," he says, then pauses, looking behind me. "Hey! Speaking of the beautiful devil herself."

I turn to see Izzy walking up to us, and she isn't alone. Layla and Izzy's cousin, Sara, are with her, one on each side. They look like a unit, like Layla's already claimed her place among them.

I think a hard day's work looks good on her.

Her cheeks are rosy, and there's a stray strand of hair dangling on the side of her face.

"Hey, boys!" Izzy announces as they reach us, jumping into Rowdy's arms and planting a sloppy kiss on his forehead. "What are we doing tonight? I think it's a full moon because I have this weird amount of energy right now."

Austin perks up. "Bonfire and music?"

"Oh, yes, great idea. But only if my girls are willing to join." She gestures toward them. "Guys, you know Sara, my cousin, and this is Layla, she's new here."

"Hi, everyone," Layla says, beaming.

"Layla, this is Rowdy, my hunky man. This is Austin, the newbie on the team. And I think you've met Leo, the captain of the crew."

Layla shakes Rowdy and Austin's hands with a polite "Nice to meet you." Then her gaze lands on me, her full lips shaping into another smile. "Hi again," she says softly, her eyes connecting with mine.

"You girlies up for a bonfire?" Izzy asks, still hanging off Rowdy's neck.

She looks to Sara, who shrugs and then nods, before turning to Layla.

"I'm in!" Layla says, breaking eye contact.

"Bonfire it is," Izzy declares. "Just give us like twenty minutes. We need chairs and blankets. I've got some in my car."

"I've got wood and beer in my truck," Rowdy says, already heading off.

I glance at Austin.

"I always have the best ideas," he says, making me chuckle.

I'd been more on Hank's page, ready to crash after a long day. But now, I'm not entirely sure why I'm looking forward to this.

The fire's going strong, Austin's music selection isn't bad, and neither is the beer I'm nursing.

Rowdy and Izzy are sharing a chair, pausing between random makeout sessions, not caring that there are four other people here—one of them being Layla, who's sitting on a woven striped blanket next to Sara.

Austin's been chatting Layla up for the last fifteen minutes.

I think he's into her, and I don't know why the thought makes me feel tense, putting a knot in the middle of my chest. He's doing his usual thing with a pretty girl, flexing his job, talking about how he lives with his grandma so he can take care of her, and slipping in how he used to play baseball and thought he'd make it to the big leagues one day.

She listens, nods, and smiles. Polite, but not impressed. I can tell it's just a courtesy.

Izzy finally tears her face from Rowdy's and stands, heading over to Sara. She tugs on her arms. "Dance with me."

Sara shakes her head and pulls away. Izzy rolls her eyes, then turns to Layla and tugs her up.

"Come on, Layla. I know *you* like to have fun."

Layla grins and jumps to her feet. The two of them spin barefoot in the sand, shadows stretching and shrinking in the firelight. Layla's hair hangs loose around her shoulders now, shifting in the breeze alongside her movements.

I notice the sprinkles of freckles across her nose, and the smile lines forming at the creases of her lips. She laughs at something Izzy says and brings a hand to her mouth, covering a smile too wide to contain. I see that her bare toes have a few freckles too, and that they are painted pink, though chipped in some places.

At one point, her eyes sweep across the fire and land on me. Just for a second or maybe even less, but it jolts through me. Makes me feel uneasy, like she caught me doing something that I shouldn't be doing. So I look away and take another swig of beer, eyes on the flames, only to find them drifting back to her.

Watching the way she moves, like fun and laughter and spontaneity are normal to her.

Her smile doesn't falter, she just stays in the moment and I wonder if she felt the jolt as well. I wonder if she, too, senses the sudden shift in the tide, in the energy.

Like something is *pulling*.

I force my gaze back to the flames, but I think it's a little too late.

The damage is done, leaving an irreparable crack running through my walls.

15

Layla

You can't have bonfires on L.A. beaches; it's against the "rules".

So this is new for me—and I *love* it. Feeling the presence of so many elements all at once: the mist from the ocean, the breeze in the air, the warmth of the fire, and the soft sand of earth beneath me. It's quite beautiful.

Like nutritious fuel for the soul.

Everything about today was good for the soul—the beach clean-up, hard work for a good cause, the fresh lemonade, the comfort of homemade cookies. And now, living in the moment, surrounded by new friends.

Sara didn't want to dance, but that's okay. She doesn't have to. She finds her comfort and her peace in observing, and I love that about her. Izzy is the total opposite. Completely energized by attention and movement.

I like to think I'm somewhere in the middle. Happy to be quiet, soft, and observant, but also happy to be spontaneous and loud.

After about ten minutes of dancing around the fire with Izzy, like witches under a full moon, we collapse in the sand, the length of the day and the exhaustion in our muscles finally catching up with us.

"I need a refill," Rowdy says, placing his hands on Izzy's hips once she settles back onto him.

"I'm on it. Anyone else?" I offer.

Austin and Izzy raise their hands. I glance at Leo, who just nods.

I grab four beers from the cooler. Sara and I decided early on to skip the drinking tonight. We'll already be tired for our shift tomorrow morning, and we don't need to add alcohol to the mix.

I hand Rowdy and Izzy their beers, then Austin, and finally Leo.

Our fingers lightly brush on the base of the bottle during the hand-off, and a warm sensation crawls up my arm, leaving goosebumps in its wake.

I don't know if he felt it, too. If he did, he's hiding it much better than I am.

"Thank you," he says.

I take the opportunity to sit in the space beside him on the driftwood he's settled on. I feel him watch me as I get myself comfortable.

"You ever get used to this?" I ask, admiring the stars above us.

"Used to what?"

"*This,*" I say, gesturing toward the open beach, the open sea. "The air, the sound, the smells. It's like it seeps into your bones here."

He studies my face for a moment before answering. "I don't think it's that simple."

"No?"

He shifts a little, straightening his posture and taking a drink from his bottle. "It's more of a gift and less like something to get used to."

"Hmm." I bob my head, letting his words stick with me.

A long moment of silence sits between us as the fire crackles, and the wind picks up.

"You've been here your whole life, right?" I finally ask.

"Born here. Raised here. Probably die here." His tone is calm.

"I get the feeling that's not a bad thing for you."

A small smile grows on his face. "You catch on quick."

I laugh, digging my foot beneath a layer of sand. "Back in L.A., people are never content. Always chasing something— usually money or popularity. You know, something vain. I don't think I know anyone back home who's talked about dying in the same place they were born."

He looks at me, the first *real* eye contact on this beach tonight. "And what are *you* chasing, Layla?"

The question catches me off guard and heat blooms in my cheeks from the intimacy of that question. My fingers tingle in my lap as I think of an answer.

"You know, I'm not entirely sure yet," I admit. "I just know I wanted to slow down a little bit."

Eyes still on me, there's a shimmer of *something* behind them. "Then maybe you did pick the right place."

That's it.

The conversation ends. I tuck my knees to my chest, telling myself it's just the chill that makes me shiver. He doesn't look at me again, not directly anyway. I just stare into the flames, pretending I'm not hyperaware of him beside me, or how close his shoulder is to mine and how if I leaned the wrong way, *we'd touch.*

We sit together silently as the fire starts to dim, the energy around us fading. Conversations around us slow until there's nothing but the crackle of the flame and low music diluting the cool night air.

16

Leo

AUSTIN'S SORRY EXCUSE FOR A CAR BROKE DOWN, AND HE needs help getting it to the mechanic.

My truck has a tow hitch, and I know the local grease monkey so it only makes sense that I'm the one to go.

Austin's a good kid, sticking around town to take care of his grandma. She raised him, stepped up when his parents couldn't—lost to the life of drugs—so he figured it's only right to return the loyalty now, in her old age.

It's admirable, really. One, he puts family first. And two, he never gave in to the same addictions that took his parents, no matter what society expected of him.

So anything I can do to help out, to keep him on that path, I will.

"Hey, man, thanks so much for helping out," Austin says, meeting me in his driveway.

"It's no problem, let's get it hooked up."

There isn't a lazy bone in Austin's body, always eager to learn, eager to do anything really. I know it bothers Hank— the high energy and constant questions—but if he keeps it up, he could very well be running his own crew sooner or later. He has it in him.

"I've had this thing forever, it's no surprise it died on me," he says as we tighten the tow line. "It's worth fixing, though. It's a Toyota, she's got another hundred thousand miles on her at least!"

We check everything, making sure nothing is loose.

"Marty will give you a good deal," I say with the final tighten, "hop in."

Austin doesn't live too far from Marty's, the only mechanic I trust with anything. So, after less than twenty minutes, we are already unhooking the car and handing Marty the keys.

"Just make it driveable, I don't need anything fancy," Austin says to Marty, "I'm on a tight budget. I got a good job, but it takes time to build up, ya know?"

He keeps rambling, and I don't have the heart to tell him Marty's completely deaf in one ear and damn near deaf in the other. So I let him talk and allow my focus to drift across the street to the docks instead. The sky is still gray, mist resting low over the ocean, most of the town still asleep and upholding the slow-living lifestyle.

But my mind is anything but slow. It won't shut up, not after last night. I didn't sleep much at all, despite needing it after such a long day.

I hesitate to admit it, even to myself, but I kept thinking about her.

Layla.

I don't do this. I don't think about women after just a couple of short conversations. There's no space for that. I'm too broken to offer myself in that way, and broken things *don't* get to want.

Broken things just learn how to survive, and yet she lingers in the back of my mind for reasons I can't explain.

"So, what do you think?" Austin asks, pulling me back to earth.

"Uh…"

He rolls his eyes. "Never mind. Whatever you just said sounds good, Marty."

Marty just smiles and nods. "Give me two days tops."

"Great, thanks so much, sir! Again, on a tight budget so —" Austin says, but I can't help but cut him off.

"Let the man do his job."

Austin darts his eyes between Marty and me. "Okay then!" He claps his hands together.

"Thanks, Marty," I say, patting the old man on the back.

Austin whistles a tune as we walk back to my truck. "Hey, let's grab a coffee," he says once we're inside.

"I don't think you need any more caffeine."

"Aw, come on, man. The Busy Bean has some breakfast sandwiches, too, they're *so* good."

"The Busy Bean?"

"Yeah, it's the best coffee in town, right?"

I narrow my eyes at him. He doesn't just want coffee; he wants to go there because *she* might be there.

"Come on, it's right there," he pushes, pointing toward the shop.

I think about it for a minute. A coffee does sound necessary.

"Fine," I grumble.

And the truth is, I can't pretend that I'm not hoping she's there, too.

17

Layla

SARA IS ALREADY HALFWAY THROUGH THE MORNING TASKS when I get to work.

The whole place smells like fresh pastries and brewing coffee. It's warm in here, too, and slightly humid from the steam of the espresso machine, a nice contrast to the light nip outside.

I wonder what it will feel like during autumn here. Sara and I can decorate for the season, keep the fireplace lit, maybe even try out a new seasonal flavor. Fall has always been my favorite time of year, and I can't wait for that cozy feeling.

"Good morning!" I say warmly.

"Morning!" she responds, focused on her snickerdoodles, which smell delicious.

I should feel rested, despite being out later than intended. I was actually getting some quality sleep, but then my neighbor decided that starting *Star Wars* at two in the morning was a good idea. So here I am, groggy as hell, rocking an oversized sweater and a messy bun. But you know what?

I'm killin' it.

I clock in and almost instantly after, the door chimes. I

always love the first customer of the day; most people are friendly here and who isn't excited for some caffeine and a morning treat?

Most days, it's one of the usuals coming in, either rushing in and out, or staying and enjoying our small seating area next to the fireplace.

That's most days.

Today is different.

Because it's not the older gentleman from the grocery store down the road. It's not the lady from the boutique across the street.

No.

It's Leo.

He's wearing a dark green hoodie and jeans, which somehow makes his eyes even more hypnotic. His jaw's tight, his expression a mystery, but he's *definitely* looking at me and not in a casual, passing-glance kind of way.

I can't tell if he's annoyed or just brooding by default. Either way, it does something to my belly. Also, I find it just a little odd that a fisherman in this town keeps his beard so well-trimmed.

It's after the fact that he's been standing at the order counter for who knows how long—*I have yet to say a word*—that I notice he's not alone. He's with Austin, who I'm pretty sure has a crush on me. He was laying on the moves a little too obviously last night.

I gather myself and greet them as I would anyone else. "Good morning," I say with a smile.

"Good morning," Leo says.

"A good morning indeed!" Austin chimes in even though Leo and I haven't unlocked eye contact yet. "Whatever that delicious smell is, I want it."

I break eye contact first and give my attention to Austin. "Sure thing. Anything else?"

"We'll take a couple of coffees," Leo says, his eyes still on me.

"For here," Austin adds, "we're waiting to see what's up with my car. We just dropped it off at Marty's up the street."

"Oh, yeah?" I say, pouring their coffees into a couple of our locally crafted mugs.

"Yep, oh, give us a couple of those breakfast sandwiches, too." He points to the display sandwich.

I exchange a look with Leo. "You got it."

"Just one for him is fine, I'm not hungry," Leo says.

"Your loss." Austin drools as Sara hands him a fresh snickerdoodle cookie. "Thanks, this looks amazing."

I grab another one and hand it to Leo. "On the house," I say with a wink.

He doesn't argue. He pays for the coffee and sandwich and then drops a ten-dollar bill in the tip jar and finds a spot at one of the tables.

Sara is beside me now and whispers in my ear, "You okay? You're salivating."

I lightly nudge her in the side. "He's just…" I pause and exhale. "Like *really* good looking."

We both take a moment to admire his physique and quickly turn away when he notices us.

"Go chat with him, you two seemed kind of cozy last night around the fire."

I think about it for a second. Yes, we had somewhat of a conversation last night, but I wouldn't even know what to talk about today. The man is not a chatty kind of guy.

"I don—" I start to say, but Sara interrupts me.

"Nope. No excuses, you gave Will my number behind my back because I needed a push. So this is *my* push for you to go make friends with Leo." She quite literally pushes me from out behind the counter.

"Okay, okay, fine," I whisper as I grab the carafe of coffee and bring it with me.

"Refill?" I ask, even though their coffees are still mostly full.

Austin quickly chugs a big gulp, wincing at the heat. "Yes, please."

"So, no fishing today?" I ask, aiming the question at Leo as I pour the coffee.

"Not today," he says, voice low and... *rough.*

"He gives us time off, sometimes," Austin teases, rolling his eyes.

"How nice of him." I giggle.

Leo looks between Austin and me. I feel Austin's eyes lingering, but mine fixate onto Leo's. Our second eye-lock of the morning, and I'm doing my best not to be the first to look away. My heart flutters, the silence in the shop suddenly too loud.

Heat flushes my cheeks, and I clear my throat, breaking the spell. "Okay, well... You two have a nice day." I turn to leave, but Austin stops me.

"Wait! What time are you off today?" He asks. "I was thinking of trying to talk Leo into a little surfing lesson. He's a pro, and it's supposed to be a pretty nice day. Since you're new in town, you should join us."

Leo glares at him. "A surfing lesson?"

"Yeah, I've been asking you for weeks. Today's the perfect day for it." He pauses and looks at me. "And Layla should join."

Leo looks between us, hard to tell whether he likes this idea or is pissed at his friend for even suggesting it.

"Alright," Leo finally says. He looks at me again, more directly this time. "Meet us at the beach by Morro Rock around two."

Austin adds, "Oh—and wear a swimsuit."

Choosing a swimsuit for a surf lesson is much harder than I thought. Do I go with a conservative black one-piece in case of any swimsuit mishaps? Or, do I lean toward a more riskier selection, like my sparkly pink two-piece bikini?

I look between the two, holding both options in my hands. Safe or risky.

I choose the two-piece.

I know Austin was technically the one to invite me, so I don't want it to seem like I'm dressing to impress him. If his apparent crush gets any deeper, I'm going to have to find a way to let him down easy. He's sweet and all, but I don't think he's my type.

And not the one I'm really thinking about.

I feel kind of silly thinking about Leo in any way outside of a mutual friend with my new friends. But between the bonfire last night and his coffee visit this morning, I haven't been able to get him out of my mind.

There's something about him, something poetic and... deep. Something that makes me want to know more.

I glance outside; the sun is high in the sky. A contrast to it's more dreary morning. Hopefully a sign that this afternoon lesson will go well.

I slip into my bikini, take a second thought that maybe I should go with the safe option, then immediately decide against it.

I check the clock, and it's already ten after two. I'll be a little late, but that'll show that I'm not too eager.

Here goes nothing.

18

AUSTIN BAILED.

Said his grandma needed help fixing a busted sink and, *"Bro, she's ancient, this is the last sink of her lifetime. I gotta help."*

I told him not to worry about it, then thought about canceling. Alone with Layla seems a little too... close. But somewhere in the back of my mind, I don't hate the idea.

So now, I'm standing barefoot in the sand, holding two surfboards, a couple of wetsuits, my T-shirt already tossed in the truck bed, and asking myself again what the hell I'm doing. This is way out of my comfort zone. I like to stick to my routine. Work, beers with the guys, the occasional barbecue, and sleep.

I don't do surf lessons with sunshine girls.

And... she's late.

I check my phone for the time again. The sun's out, the heat is welcome, offsetting my growing anxiety. Though the warm sand is a nice distraction, it feels good on my feet. Not too hot, not too cool and despite the time of day, the waves look mellow, but decent enough for a beginner.

I wonder if she decided to bail, too. I wouldn't be

surprised. It's obvious she's the happy-go-lucky type, but meeting two guys for an afternoon of surfing—well, now just one guy—I'm not sure that's up her alley. I could head home, take a nap, maybe get some laundry done.

But then, I see her.

She's walking toward me, slow and barefoot, her sandals dangling from her fingers. She's wearing cutoff shorts and a sparkly pink bikini top, her hair now loose from the messy bun she wore earlier.

Damn. She looks *good*.

I couldn't look away even if I wanted to.

"Hey," she says, standing in front of me now, wearing the same smile she always does.

"Hey," I say back, dragging my eyes away from her lips, then hesitating for a moment before announcing, "Austin had to bail. It's just us."

"Oh, one-on-one lesson, lucky me." She winks.

I try to read her expression, wondering if she's just being flirty, or if she's disappointed—which I don't think is the case, but I need to do something to distract me from her body, so I hand her a board.

"Ever been surfing?"

"You know, it may seem like I should have, growing up in L.A. and all, but no. I've never even touched one." She admits it without a hint of sheepishness.

"No problem, it's easy to learn."

"Says the guy who has muscles on his muscles." She giggles, eyeing my shirtless body.

I can't help but chuckle. Haven't heard that one before.

We make our way closer to the water, stopping with enough space to run through the basics before jumping in.

"Okay, so basically, the main thing is to keep your balance and roll with the wave."

"That's it? That easy?" she teases.

"In theory."

She stands there holding the board like it might bite her if she makes any sudden moves. It's kind of cute, and something in her expression makes me want to laugh and protect her at the same time.

"Okay," I say, setting my board down on the sand. "Feet about shoulder-width apart, knees bent, balance centered. Don't lean too far forward or you'll eat it. Eyes up, where your head goes, your body follows."

I motion through the stance as I talk, then drop down onto the board, chest flat.

"From here, pop up quick." I push myself upright into position again. "Always keep your nose pointed toward the shore."

Her eyes whip from mine to the ocean.

"Come on," I say, tipping my chin toward the water. "It'll be fine."

She follows quietly—the first time I've seen her without her usual smiley, bubbly energy.

We carry the boards to the shoreline, going through the basics one more time, but I can tell she's not really listening. Her eyes aren't on the board.

They're on *me*.

And yeah, I notice.

I'm not blind.

When a beautiful girl is sneaking glances at your abs, you notice it. I'm actually starting to feel grateful that Austin isn't here.

The heat of the sun's catching up with me. A bead of sweat runs down my chest as I watch her try the pop-up. I step in to adjust her stance, forcing our proximity.

"Think you got it?" I ask, backing away.

"Uh… Not even the slightest bit."

I laugh. "Just give it a try."

"Alright, but if I die, *you* have to be the one to call my mom."

"Deal." I nod, grabbing one of the wetsuits from where I set them down earlier and hand it to her.

"Thanks." She grins, already pulling down her shorts, revealing more of her toned legs and the curve of her hips. I try not to stare and fail, miserably.

She slips into the wetsuit—more gracefully than I do— grabs the board, faking some confidence, and strides toward the water.

"Let me embarrass myself a bit before you come out and save me, yeah?"

I follow a step behind, still trying to get my head on straight, watching as she paddles out, misses one wave, then another. She tries to catch one, stands up, and immediately wipes out. Tries again—wipes out again.

She's determined, I'll give her that. But if she keeps this up, she's going to wear herself out. So, I swim out to meet her.

"Okay, okay," she says, spitting out seawater with a laugh. She treads water in front of me, one arm hooked on the board. "This is *not* my sport."

"You're not doing too bad," I lie. "I'll help."

We climb onto the board together, careful not to knock each other off. The board wobbles beneath us, her elbow brushing mine as she shifts. I steady her waist for balance, then pull her in front of me. She fits there naturally, her back pressed to my chest, her suit cool from the water, her hair wet and heavy with salt, her breath uneven from the exertion.

The waves rock us gently, and I can feel every movement of hers against me.

I steady us with my knees and cage her in with my arms. "Like a bird," I murmur near her ear, guiding her arms out.

She shivers.

It's not cold.

"You're too tense," I say.

Can I blame her? She's pressed against me, every movement and breath impossible to ignore, and I'm doing a terrible job pretending I don't feel every inch of her.

"Yeah, well, I could say the same about you when you're anywhere but here... apparently." She giggles.

I laugh because it's *true*.

For a minute, we just sit there. Quiet. Floating. Her back flush with my chest, the board rocking gently with the sea.

It's peaceful.

It's perfect.

It's *dangerous*.

And ironically, it's making me feel... relaxed.

"Alright, here comes a wave," I say, feeling the swell behind us. "You ready?"

She nods quickly. "Yes!"

We rise slowly. My hands secure her hips. The wave hits, and I keep my arms loosely around her, guiding her through the motion.

"Balance with me. Just follow the water."

She does.

We ride it in together. She yips with excitement, and when the wave dies, we tumble into the water. She surfaces after me, water streaming down her face from her wet hair, grin wide.

"That was so much fun," she says out of breath.

I can't help but smile back.

"Yeah?" I say, pulling the board toward us.

"Let's go again."

I happily oblige and after a few more mostly successful rides, we're spent. Layla suggests heading in, and I'm glad she did, because I'm not sure how much longer I could handle her sitting in my lap like that. It's not every day you've got a wet woman in a tight wetsuit with a little bikini underneath pinned against you and well, I'm a man.

We peel off our wetsuits and drop onto the sand. The sun's still bright, the waves choppier as the wind picks up. She leans back on her elbows, face tilted toward the sky, the breeze teasing her hair.

"That was too much fun," she says, eyes closed, soaking in the rays. "Thanks for teaching me."

"No problem."

She looks at me now. Full smile, chapped lips. "You always this serious?" she asks.

"Only when I'm thinking."

"You must *always* be thinking," she teases.

"Maybe so."

"What are you thinking about right now?"

I meet her eyes. They are locked onto mine, waiting for me to admit what's been in my head all afternoon.

"The truth?" I ask.

"Always."

"I'm thinking I'm glad you came today," I admit. "I didn't think I'd want company… Turns out I didn't mind yours."

She faces the sun again, eyes closed, and says quietly, "I don't know if that was a compliment but I'm taking it as one anyway."

I chuckle. "It's still early, you hungry?"

She pops one eye open and winks. "Starving."

19

Layla

THE LOCALS STARE AS LEO AND I WANDER TOWARD Dockfront, the waterfront restaurant tucked along Embarcadero Street.

We left the towels and surfboards in his truck. The wind has picked up, and I'm wrapped in Leo's hoodie. His offer after my not-so-smart decision to think a bikini top and daisy dukes would be enough for the day.

Sara told me that she hasn't seen Leo date. Not that *this* is a date, but to the locals watching us right now, it probably looks like one. I'm starting to think there's some truth to what she said based on their stares and whispers.

Dockfront is a cute little place with a perfect view of the harbor and Morro Rock. According to the sign out front, their Bloody Marys and crab cakes are *always* the special of the day, which both sound extremely appetizing after a couple hours of surfing with, for lack of a better description, a *hunk*.

In fact, the goosebumps that broke out the moment he pulled me practically into his lap on the board still haven't faded—and I'm not sure if I want them to.

Leo opens the door for me and follows me in. It's crowded, which makes sense for happy hour.

"Leo!" a tall, round man with dark hair, about the same age as Leo, calls from the kitchen. He makes his way over, wiping his hands on his apron.

"Hey, Nate." Leo greets him with a fist bump. "This is Layla."

"Ah, finally getting to meet the new girl in town," Nate says, turning his attention toward me. "Welcome to Morro Bay! Hope it's been treating you well."

I extend my hand for a handshake but am a little surprised when he pulls me into a hug. "I'm a hugger. A friend of Leo's is a friend of mine."

I enjoy the embrace, though he does smell a little like crabmeat.

He releases me and leads us to a table next to a large window overlooking the docks. "So, Leo, are you being chivalrous and showing the new girl around, or are you staking claim?" Nate teases.

Leo doesn't seem to find it that funny; he just rolls his eyes.

"Maybe *I'm* the one staking claim," I joke. "Just kidding."

Nate belly laughs and even Leo smiles at that one.

"That's good, Layla. See if you can get this dude to crack. He's a tough one."

So I've noticed.

"So, what'll it be?" Nate asks, clapping his hands together.

I look to Leo. "You're the local, why don't you order for us?"

He nods. "Let's do some crab cakes, some fish tacos, and a few grilled shrimp skewers."

He must be just as hungry as I am.

"Coming right up." Nate grins and hustles back into the kitchen.

I take in the ambience of the restaurant. Like Taboo, it's

decorated in coastal trinkets. Random lengths of netting and what looks like taxidermied tuna heads. It appears much smaller from the outside than it does inside. Natural light streams in through wide windows, and every table has a view, except for the counter lined with worn wooden barstools where a few locals sip those special Bloody Marys.

My eyes finally land back on Leo, who is now chugging down a glass of water a waiter just brought. He's gulping endlessly until his eyes meet mine. Then he sets the glass down, and wipes his mouth with the back of his hand.

"So," I ask, breaking the silence, "what happened with Austin today?"

"His grandma needed help," he says with a shrug. "And we took his car to the shop, so he's kind of stuck for now."

I smile. "He's lucky."

Leo raises a brow. "To have a broken car?"

"No," I laugh softly. "To have you. Someone to help him out."

He glances away, looking a little uncomfortable. "It's just the right thing to do."

"Maybe," I say, taking a sip of my own water. "But that doesn't mean everyone does it. Some people talk. You actually *do*."

He doesn't respond, just looks at me with a composed face.

"I've heard you're the kind of guy people can count on," I add.

I catch the slightest blush creeping up his neck. "Well... Don't believe everything you hear."

"Something tells me this one might be true."

He looks down, fighting a smile.

"Ooh! Food's here," I say, rubbing my hands together.

My intention isn't to make him uncomfortable, but Nate gave me the challenge of cracking Leo open, so maybe I'll push the limit.

Just a little.

———

The food is amazing.

Like really amazing and *so* fresh. I order a Bloody Mary for dessert, and it tastes like the garden gods hand-delivered the tomatoes and garnishes themselves.

Leo shares a bit of Dockfront's history, telling me it's one of the oldest buildings in Morro Bay. Nate inherited it from his grandfather, who passed away a few years ago. Back in the day, it was the go-to spot for the old-timer fishermen, the special always being the crab cakes.

"Can we split it?" I ask as the waiter drops off the bill.

"No, no. I got it," Leo says, already reaching for his wallet.

"It's the twenty-first century," I tease. "Women are allowed to help pay the tab."

He looks at me, stoic but with a hint of amusement in his eyes. "I'm aware. But I'm still paying."

I smile, leaning back slightly. No sense in arguing, and if I'm being totally honest, I kind of like a man who insists on picking up the tab.

Chivalry doesn't have to be dead.

"Where'd you park?" he asks as we step out of Dockfront, the evening air cooler now, the sky streaked in gold and lavender.

"Oh, I walked," I say, my fingers reaching for the hem of his hoodie. "My place isn't far."

I start to pull off the sweatshirt, but he stops me with a shake of his head.

"Keep it for the night. It looks better on you anyway," he says with a half smile that makes my cheeks warm. "It's chilly. I'll walk you home."

I should tell him it's unnecessary and that I'll be fine

walking alone. But I don't. Because the truth is... I like the idea of him beside me a little while longer. I like the way his hoodie smells like sea salt, driftwood and a hint of manly cologne.

And I like how... *just maybe*... he doesn't want the night to end, either.

20

Leo

THE SIGHT OF LAYLA IN MY HOODIE IS KILLING ME.

It swallows her whole. The sleeves hanging past her hands, the hem brushing her thighs, with only her legs and sandy toes showing.

It shouldn't be taking my full attention, but it absolutely is.

I try to shift my focus to small talk. She tells me a little about her life back in Los Angeles. About her parents, still married after twenty-five years. A fact that shouldn't sting, but does. She says she liked the chaos of city life when she was younger, but eventually it all felt hollow, and that's why she came here.

Which is only starting to make a little bit of sense to me.

She could be anywhere. Somewhere always warm, somewhere with a better balance of pace, somewhere a little more energetic. Somewhere that matches *her*.

And yet, here she is, wrapped in my hoodie, walking beside me like this little town is plenty.

She fills the silence between us as we walk the few blocks to her apartment. Her hair is still damp, smelling like the sea. I wouldn't know how to lead a conversation like she does. I wouldn't know how to make someone feel at ease just by being near them.

She's a natural at that.

All sunshine and no rain.

I feel like I'm the storm that most people avoid, and I wonder if her being around me will wear on her. If my heaviness drags her down without her realizing it. Some people soak up whatever energy is in the room.

I think she's like that, an empath.

She points out her building from down the street. One of the older apartments in town, tucked into a quiet nook.

She's still talking. Now about her friends back in L.A.: a girl named Mel, the sweetest person she knows, and another who drinks tequila much too often. I soak in every word, every giggle. Let her words take up the space around us.

But in the back of my mind, I wonder how long this lasts. How long before she gets restless. Before she realizes this town can't give her anything that she's used to.

We reach the bottom of her stairs.

"Thanks again for today," she says, turning to me with that same damn smile. "It was nice to get out and do something a little different."

"It was no problem," I say, matching her smile the best I can.

"I'll find an old surfboard and start practicing for next time."

"Next time?" I repeat.

"Yes, next time." She nudges my arm with her elbow. "This town's small, Leo. You're gonna have to share the ocean with me."

Another idea I don't hate.

"I suppose you're right about that," I say quietly.

She twists her lips into a grin. "You should really try showing some enthusiasm sometime. I'm all for the stoic charm, but you could break character once in a while, you know. It wouldn't kill you."

I laugh under my breath. "I'll try."

She grins again, glances at my lips at the same time I'm looking at hers. She lightly bites her lower lip then takes a deep breath.

"Well, goodnight," she says.

I feel stuck in a trance, a foreign urge to reach out and touch her, and I think she might feel the same.

I watched her gaze dip to my lips. Mine mirrored... If I wasn't so reserved, she might have kissed me.

But by the time I come back to reality, she's already halfway up the stairs, tossing a goodbye smile over her shoulder.

I watch her until the door clicks shut.

A feeling I don't recognize washes over me. Like her light is up against my shadow, and she's winning. Pushing me outside of my comfort zones by simply being herself. Unsettling me in ways that feel less like chaos and ache and more like peace.

And for the first time in a long time, I feel good.

I feel excited.

⸺

The house feels extra empty tonight.

Maybe it's because it's almost midnight and I'm still awake. I'm supposed to be sleeping, supposed to be resting for an early morning.

I thought a beer and a mind-numbing movie would do the trick, but the unexpected excitement from earlier has my adrenaline running a little too high that I can say goodbye to a full night's rest.

Again.

I glance at my guitar, still in the same spot, now with another layer of dust. I've been promising myself I'd restring it; I guess now's as good a time as any.

I open my junk drawer, finding the envelope of coiled guitar strings, and get to work. It's a therapeutic job with each turn of the peg tightening beneath my fingertips, each testing strum sending a vibration through my arm.

It takes about thirty minutes to restring and tune the guitar. Great if you don't want to spend too much time on the task, not so great if you're trying to kill the time.

I strum for a bit, trying to loosen up my rusty fingers.

It feels good to play again, kind of like saying hello to an old and dear friend. I'm out of practice, but if I pick it up a few times a week, I should sound pretty decent again. Maybe even make Mrs. Walker happy by playing down on Embarcadero at the next festival.

We'll see. For now, I'll play in the comfort of my own home.

My phone buzzes on the coffee table in front of me, a reminder of the text I missed from Nate earlier when I was walking Layla home.

I set my guitar back in its spot, now dustless, and check my phone.

> Barbecue at my place Sunday night. Bring the new girl.

I smile and think that I just might be able to do that.

21

Layla

It's been two days since my surf lesson with Leo.

Two *painfully* slow days. I feel like the art geek crushing on the prom king, finding myself glancing at The Busy Bean's front door every time it chimes, hoping a tall, strong, bearded man might just stroll in.

He hasn't stopped by. At least, not on my shifts.

I know the days get busy for those guys—sometimes the days even morph into one—so I'm trying not to think pessimistically. Trying not to think that I did something wrong or turned him away before I even had the chance to maybe bring him a little closer.

But then again, it really was *just* a surf lesson. One that was supposed to be more casual, with both him and Austin. The two of us spending that time together was an accident. It wasn't planned. And despite the obvious attraction between us, and the fleeting thought of kissing him, it's very likely Leo hasn't been thinking about it nearly as much as I have.

Probably not thinking thoughts like: *there is absolutely no way, not even the teeniest, slightest possibility, that I will ever, ever be able to erase the image of him standing on the beach next to two perfectly propped, colorful surfboards... shirtless, literally glistening in the sun.*

He also has a scar on his V-line—a very sexy and welcome image now branded into my brain.

All the closeness, the touching, the holding while he taught me to surf doesn't help, either, and all of this overthinking has amounted to me accidentally oversleeping this morning, making me late for work.

"Hey," I say, breathless, rushing through the door. "I'm so sorry I'm late."

Sara doesn't say hi. She just stands there with a giant, cheesy grin on her face.

I stop halfway from the front door to the counter. "Did I miss something? Someone win the lottery?"

"No." She giggles. "But *you* might have won the *man* lottery."

She marches from behind the counter and hands me a small folded piece of paper.

I open it:

I'll pick you up at your place at 8 - Leo

"He stopped by maybe fifteen minutes ago, asked if you were here, obviously you weren't, so he left you the note," she says, her smile still ginormous.

"Damn. Wrong day to be late to work, huh?" I laugh, feeling my cheeks flush as I stare at Leo's messy handwriting.

"There are going to be some really jealous girls around town." Sara laughs. "I don't know what you're doing, but keep it up. Leo Anderson has his eyes set on you."

The day drags on.

Normally, I'm happy to be at work. Happy to meet new people, hang out with Sara, and chit-chat with the locals I've grown familiar with.

But today is different. I can't *wait* to get out of here and get ready for my eight o'clock rendezvous with Leo.

When closing time finally comes, I don't stick around. On my way home, I stop by the corner market for a few necessities —milk, apples, bananas, eggs, the essentials.

The doorchime gives me away the second I step inside. I've been here a few times over the last month, but mostly I've been surviving on the free coffee and breakfast sandwiches at work.

I head for the dairy aisle, passing a couple of people I haven't met yet. I offer polite smiles but don't stop for small talk; I'm too eager to get home.

"Good evening!" the cashier calls from behind the counter. "Holler if you need help."

Two women by the produce section glance my way and whisper, loud enough for me to hear, "That's the girl Leo has been seen with."

Heat creeps up my neck and I pretend not to hear, biting back a smile as I suddenly become very interested in a carton of strawberries. Back home, no one cared what you were doing or who you were with. Here, it feels like every look is through a magnifying glass.

When I head for the register, I can still feel their eyes on me. I pay for my groceries, step outside, and hope the cool air will chase away the pink in my cheeks.

The girl Leo has been seen with. I laugh to myself. Word gets around fast in a small town—especially when it's about the most off-limits bachelor.

Once I'm home, I put away my groceries and throw a load of laundry in. I glance at the clock.

Damn. Still a couple of hours to kill.

I take my time in an "everything" shower—legs, bikini line, and pits shaved; hair washed; eyebrows plucked; feet exfoliated—though I think the sand has been doing a great job of that already.

I let my hair air-dry, scroll on my phone, send a quick text to a couple of my friends back home, my sister, then my parents. I stare at the ceiling for what feels like forever until seven p.m. hits.

Time to get ready.

I wear my hair down in its natural waves and put on tinted moisturizer, a light layer of concealer, some highlighter on my freckled cheeks, and nude eyeshadow followed by a few swipes of mascara.

I slip into my favorite ripped jeans, a skin-tight black T-shirt, and a light-weight jacket.

There's a knock at my door—eight o'clock, on the dot. I try to ignore the butterflies in my stomach and apply a quick layer of lip gloss, give my hair a once over and then head to the door.

"Right on time," I greet him.

"I'm always on time," he says with his deep, scruffy voice, offering a small smile.

My cheeks flush. *Again.* Suddenly, it's way too warm for this jacket.

"So, what's the plan tonight?" I ask, grateful for the cool draft drifting in from the door.

"A barbecue at Nate's house with the crew."

"Oh good. I was hoping food would be involved." I smile.

Sure, I'm hungry, but mostly I'm banking on food to smother the flutter in my belly.

I lock my apartment and follow him down the stairs to his seafoam-colored truck. An old, single-cab Ford pickup. He opens the door for me, I scoot in, and he closes it behind me, leaving a trail of his cologne.

Is that new? I haven't smelled that on him before. It's nice... but I think I like the salty wood aroma better. It's more *him*.

"You look nice," he says once inside, shifting in his seat a little. This time, he lets himself smile fully.

"Oh. Thanks." My cheeks burn hotter. "So, what's the occasion?"

"No occasion. Just something we do here and there."

I like that. Spending time together just *because*.

"Well thanks for including me," I say, softer this time.

He glances at me, presses his lips together and nods. "Of course."

Silence stretches for a minute before I blurt, "So... Busy at work?" I ask, trying not to give away that he's been on my mind for the last two days.

"Yeah, we're transitioning into the next season. It's been busy," he says, eyes on the road. "Boat's just about prepped, though. We'll get a few days off before we're back out there. Easy to get burnt out."

"By the looks of all the gear on the boats, I believe it."

"Our mornings will get busy again soon," he notes, looking over at me, "but evenings are open."

Evenings are open, huh? A hint at later shenanigans? Am I cracking through those stoic walls?

"Well, my mornings are busy, too. Sara and I like to tackle the rush together," I say. "Obviously, my job is nowhere near as busy or dangerous as yours, but if Ol' Gary doesn't get his morning latte, I hear he's a menace."

Leo belts out a laugh. "Gary's a menace with or without his latte." He turns down a road, the sun completely gone now. "And if he gives you any trouble, you tell him to come talk to me."

I giggle. "Gary loves me."

"Well, you're the only one, then."

A few minutes later, we pull into the driveway of a small, plain yellow house with a gravel pathway. Wind chimes sing in the breeze, and warm yellow lights glow from the windows.

Once we're out of the car, I realize I should've brought something. If I'd known it was a barbecue, I would've grabbed a dish or a bottle of wine. I hate showing up to places empty-handed.

"You good?" Leo asks, noticing my hesitation.

"Yeah, I just wish I had something to contribute."

"Don't worry about that, you're with me," he says, winking. "I caught most of the food they're cooking."

Oh.

The words spark something inside of me. *You're with me.* It's nothing, probably just Leo being casual, but still; it makes me see him in a different light. A little less broody fisherman, a little more… sweet.

Leo doesn't knock. He just opens the door and lets me step inside first.

Into the warmth of his friend's home.

Into his world.

22

Leo

THE MOMENT LAYLA AND I STEP INTO THE ROOM, ALL EYES ARE on us.

I can't help but feel a touch of pride having her right next to me, her arm just barely grazing mine. I'm not one for attention, but catching the subtle look of defeat on Austin's face feels like I just won a hand of cards. The hint of jealousy I'd felt at the bonfire the other night is gone now.

Now that she's here with me.

I smirk. I love the kid, but—*shouldn't have bailed, man.*

Nate's the first to greet us. "Hey, you two!" He pats my back and pulls Layla into a hug.

She hugs him back and then makes her way through the group, saying hello, shaking hands. First Rowdy, then Izzy and Austin and finally Kyle, who I'm somewhat surprised to see here.

"Nice to see you again, blondie." Kyle's eyes rake over her from head to toe like daggers, I'm sure stripping her bare in his mind.

A sudden rage ignites in my chest.

Kyle's always been a wild card, never sure if he's truly

on your team or just playing along. We tolerate him, but that wouldn't stop me from putting him on the ground if I had to. He's known to treat women like objects. Using them to his advantage and then tossing them aside for the next one.

I glare at him, the same way he's glaring at her.

His is lust.

Mine a warning.

He meets my eyes for a second before quickly shifting his focus back to his phone.

"Thanks for having me over tonight," Layla says to the room, breaking the tense quiet between Kyle and me.

Her voice, her smile—they bring ease back into the space.

"Sorry I had to bail the other day. My grams needed some help," Austin says.

"It's no biggie. Leo and I had a good time." She glances at me and winks, sending a warm rush through my body.

"Ugh, Layla, every time I look at you, I immediately get jealous. You're way too pretty to be hanging out with that smelly ol' fisherman," Izzy comments.

"Me? I would absolutely say the same about you." Layla grins, definitely earning points with Izzy.

"You must be something special," Hank murmurs. "Leo hasn't had female company in… who knows how long."

I want to say something back, something to shut him up, but I don't. Part of me welcomes the idea of Layla seeing I'm not some fuckboy. Not someone like Kyle.

She looks at me, smiles, then says, "He's just showing me around. Being the new girl in a tight-knit town isn't exactly the easiest thing."

"Mhm. Sure." Hank hands her a cold beer bottle. "I'm Hank. Here's a beer."

She takes it graciously. "Thank you."

"Let's all head out back. I'm just about done searing some

tuna, but the salmon's in the smoker," Nate says, clapping his hands together.

The crowd drifts outside to the backyard, and the air is heavy with the scent of smoked salmon. Nate inherited both his restaurant and this house from his grandparents, so it always feels a little nostalgic when I'm here.

We'd spent countless summer days and nights here as kids. His grandma made the best desserts—strawberry shortcake, specifically—and his grandpa had the best war stories. Nate even lost his virginity in the treehouse that is still clinging to the old oak. Broken and unstable now, but still carrying the same charm it had all those years ago.

Nate likes to get us together here as much as possible. It's healing for him, healing for all of us. Keeping those happy memories alive, even as time moves on and people leave this earth.

It's strange, living in the same lifetime as the people we love… only to have them taken too soon. Nate lost both grandparents to cancer. First his grandma, then, a year later, his grandpa. When his grandpa was diagnosed, he refused treatment. Said he didn't want to spend his last days sick in bed, that he'd rather go happy, ready to be with the love of his life again.

A love like theirs is rare.

My parents were each other's first loves, and their last. My dad once told me that when you meet that special person, you have to be capable of falling in love with them all over again in each phase of life. People constantly change, he'd said, and love is both a feeling and a choice.

He chose my mom—chose to love her, chose to learn her, every time she shed a shell and grew into someone new.

When my dad passed, my mom changed. She became dim, tired. Shedding the shell of the woman loved by a true man, and growing into the woman left behind by losing her true love. He was her everything, and without him, she was hollowed out, like someone had carved the center from her.

She does better now. She functions, stays busy with new friends, a new life. She keeps the grief tucked just beneath the surface. But it's never gone. You can see it in her eyes, in the way she stares off sometimes, like she's looking for him. And maybe that's the part that hurts the most. Knowing she'll always be searching for something she'll never find, holding onto a grief she'll never let go of.

Neither will I.

He was my best bud. He was everything to both of us, taught me all that I know about… well, *everything*.

"Where'd you go?" Layla's soft voice pulls me out of my thoughts.

I look at her. The backyard lights glint in her blue eyes, freckles scattered across her cheeks, her sweet smile patient, waiting. She knows my mind was somewhere else.

"Sorry. Just… a lot of memories in this place."

"It's good to reminisce," she says, pressing the beer bottle to her lips and taking a small drink. "Keeps us from falling too far forward in our thoughts."

She doesn't look at me when she says it. Just drinks her beer, casual, like her words aren't gut-punching. But she's right. Living in the moment while basking in happy memories is far more fulfilling—more soul-filling—than thinking too far ahead.

And she's kind of like that. *Soul-filling*. It's new—and I don't quite know what to do with it.

The night moves around us, both laughter and bickering spilling from Izzy and Rowdy, the scent of smoked salmon even stronger now.

But all I can focus on is *her*.

23

Izzy has handed me three beers now, but I'm still on my first.

One: the girl can drink. Two: she's beautiful.

Rowdy hit the jackpot, because even though he's fit and has the whole scruffy-and-tattooed look down, she's an eleven and he's maybe a seven.

She's keeping me company while Leo joins Nate and Hank inside to make our plates. Normally, when I think of a barbecue, I think of burgers and hot dogs, not tuna and salmon. But I guess I'll have to get used to more fish-based meals living here.

Blues music drifts from a speaker propped in the open kitchen window, the clear night sky letting the cool air roll in. Thankfully, a fire pit is full flame, providing some nice warmth.

"So, you two look cozy," Izzy says, scooting closer to me on the picnic bench. "I know you said he's *just* showing you around town, but I think we all know better."

I laugh. "Honestly, I wish I had more information to give you. He's a tough one to read."

"That is so true. Oh, I tried to get Sara out tonight, but she said she was binge-watching one of her comfort shows."

"That sounds like Sara."

"By the way, the shopping here is shit. So, I'm taking you to SLO soon for a better shopping experience." She takes a swig of her beer. "Rowdy says I have a shopping problem. I say I have a healthy outlet."

"Cheers to that," I say, clinking my bottle to hers.

"We're all really close—like *family* close," she continues, popping open another bottle. "Most of the guys have known each other their whole lives. Hank was close with Leo's dad; he worked under him his entire fishing career until Leo took over."

My heart stings. I'm learning that Leo's father was a very big part of his world.

"Does Leo ever talk about what happened with his dad?" I ask, not sure how to get the information without sounding insensitive.

"I'm sure he'll tell you about it sometime. It's a touchy topic. So yes and no, to answer your question."

Understood.

Nate makes his way outside after prepping a pasta salad, followed by Hank and a woman about my age, with a blonde pixie cut, who must have just shown up.

"Ugh, gag. *Charlie's* here," Izzy says, rolling her eyes.

"Charlie?"

"Yeah, that girl." She points to the woman with Nate and Hank, now caught up in conversation with them. "That's Charlie. She's harmless, but she's annoying. She's a local, works at one of the boutiques that her mom owns, never really had any ambition to do more than that, and she's had this major crush on Leo since forever." She rolls her eyes again. "Total waste of time. Leo's only ever seen her as more of a distant little sister."

"I mean, I can't blame her. Leo is... Well, he's easy on the eyes," I joke.

"Ha, good point!" she says, standing. "Now go give your guy some attention before Charlie follows him around like a lost puppy."

I don't think I need to worry about Charlie. She's been in his orbit a long time and hasn't been able to reel him in. That speaks for itself, but I won't pass up the chance to be near him.

Almost like the universe agrees, the sliding glass door opens and Leo leans out, tipping his chin toward me. "Want to come in and tell me how much you want on your plate?"

I nod and make my way to the kitchen, finding him standing in front of a buffet-style spread of food on the beige-tiled counter.

"Wow, this looks amazing. Nate made all of this?" I ask.

"He did—he's a pretty good chef." He pauses. "I wanted to bring you a plate, but I, uh... wasn't sure how much to put and didn't want to seem rude if I put too much or too little or something."

I want to laugh at how precious that is. But it's sweet and thoughtful. And the last thing I want is to make him shut down again when he's finally starting to open up. So I swallow the giggle and let it stay mine.

"I think I'll just take a little bit of everything," I say, turning to reach for a plate. But Leo turns at the same time, and our shoulders collide.

His breath catches.

Mine follows.

Our hands land on the same plate, fingers brushing, neither of us pulling away.

Neither of us *wanting* to.

We're close. Face-to-face, close enough to see the tiny flecks of gold hidden in his deep green eyes. Close enough to feel the warmth radiating off of him, to breathe in the salt and salmon smoke clinging to his skin. Close enough to witness the plump of his lips.

His chin dips, gaze moving down to my mouth.

He swallows. My lips part. My throat desert-dry.

The world holds still, my pulse hammers, and every nerve in my body begs me to just woman up and kiss him.

And then—the kitchen screen door screeches open.

"Oh, sorry." Charlie stumbles over her words. "I was just going to ask you to grab some more beer from the fridge."

She's talking to Leo. Not me.

Leo lets out a heavy sigh, eyes still locked on mine. "Yeah, I'll grab some."

Silence lingers. She's still standing there, clearly fishing for more, but Leo doesn't bite.

"Charlie, right?" I say, finally breaking the unbearable silence and turning to face in her direction.

"Yeah."

"I'm Layla." I pause, feeling Leo's gaze slip away. "I like your hairstyle."

"Thanks," she mutters, rolling her eyes before heading back out.

I look back at Leo; he's still close, but already focused on loading up two plates. He hands one to me.

"Here. A little bit of everything." He gives me a small smile, then carries his plate outside.

I stand there for a second, letting go of a heavy breath. Then I follow him out, sliding into the seat beside him.

We eat in silence, the charge between us still *very* much present.

⁓

Leo was right, Nate can make good food, and I haven't had a

home cooked meal in quite some time. So this is just what my body needed.

Leo and I are still side by side, bellies full of food, but I somehow have room for another beer. I'm not much of a constant beer drinker, but maybe that's just another change I'll have to get used to here. Besides, I think I might be learning to like it.

"So…" Charlie cuts in, and for a second I brace for an awkward moment at my expense. Instead she says, "Sam's on his way. Hope you don't mind me inviting him."

Leo tenses immediately next to me, and I can almost feel the flex in his muscles.

He turns to her slowly. "*What?*"

Everyone goes quiet. Hank sparks up a cigarette, Austin looks confused, Rowdy squeezes Izzy's hand and Kyle shifts uncomfortably.

"What did you just say?" Leo asks, clenching his jaw.

Charlie talks quieter this time. "I said Sam's on his way."

Leo bolts up, visibly angry. "Are you fucking with me right now? *Why* in the hell would you invite him?"

She looks ashamed for a brief moment, but still holds her ground. "People change, Leo. Give the guy a chance."

"A chance? You're fucking with me, right?" He clenches his fist. "He has brought a lot of people a lot of fucking pain. He's wrapped in some shit, Charlie—you don't need to be messing around with him."

Leo turns to Nate. "Did you know he was coming?"

"No, man," Nate says, looking just as surprised as Leo. "I wouldn't have been okay with that. I'm *not* okay with it."

"Like I said, I invited him," Charlie says, picking at a fingernail. "Kyle didn't think it was an issue."

Kyle flinches at his name. "Leo, calm down. We're adults, remember?" His gaze slides to me. "No reason to be rude in front of your new friend."

Leo's face turns red. "Leave her out of this. And you know damn well what the problem is."

Nate stands up and claps his hands together. "This conversation is over. Charlie, uninvite Sam. Kyle, I think it's time you go home."

"Seriously?" Kyle contests. "What did I do?"

"Honestly, I don't know, but I feel like you're stirring the pot here," Nate says.

Kyle scoffs, shaking his head. I stay quiet, my body tense. I can feel the anger, the resentment. Charlie glances at me quickly, then looks away.

Before anyone else can chime in, a tall, gangly man with hollow cheeks walks through the side gate.

"Hey, heard my name," he says with a scratchy voice, smirking.

Leo's face falls. My heart beats quicker.

This must be Sam.

24

Leo

"We're leaving," I say to Layla, who looks completely lost. "Sorry, Nate. You know I can't be here right now."

Nate starts to respond, but Sam cuts in over him. "That bad, huh?"

His voice is smug, knowing exactly what he's doing, daring me to snap in front of everyone.

I ignore him and hold my hand out to Layla, hoping she can read the room. "We are leaving."

Her eyes dart from me to the others, but she doesn't argue. She takes my hand and offers a quick goodbye to everyone— everyone except Sam, Charlie, and Kyle. The silence behind us heavy as the side gate bangs shut a little too loud.

By the time we get in my truck, my pulse is pounding. I'm gripping the wheel, fighting the urge to turn around and put Sam on the ground like I've wanted to for years but the drive stays quiet. Just the dark stretch of road in front of us as I try to focus on anything other than him.

I tilt my head back and catch a glimpse of the crescent moon hanging in the sky.

To my left, shops line the street with fleeting gaps of dark sea between them. When I look to my right, the faint scent of Layla's shampoo drifts toward me as she looks back, catching me staring. She offers a polite smile.

Ten minutes later, we're almost back to her place. She's been quiet, probably trying to gauge just how mad I am.

"I'm sorry," I finally say, my voice rougher than I mean it to be. "Sam Murphy is bad news. I just… can't be in the same place as him."

She nods, her hands folded in her lap. "I figured it was something like that."

I exhale hard through my nose, pulling onto her street and putting the truck in park in front of her building. "I know you probably expected to stay longer."

"It's okay," she says, then twirls a piece of hair around her finger. "Just because we left them doesn't mean we can't hang out a little longer."

I feel a smile creep onto my face, contrasting with what I was feeling just moments ago.

"Yeah?"

"Come on," she says, opening the door and hopping out with a playful look over her shoulder. "I have Scrabble."

I'm not sure how this woman redirects my mind so easily.

One minute, I'm face-to-face with her in a kitchen, seconds from kissing her. The next, I'm staring down Sam Murphy. And now, somehow, I'm playing Scrabble and eating a bowl of popcorn mixed with chopped pickles.

If I wasn't with her, I'd be home right now, trying to distract myself from driving back to Nate's and showing Sam how I really think things should be handled.

He's a poison. A toxic presence. He was supposed to be in jail—supposed to stay there for manslaughter after he pumped too much of that shit into his "buddy's" veins, causing an overdose. But now he's back, and from Joey's relapse, it looks like he's back in business, too. Pulling Charlie and whoever else down with him.

"Dang, twenty-point word. How you gonna beat that, *Captain?*" Layla's voice snaps me out of it. A sunny smile, even though it's almost midnight.

"I probably *can't* beat that," I admit.

"I like a humble man." She giggles. "I think that score means I win."

"You've earned it. It's yours."

She stands up and takes a dramatic bow. "Thank you, thank you."

I laugh. Damn.

She's way too fucking cute.

"Winners need hydration, so I'm grabbing some water. Losers, too. Thirsty?"

"Water sounds great," I say, clearing the Scrabble board and leaning back on the couch.

She grabs a couple of water bottles from the fridge and drops in the seat next to me.

"I'm sorry again for earlier," I say, still feeling bad about Nate's barbecue—especially after he texted me to say he'd kicked Sam, Charlie, *and* Kyle out just after we left. "Sam has caused a lot of trouble in my circle of friends. I thought he was gone for good, but clearly, that's not the case. So I guess I'm just... I don't know."

"Adjusting?" she offers.

"Exactly."

She sets her water bottle on the coffee table, scoots further up on the couch and sits cross-legged.

"I don't know him," she says, "but I know the type. Guys like that don't stop because you fight harder. They stop when they destroy themselves, and they *always* destroy themselves."

She leans forward, eyes locked on mine.

"You can throw punches, and you can lose sleep and carry that weight like it's all yours to hold. But it's not." Her tone becomes more sincere. "You said he's poisonous. And if you keep letting him take up space in your head, he'll poison you, too."

"I wish it was easier to ignore," I admit.

She leans back again. "I think you should let karma do what it does best. People like him always end up on their knees, begging the world to save them from the mess they made." She sighs. "You don't have to be the one who cleans it up every time."

I can't argue, because she's… right.

"I mean," she continues, "unless the universe hands you the perfect chance to put an end to this for good, you're probably better off just being there for your friends and letting the rest fall into place."

"Besides," she adds, "you have more important things to focus on. Your crew, your boat, the new season rolling in, and —" she pauses, the smile growing on her face, "—maybe even the new girl in town who will likely continue to kick your ass in Scrabble."

Fuck.

That smile. Those freckles. That damn sweet voice.

Every word out of her hits me. Things I need to hear, leaving her mouth so effortlessly.

She can't be real.

No one has ever challenged me like this or verbalized permission to let things just *be.*

As if she's some kind of angel.

That's the only explanation. Dropped here to throw my world off balance with her charming smiles and deep blue eyes.

I sit up, turning toward her, trying to find something clever to say, but I come up empty. She's watching me now, like she knows what I'm thinking and she's already decided not to stop me.

I could kiss her.

Right now.

I want to.

I need to.

Fuck it.

I lean in slowly, allowing her enough time to pull away, to say no, to tell me I'm reading this wrong. But she doesn't move, she just studies me. So I close more of the distance between us, our breath mingling now. A strand of hair drops from behind her ear and dangles in front of her lips. I tuck it back, the coarse skin of my finger offset by the smoothness of her.

Her breath swells in her chest, lifting her softly as her perfect lips fall open.

It starts in our eyes, before our lips even touch. A look that can only be explained in poetry. The kind that doesn't make you wonder, the kind that isn't open for interpretation.

So... I kiss her.

God, I kiss her.

25

Layla

His beard smells like barley and salt; his tongue tastes like it, too, but better.

Sweeter.

His mouth claims mine, lips parted just enough for a teasing tongue. Our lips move in sync with each movement. He tilts his head slightly one way, allowing more room for his nose to press into the curve of mine, his tongue slipping in deeper.

He takes one of his hands and rests it on my waist; the other finds the small of my back, pulling me closer to him. The swell of my breasts press against his powerful build, making me more hungry for him. Making me want to rip off his shirt and touch the bareness of his chest.

Heat rushes through me at the thought, my heart races and spreads tingles down to my belly, then my legs, even my toes.

His kiss deepens as his fingers dig deeper into my side, into my back. I lift my hands to his face, cupping each side of his jaw with my palms, absorbing the softness of his beard.

I move my fingers to his hair and tangle them with it,

pulling lightly. An almost quiet sound escapes his lips, proof of the pleasure he takes in it.

His movements start to slow, and gradually the kiss ends.

Gone much too soon.

I open my eyes just as he opens his and he drinks me in.

He starts with my eyes, moves to my swollen lips, the nape of my neck, and finally the curve of my breasts. His eyes dart back to mine, and he takes a deep breath. Fighting himself.

He exhales heavily. "I should go." His voice is raspy and broken.

"Okay," is all I whisper.

Because I know he's leaving to be a gentleman. Because he knows if he stays, there's no way either of us would stop before things maybe went a little too far. That kiss, full of yearning and lust, was enough to show us both what's coming.

He stands up and offers a hand. I place mine in his, and he pulls me up gently. His thumb brushes over the top of my knuckles, distracting me from the shake in my knees.

He licks his lower lip before bending down and planting a soft kiss.

For a minute, I think he's changed his mind, that maybe he'll stay and we'll see this night through. But he is a man of his word, so he lets my hand go and steps toward the door.

"Sleep well, Layla," he says with his husky voice.

Our eyes stay fused together, until he's outside and closing the door behind him.

The click echoes through the silence, leaving me alone in the midst of everything we didn't say. My fingers brush my lips, still buzzing with the ghost of his kiss. My heart pounds beneath my palm, unable to catch its breath.

There's no way I'm just crawling into bed after that. After *him*.

I allow myself a minute to compose, replaying the kiss over

and over until it's etched into my brain, making it impossible to ever forget.

Then I exhale and shake it off, slip into a big, comfy T-shirt before curling beneath the patchwork quilt my grandmother made. I pull my sketchbook from under the bed, grab the trusty pencil that always waits in my nightstand, and start to draw—a habit I've kept since I was nine.

First, the docks, making sure that every board is etched perfectly, then the boats, tired from years of working the sea. My pencil moves easily.

Then, I find myself drawing a man.

A man with broad shoulders, thick hair and deep green eyes full of tragedy and tides. My pencil lingers there and at some point, the lines blur, and the sketch fades beneath my heavy eyelids.

The alarm on my phone buzzes, pulling me from a dream where Leo Anderson was on my couch, kissing me.

Except it wasn't a dream.

In fact, I can still taste him every time I run my tongue over my lips.

I officially can't remember the last time I got a full night's sleep. Because here I am again, making minimal effort in an oversized crop top and some old leggings. I did, however, manage to brush my teeth, my hair, and wash my face.

It's okay—last night was worth it.

I skipped my jog this morning, opting for an extra hour of sleep before my shift. Luckily, it's not the earliest one. But I know the guys were working on the boats, so I probably missed my chance to catch a glimpse of them.

A glimpse of *him.*

No time to dwell, I have to get to work.

I waltz in, on time to my surprise. The place is empty, besides Sara, who is scrolling on her phone on the barstool behind the counter.

"Girl, I have so much to tell you," I say, clocking in.

"Um, spill the tea!" she squeals. "Hold on, I'll make us some coffee."

She throws together a couple of hot lattes and sits in front of me like I'm about to present a speech. "Spill."

"We kissed," I blurt.

Sara's jaw drops. "You kissed... *who?*"

I roll my eyes. "Sara."

"Just clarifying, because that is going to be hot news around here."

I take a sip of my latte, the warmth running down my throat feeling extra cozy today. "Not everyone needs to know. I think Leo likes to lay low, right?"

"Don't worry, I won't go blabbing, but if you guys spend more time together, people are *definitely* going to put two and two together."

"I'm kind of hoping that happens." I wink.

"So, what else did I miss last night?"

I almost forgot about Nate's barbecue and my semi-introduction to the town's snake—Sam. It all seems so insignificant after the kiss.

"That Sam guy showed up and as soon as he did, Leo and I split," I say, remembering the look on Leo's face when Sam walked into the backyard.

"Oh no, that's not good. They've had beef since forever. No one wants Sam here, and the only person who's ever been willing to step in is Leo."

Of course he's the one to step in.

"Well, I'm hoping this situation stays quiet—" I pause, taking another sip, "—because I'm planning to take most of Leo's attention."

26

I'm taking inventory of the boat, making sure everything's ready for the next haul in a few days. Plus, we have an overnight trip coming up that we need to be prepared for.

My eyes sting from lack of sleep; I didn't get one damn wink last night for two reasons.

One, because Sam Murphy showed up knowing it would be a problem, like the piece of shit he is.

And two, because... Well, *fuck*. That kiss with Layla nearly did me in. One more second in that apartment and I would've been ripping her clothes off, doing things that neither one of us could come back from.

I want her.

Bad.

She's the distraction I didn't see coming. The kind I haven't allowed myself to want in a long time, and yet—*God help me*—I feel it now. I want to take her advice and focus on my life, my crew and the next trip out. Focus on keeping my head on straight, even if my mind keeps drifting back to her and that fuckin' kiss.

I saw her in a different light, more than just the sweet new girl. She was raw and unguarded with me, and I don't know if I deserve it. I don't know if I deserve *her*.

We haven't even exchanged numbers yet. Old-school, I guess. But I kind of like the idea of having to earn it. I'll figure out a way to see her again, something creative, something that'll make her smile.

I've had flings before, maybe too many. It's an easy thing to get wrapped up in when you have tourists hanging around in the summer. Easy to meet someone without promising commitment.

But Layla isn't a fling. She can't be, she's too good, too rare. Already much closer than I meant to let her get.

And I don't think I want to stop it.

"Looks like everything's here, boss," Austin says, walking up behind me, bringing me back to the present. "We could probably add a couple bait bins, but otherwise, we're lookin' good."

"Great. Thanks, Austin."

He grins. "Oh, and thanks for takin' me to Marty's. He gave me, like, an insane deal on my car. I mean, stupid cheap. I almost felt bad walking out of there."

Yeah, because I paid about seventy percent of the bill. Austin's on a tight budget, taking care of his grandma. But there's no need for him to know that.

"Glad it worked out," I say. "If you're done here, feel free to head home."

Hank and Rowdy wander over, stomping their boots and smelling like smoke.

"Lookin' good, Cap," Rowdy says, sticking a cigarette between his lips.

"Agreed," Hank mumbles, stealing the cigarette. Rowdy lets him have it and lights another.

"I'm gonna run one last check, maybe take her out for a spin," I say, holding my clipboard. "You guys can head out."

Hank nods and leaves, but Austin and Rowdy linger, watching me like I'm forgetting something.

"What?" I ask.

They exchange a look. Austin giddy, Rowdy puffing.

"What?" I repeat.

Rowdy speaks first. "Izzy's got a soft spot for Layla. So if you're not planning on keepin' her around... It might be a problem."

Ah. There it is.

"Sounds like a *you* problem," I say with a smirk. "Not a *me* problem."

"I'm just sayin', this is new for all of us, so give me a heads-up if this is just some kind of hookup thing you got going on."

I expected some prying from Austin, but Rowdy?

Austin leans in. "Come on, man. Just tell us. You like her?"

"Go home," I mutter, hanging the clipboard on the hook.

Austin mumbles something about missing his chance on his way off the boat. Rowdy stomps out his smoke and follows.

Finally.

Peace.

I need a minute. Just me and the ocean. The only place that doesn't expect me to talk or lead or solve. Where I don't have to pretend I've got it all figured out.

I welcome the familiar and comforting sway of the boat rocking beneath me. The sea is the only place I've really felt like myself since Dad died. Out here, I can still hear his voice walking me through a bowline knot or yelling about rust on the railings.

It's not the same without him. It never will be. But somehow, being out on the water makes the ache just a little bit quieter.

Like the tide pulls some of it away.

27

JUST AS I'M CLOCKING OUT, I GET A CALL FROM A NUMBER I don't recognize.

"Hello?"

"Hey, it's Iz. Where are you?" Izzy's high-pitched voice on the other end of the line makes me happy.

"Just about to leave work."

"Stay there, I'm picking you up."

Before I can ask any questions, she hangs up. Sara probably gave her my number.

Speaking of Sara, she already went home for the day. After I spilled all the juicy gossip, we had some lunch, and then she went to take a nap. Dan is manning the fort until closing time.

I wait on a bench in front of The Busy Bean. A few minutes later, a shiny black convertible pulls up.

"Hey!" Izzy calls from behind extra-large sunglasses. "Get in, we're going shopping."

Right. Her kryptonite.

"Oh, I don't really need anyth—"

"Nonsense. You always need something new." She glances

over my outfit, and lowers her sunglasses down her nose. "Obviously, you're beautiful and all, but we can probably find something more fun for you to wear."

I laugh as I slide into the front seat. "Hey, I'm tired. Last night was a roller coaster, I chose an extra hour of sleep instead of style today."

"Well, you didn't miss much after you guys left. After Nate made the troubled trio leave, we all kind of trickled out. The vibe was killed."

I'm glad Nate made them leave—their presence was clearly unwelcome. Then I smile to myself, remembering what happened *after* the drama.

For now, I decide to keep it hush from Izzy.

"That Sam guy is… creepy."

"That's an understatement, but definitely steer clear of him, Lay," she says with a soft smile as she drives us out of town. "Is it cool if I call you that?"

"I love it. Nice ride, by the way."

"Rowdy got it for me," she grins. "He buys me anything I want. All I have to do is love him."

I laugh at how casually she says it. "Is he easy to love?"

"Oh, dear God, no. These guys love the ocean more than anything, so you have to learn that you will never be number one," she says, driving faster. "I've accepted it."

"By the looks of you two, it seems to be working out. I bet the cars and clothes are a perk."

"I do love him a lot. It's not *just* about the stuff he gets me." She winks. "He buys nothing for himself, like *nothing.* He still wears the same three pairs of jeans he's had for, like, seven years or something."

"Oh, no."

"Honestly, I make decent money. I bought the house we live in. He is by no means a sugar daddy. If it weren't for my income, we'd be living like the rest of the fishermen do out here."

"Like Leo?" I ask, my ears perking at the word *fisherman*.

"Yep. He has his own place on the outskirts of town," she says as she merges onto the freeway, talking loudly over the wind. "Hank lives down the road from him. They like their space."

I've noticed.

"But both beautiful souls," she adds. "Hank is just old and grumpy. Leo is more… poetic, I guess. More sensitive, even though he doesn't like to admit it."

"Poetic?"

"Yeah, he writes songs and plays the guitar and shit."

Oh. Well, if that didn't make him more desirable, I don't know what will. "I'm going to have to see this for myself."

"I'm sure you will." She winks.

———

"Here we are," Izzy says as we pull up to a clothing store.

She drove us out to San Luis Obispo—not too far from Morro Bay, but just far enough to have more shopping options than the local boutiques.

We spend about an hour rummaging through the store, making small talk. Izzy grew up in Morro Bay, got a work-from-home sales job a couple years after high school, started dating Rowdy shortly after, and has been with him ever since. He's older than her by eight years, which she likes because, in her mind, any man closer to her age is at least ten years younger in "man years."

She helps me pick out a new pair of jeans, a burgundy sweater with a little heart stitched into the sleeve, and a beautiful, long, navy maxi dress.

She also finds a nice pair of sandy-colored wedges. "Here

—these will match literally anything, and you need to have them."

I agree. They're gorgeous *and* on sale.

"Oh! They have throw blankets here, too! Here, this looks *so* cozy," she says, tossing a dark teal throw into our cart. "You can hang it over your couch."

Again, I agree. It would look great on my couch.

Couch.

Leo.

Leo kissing me *on* my couch.

I can't help but think of him and wonder what he's doing right now. Out on the water, where he belongs. Sharing a bite and a beer with the boys. Or maybe drifting into a nap after a long, bone-tired day.

"Earth to Lay?" Izzy appears in the aisle where I'm zoning out. "I asked if you were hungry."

Oops.

"Actually, yes. Very hungry."

She nods and leads the way to the checkout. "This is on me today," she says, handing her credit card to the clerk.

"What? No way, I couldn't let you—" I start, but she cuts me off.

"Yes, you can and you will." She smiles. "We take care of each other here."

My heart warms. *We take care of each other here.*

This—*this* is exactly why I wanted to live in a smaller community. People like Izzy, dynamics like *this.*

"Well, thank you. Very much." I give her a hug, enjoying the scent of her citrus-y perfume.

"You're welcome." She smiles as we head back to her car. "Let's go get a bite to eat at Dockfront. Nate will hook us up."

She revs the engine, cranks up the Indie pop music, and speeds away.

28

Leo

THE OCEAN IS CALM TODAY, JUST HOW I LIKE IT. THOUGH, I don't mind tangoing with the sea here and there.

Man vs. Nature.

Nature will always win, so I may tease it a little, but will always surrender, because the ocean knows no mercy.

I should have thought ahead and brought my guitar, now that it's restrung and ready to go.

I learned to play out here. Dad would teach me on our overnight trips. He'd play a lullaby for the water, or some kind of fun sea shanty that we'd sing together until the night grew dark.

If you listen real close, the ocean sings back to you, he would say. I swear, I hear his voice ride in the waves some days. *If you give a gift to her, she will always repay you.*

I never knew exactly what he meant until I was older. As a kid, I thought he was talking about tossing a fish back or something. But Dad meant more than that. He meant respect and patience. Knowing when to take, and when to walk away with empty hands.

Sometimes we'd leave an extra crab pot untouched, or

release a haul if the season felt thin. Sometimes it was a whisper of a thank-you, speaking to someone I couldn't see.

He really was my best friend. A true man, a genuine and gentle soul. A great father and husband.

I was lucky to have parents like mine—summer camping trips, weekly boat adventures, and home-cooked meals almost every night.

We never really had much money. Dad was top of the chain when it came to fishing, but the haul didn't always profit much. He often donated a portion of his catches to the local grocers and shelters, making sure everyone ate, though it left himself with less than half. Still, he took care of us. We always had a roof over our heads, and we never went hungry. Never went without.

He took care of everyone.

I think about that now as I lie on the floor of my boat. A boat that used to be *his*. My face toward the sky, the sun just past its peak, still offering its rich vitamin D and energy.

The boat rocks, creaking with every roll, syncing with every wave.

Sam doesn't exist here; he can't poison these waters.

I close my eyes and try to enjoy my happy place, but I find my mind wandering.

What's typically blackness, empty thoughts, and meditation with the sounds of gulls and a cool breeze is now infiltrated with… *her.*

Her bright eyes, wavy hair.

Her big smile and ethereal laugh.

Her fragrance, her body.

Her *mind.*

Is now consuming mine.

And for the first time in years, I don't really feel like being alone.

I feel like being closer to her.

I pull up to The Busy Bean. I'm not entirely sure if she's still here this late—pretty sure they're closing soon, actually, but if luck's on my side, she's on the closing shift, and maybe I'll get to steal her away for the night.

Walking inside, I feel a little let down. She's not here. Just a picture of her and Sara pinned to the bulletin board behind the counter.

"Hey, Leo. Late in the day for a cup. Must have been a day, huh?" Dan, the owner, greets me.

"I was actually looking for—"

"Layla," he finishes with a grin, pouring a cup of coffee. "Here, on the house. Have a seat."

I suppose I could stay for a minute.

"Thanks, Dan."

"No problem." He sits down on the barstool behind the counter. "Getting ready for the next season?"

"Oh yeah, we're ready. We've got a couple more days of freedom, then we're back at it."

"I have a feeling it's going to be a profitable one," he says, drinking from his own cup.

"I hope so. The boys need it."

There's a moment of silence. Just two men drinking plain black coffee. It's nice, but it's not why I came here.

Dan is the first to break the quiet. "She's a good one, you know—Layla. Customers really like her."

I hide a small smile behind the rim of my mug. "Yeah, I can see that."

He smirks. "Anyway, she hopped in a black convertible earlier. Few hours ago, maybe."

Black convertible—Izzy's new ride. She must have taken

her out. I warm at the thought of my world merging with Layla's.

I gulp down my last bit of coffee and bring the mug to Dan. "Thanks, Dan. I'll bring you a cut from our first tuna haul."

"Can't wait," he says with a semi-toothless grin, taking my mug.

If Lalya and Izzy have been out for hours already, there's a good chance she'll be back soon. But I can't show up at her place smelling like my boat—fishy and musty.

I'll run home, shower, and change.

Then, I'll go to her.

29

Layla

We park along Embarcadero, right in front of Dockfront. Izzy's speedy driving got us back in record time; she wanted to beat the rush to make sure she could get her hands on some crab cakes.

Nate's expression, as he spots us walking toward the front of the restaurant, catches me off guard. The usual brightness in his smile is absent.

He stops us at the door. "Not a good time, ladies."

"What? Why?" Izzy asks, sounding aggravated. "You're not closed, are you?"

Nate mumbles that it's not a good time and he'll explain later. I look past him as he and Izzy hash it out. Most of the tables are empty—except for one.

Sam.

My stomach drops. I tug gently on Izzy's arm. "Izzy… We can just eat somewhere else. It's no biggie."

She doesn't seem to notice Sam, she's too focused on Nate. "Fine, but I'm pissed. I was really craving those crab cakes."

"I'm sorry," he says, watching us walk away, his expression

apologetic but turning his focus to the crowd entering the restaurant.

"Sorry about that. I know another place down the street. But it's small, and they don't have a bathroom," she says. "Hang tight for a minute. I really need to pee."

She heads toward the public restroom right across the street before I can mention spotting Sam. I find a bench to wait at, still feeling uneasy knowing he is so close.

Like clockwork, I sense a presence—aware I'm no longer alone.

He must have slipped past Nate, or maybe found a side door, because now he's at the bench, hand outstretched, introducing himself like I don't already know who he is.

"Sam Murphy."

I'm not sure if I should pretend I don't know he's a snake, shake his hand, or make a run for it toward the bathroom. My body tenses, my brain on high alert.

"Cat got your tongue?" He chuckles and sits down next to me, resting his hands in his lap.

Sam is tall and skinny but still muscular. A rat-shaped face, big, beady brown eyes and all.

"Hi," I say, wishing Izzy wasn't taking so long.

"I saw you with Leo at Nate's. You his girl or something?" he asks, tucking chewing tobacco along his gumline.

"We're friendly," I say, keeping my words to a minimum.

"Friendly? *Cute.* Where is he, anyway?"

"Not sure. I'm with another friend today."

Thankfully, Izzy re-emerges from the bathroom, notices Sam next to me, and picks up her pace.

"Sam," she says smugly once she reaches us, "can you do us all a favor and crawl back in the hole you came from?"

"Izzy," he snickers, "always a pleasure to see you."

"Let's go, Lay," she says, grabbing my hand and pulling me away from the bench—and from Sam.

He watches us leave, unbothered, still smirking.

"Why is he here?" I ask quietly. "I saw him inside the restaurant, I thought Nate wasn't a fan."

"Who knows and no, Nate is *not* a fan, but I'm sure he'll fill us in later. Now it makes sense why he turned us away," she says as we walk down the street. "Sam's fucking scum. We hooked up once when I was much younger, before I met Rowdy, obviously, and before he got into the drug bullshit. Biggest mistake of my life."

She pauses, glancing back at the bench where Sam still sits. "He wouldn't leave me alone for months after. Rowdy had to step in, that set him straight." She opens the door to a small café. "That's how Rowdy and I bonded, actually. He was my knight in shining armor."

"Leo was there, too," she adds. "He always is. That guy is just everything good."

I smile, warmth replacing some of the tension in my chest. "I'm starting to see that."

"He might be this borderline-grumpy, minimal-words kinda man," she says with a light chuckle, "but he *always* shows up."

Her expression shifts, sadness slipping in at the edges. "Just like his dad used to. He was always a friendly face."

I have questions. Questions that will help me see even deeper layers of Leo. But I don't want to push. If he wants me to know more, he'll tell me when he's ready.

"They were really close," she says. "Like, *really* close."

"I get that," I say gently. "I'm close with my parents, too, more so when I lived at home, but I honestly don't know what I'd do if something ever happened to them."

"Well… Leo didn't know what to do, either. Still doesn't." Her voice lowers. "He disappears sometimes. A few hours, sometimes days out there in the ocean on his boat. I don't think he ever got the closure he needed."

"That's awful," I whisper.

We move forward in line, now standing in front of the register. The teenage guy behind the counter is ready to take our orders.

Izzy looks at me. "Leo likes you, Layla."

I feel myself blush. "Yeah?"

"He's never introduced us to anyone before—not before he lost his dad, not ever. And I've known him a long time." She smiles, then leans in a little. "I mean, sure, we all know he's been with women. He's a man, after all. But none of us have ever met any of them. He always says he's too busy, claims he's emotionally unavailable." She rolls her eyes. "I call bullshit. He just hadn't met the right one yet."

I don't say anything. My heart is beating way too fast.

"He doesn't let people in easily," she continues. "And he definitely wouldn't have brought you around us if he didn't see something in you."

She reaches out, giving my arm a gentle squeeze.

"We're family," she says simply. "A very selective one. Which is why we'll have to bring up the Sam sighting today. The boys won't be happy about him approaching you."

Emotion swells in my core. That pull toward Leo, the intensity I feel when I'm near him, and now this. It all confirms it's not one-sided.

"Well, I like him, too," I say quietly, letting the Sam comment linger but pushing it aside for now.

Izzy beams. "Oh, sweetie, I know. It's written all over your face."

I laugh through my burning cheeks.

"Um... Are you guys gonna order?" the teen behind the counter asks, red-faced and clearly overwhelmed.

Izzy drops me off at home.

"Thank you so much for spending the day with me," I say, hugging her. "And for buying me all these beautiful clothes. I wish you would have let me pay for lunch, you're really too generous."

"No such thing," she answers, hugging me back. "You have my number, so call me anytime. We'll drag Sara out of her cave for the next shopping spree!"

"Sounds perfect," I say, stepping out. "Drive safe and tell Rowdy I say hi."

"Will do!" she squeals, pulling away.

Once inside, I put my new clothes away, already planning when and where I can wear them. Maybe a date with Leo. Perhaps I can talk him into grabbing a coffee and walking around the farmers market with me. I don't know if he's the farmers market kind of guy, but something tells me if anyone could persuade him, it might be me.

I fold up my new jeans and place them in my dresser when there's a knock on my door.

It could only be a few people. Maybe I left something in Izzy's car and she's coming back to return it. Or Sara's stopping by, finally pried away from her baked goods and re-runs. Or it could be... *Leo*.

My heart rate spikes, hoping for the latter as I swing the door open.

But it's not Leo.

It's not Izzy.

It's not Sara.

"What are *you* doing here?" I ask, starting to close the space in the door.

Sam stops me, shoving it open as far as it will go. He still hasn't said a word—just stands there with a creepy smile stretched across his face. Fear prickles down my spine, my pulse pounding for an entirely different reason now.

Trembling, I start to retreat further into my living room. I'm blocked. I can't run past him. He must have waited for Izzy and me near the café, then followed me.

Now he's here, in my home.

He creeps forward. "I'm just welcoming the new girl in town, that's all."

I'm paralyzed, unable to speak, unable to move.

"You know," he says, taking another step toward me, "it's no secret that Leo and I aren't friends."

Closer.

"He likes to stick his nose in my business, and I'm getting pretty fucking sick of his little tantrums."

Closer.

"I need to send him a message." His gaze locks with mine. "Show him what happens when he keeps fucking my shit up."

"Back up, Sam!" I scream, breaking the paralysis.

He ignores me. "It's quite clear he's protective of the people he cares about."

He's face-to-face with me now, and I think I might vomit.

"It's also quite clear that you may just be one of those people." He sets his hand on me and squeezes my left bicep. "Messing with his pretty little thing would drive him insane."

Tears involuntarily start to stream down my face. All kinds of things run through my mind. What is he going to do to me? Is my neighbor home? Will he hear me scream?

"Let go of me!"

His face is inches from mine. The foul odor of chewing tobacco, liquor, and something sour I can't place stings my eyes.

"I'm not going to hurt you, honey," he whispers, leaning in close. "Fear lasts longer than pain."

30

Leo

I DECIDE TO STOP BY DOCKFRONT ON MY WAY TO LAYLA'S place. Nate's inside, pacing.

"Hey, bud," I say, walking in.

"Leo, man—I've been trying to call you."

"My phone was off, like it usually is when I take a solo trip out." Panic starts to creep up on me. "What's going on?"

He exhales and starts talking with his hands. "Sam was here earlier. Offered me a cut of sales if I let him use this place as a 'front' for his deals."

My jaw clenches. "*What?*"

"I told him no way in hell. Then—" He hesitates, dragging a hand through his hair. "Layla and Izzy showed up while he was still here. I had to turn them away."

Ice slides down my spine. "Did he see them? Talk to them?"

"I'm not sure. A crowd came in right as they left, and when I looked again, he was gone. Slipped out on me."

"Fuck."

Pressure builds in my chest. The thought of Sam anywhere near Layla causes rage to flood through me.

Nate shakes his head. "I don't know what his end game is, but he's sniffing around, trying to plant roots. I'll keep my eyes and ears open."

"Thanks. I need to check on Layla, make sure Sam didn't go near her."

He nods, grips my shoulder, his face carrying concern. "Be careful, brother."

I say goodbye to Nate and hop in my truck. As I pull onto the street, Izzy's convertible zips past in the opposite lane, music blasting. She flashes me a smile and a wave.

Relief rushes through me—if she's alone, then Layla must be home, safe.

I park in front of her place a minute later. The ease I felt just a moment ago immediately evaporates, replaced by a sudden surge of adrenaline.

A scream.

Fuck. Was that Layla?

Instinct takes over. I'm up the stairs, three at a time, ready to pound on the door, but it's already open. My vision burns red when I see Sam gripping Layla's arm, tears streaking her face.

In a millisecond, I'm behind him. One arm around his throat, dragging him off Layla. My bicep locks, crushing his windpipe as I haul his body toward the door. He claws at my arm, making a guttural choke.

"Wrong. Fucking. Move." My growl rattles through me. His face darkens, turning purple under the pressure.

I squeeze around his neck harder and dig my knee into his back. White noise fills my head. Nothing but static. Nothing but *rage.*

Until—her voice.

"Leo!" Layla's scream cuts through. "You're going to kill him!"

Sam's eyes bulge, bubbling spit leaking from the corners of his mouth. He's seconds from being out cold.

I release in just enough time for him to suck in air, then rip him up by the front of his dirty shirt. My fist twists the fabric, knuckles pressing into his throat. It would be so easy to end him. One solid shove down the stairs. One good crack to the skull.

I want it. *God,* I want it.

But I won't ruin my life for his.

So I drive my fist across his cheek instead, catching his nose at the end of the swing. His bone crunches and blood splatters across the concrete.

"What the fuck is wrong with you!?" he spews, spitting out blood and trying to grab the stair banister to steady himself.

"Get the fuck out of here, Sam," I demand. "*Now.*"

He manages to catch his balance, holding his shirt to his face as he stumbles down the stairs. "You'll regret this, you motherfucker!"

And with that, he's running down the street, grunting in pain.

My focus moves to Layla immediately. "Are you okay?"

She nods her head slowly. "I'm okay."

But she's trembling so hard, it shakes through me when I pull her close. I cradle her head against my chest.

"Are you sure?"

"You came just in time," she sniffles.

She's quivering, her breath shaky. I slide my hand to the back of her head, run my fingers through her hair to soothe her, to let her know she's safe.

To make myself believe it, too.

Her breath starts to steady after a minute, syncing with mine. I guide her to the couch and settle her onto my lap, her small frame molding perfectly against me.

"This is all my fault. I'm so sorry."

She squeezes my hand, now intertwined with hers, and shakes her head. "It's not your fault, Leo. This is *Sam's* fault."

I look at her, eyes now free of tears but slightly bloodshot.

"He wouldn't have been here if it weren't for me." I pause, trying to contain my guilt and suppress my anger at the same time. "I'm so sorry."

She doesn't say anything. She's not going to let me take the blame.

"You can't stay here tonight," I add quietly.

She nods her head in agreement. "I'll call Sara."

"No," I breathe. "You'll stay with me. Pack a bag. We're getting out of here."

She gives me a fragile smile, and I watch her walk toward her room. Shoulders slightly slumped, trying to piece a little bit of calm back into herself after what just happened.

I tuck my head into my palms, feeling the anger rise again. If I had been one minute later, who knows what would have happened? Who knows how far Sam would have taken it? I try to push the thought out of my mind, try to stow it away and save it for the day I plan to properly confront him about this.

Layla *could* stay with Sara, or even Izzy, but I wouldn't be able to stop worrying. I need her where I can see her. Where I can ensure nothing bad touches her.

She walks back in, the tension easing in my shoulders as she moves toward me with a small duffel bag. I stand and take it from her, setting it down by the door before returning to her, and holding her tight once more.

"You're safe now."

"I know," she whispers, holding me back.

And there it is—the current sparking from her heart to mine, something deeper than simple attraction.

Something *so much* deeper.
Not even the scum of the earth could break her light.
And God help anyone who tries.

31

Layla

THE DRIVE TO LEO'S HOUSE IS SILENT, AND DESPITE THE SCENE we just left behind the ride is peaceful.

Oddly peaceful.

Sam couldn't get his claws too deep into me before Leo barreled in. I'm still shaken, wondering how far he would have taken it.

He wanted to rattle me, wanted to push me to a breaking point to scare Leo. I want to believe he wouldn't have done the unthinkable. But I don't know him... and by the hatred others have for him, I wonder if he is someone who could really hurt me.

Or Leo, for that matter.

Who is now visibly distraught.

I know he blames himself, that *he's* the reason Sam sought me out, and that seeing us together at Nate's gave the enemy a chance to strike at his weakness.

His people.

I might be petite in size, positive in personality, but I don't let fear make me shy away. I try to see the good in people, the good in *all* things. And even though I'm still feeling shaken up and uneasy about what just happened, I'm grateful to have Leo nearby, taking me to his home.

A home that holds him every night. A home that keeps his comfort and carries his solace.

The Pacific Coast Highway is beautiful, wild and endless, stretching like a bridge between land and sea. The ocean is to the left of us, catching the setting sun. Each wave rolls in with sparkles, setting the perfect backdrop to Leo's captivating face.

A comment Izzy made comes to mind. Something about them loving the sea more than anything, and having to know *you'll never be number one.*

He belongs to the ocean, even if it's haunted by loss. And with his face outlined against the horizon, I understand.

I glance at him again—something I find myself doing often. And yes, the sea, the salt, the sky are all picture-perfect things to stop and enjoy. But I'm starting to see the *deepest* kind of beauty in the man sitting next to me. The man who, according to his friends, *always* shows up.

And he did.

My bicep throbs a little. Fingerprint-sized bruises are slowly starting to form.

"You okay?" Leo asks, noticing me inspecting the marks.

"I am," I say confidently.

Because I *am* okay. Thanks to him.

"I'm so sorry. I can't believe this—" he starts.

"Please stop blaming yourself," I interrupt, setting a hand on his knee. "The best thing... The *only* thing we can do is move on from this."

Leo doesn't respond right away, his gaze distant. Then he gives a small nod, not quite agreeing, but not dismissing me either.

He carries things. *Deeply.* So this may take some time for him to let go.

He turns off the highway, down a road lined with trees. Monterey Pines, I think.

"I was the one responsible for his last arrest," Leo says, the sun nearly set now. "I'm sure you've gathered he's involved with drugs and has brought some people down with him. Like my friend, Joey."

I listen as he turns down another road.

"He was using the docks to bring in his goods from San Luis Obispo." He turns again, and the road becomes more like a driveway the further we go. "I shut that down once and now he's looking for another place to do it."

"Why don't you get the cops involved again?" I ask the obvious. "Why didn't *we* just get the cops involved? What just happened was… assault."

He cringes at the word. "We could try, but his dad was in the police force, very high up the chain. Retired now, but still has a lot of pull."

I consider calling the cops now, a thought that hadn't even crossed my mind in the midst of the chaos. We could go to the station, tell them what happened, but it would be our word against his. And if Leo already has history with Sam in the system, who knows which one of them would end up in trouble.

Especially since Leo just nearly rearranged his face.

He puts the truck in park in front of a beige home lined with large windows and surrounding trees. He leans back in his seat, hands resting in his lap.

"I saw Nate for a minute before coming to you today. He said Sam was there trying to get him to agree to use Dockfront as a front for deals or something."

He turns toward me, still carrying that distraught look. "Sam knows Nate and I are tight. He knows I've got his back —and that gave Nate the courage to say no." His eyes trail from mine to the floorboard. "I'm assuming that's why he targeted you. To send a message that he's not going to quit."

"Joey came to Taboo the night you and I first met. He told me I should just let Sam do his thing, that it'd be easier that way." Tightness strains his jaw as he looks back up. "So I punched him and said, 'No fucking way.' That was *my* way of sending a message."

"Thing is... Joey left town again. His mom took him away to get him sober, and without Joey around, Sam's got one less way to reach me." His eyes flash to mine, full of worry. "So going after you makes perfect sense. He's not stopping until he breaks somebody."

I scoot closer to him, feeling the anxiety ripple in his body. "I know Sam's dad has a heavy hand with police politics, but is there really no way to take it above him?" I ask.

Our bodies touch slightly, sending a tiny shockwave through my system. His body feels warm despite the cold look on his face.

"We've tried. *Daddy* bails him out. Some people see drug dealing as a victimless crime, so it's not exactly a high priority, I guess."

Leo's face goes from cold to glacial.

"Also," he adds, "Sam's dad gets a percentage of his deals. He's actually been in the business much longer than Sam. He's moved down to Santa Barbara now, but still quietly has his hand in the pot."

He sighs. "Sam's father, Victor Murphy, was in cahoots with the old Harbor Master, too. When my dad was alive, he did his best to keep the docks clean. It pissed off both the Harbor Master and Victor. Probably why they denied the flotilla memorial Mom and I wanted for my dad—something more than *half* the town wanted for him. They even told us a paddle out wouldn't be approved. It broke us to the point where we didn't even want to try anymore."

"We did our own little memorial at home with family and friends. It wasn't how we truly wanted to say goodbye, but it was better than nothing."

My heart breaks into pieces. It isn't a secret that Leo and his father were closer than anything. That his dad was his hero, the one who taught him everything he knew, the man he still strives to be like.

"Oh, Leo," I whisper.

"My dad died out there in the ocean. Something happened with the cables on one of his personal boats, and he must have lost control. It was a fluke thing. My dad was always so on top of safety except he ignored the golden rule—never fish alone at sea."

There's nothing I can say to ease that pain, to erase that memory. His face is emotionless, like he's lived through this a hundred times before.

"It benefited the Murphys, devastated the rest of us. They found his boat days later on the beach, after Mom and I had searched the waters until we couldn't anymore. But we never found him. The ocean gave back the vessel, but not my dad."

"I'm so sorry," I whisper, knowing there's nothing else to say.

"Thank you," he says, offering the tiniest smile. "It ruined me, losing him. Even now, I've never gotten over it. Never found closure. Never got to say goodbye."

He pauses, then adds, "But there's one thing I do know— outside of being with Mom and me, there isn't a place he'd rather be than lost at sea."

The windows start to fog, our warm breath clashing with the cool, humid air outside. My hair starts to curl with the moisture, framing my face. His eyes don't leave mine, the faintest smile still lingering around his lips.

"Come on," he says quietly, opening his truck door and holding my hand as he guides me out from the driver's side.

He leads me to his home—a rock-lined pathway from the driveway to the front door. The large windows take up most of the front wall, offering a glimpse inside. He opens the door with a jiggle of a key, stepping into a large living room. Simply decorated with a big L-shaped couch, a coffee table, and an old TV.

Two large paintings hang on the walls. One of Morro Rock, the other of a ship with the name *Norma* painted on the side. The open-concept space has the kitchen to the left, dressed in navy blues and dark wood. An island counter sits beneath a low light, an old beer bottle and a dirty coffee mug planted next to the sink.

Leo grabs the bottle and tosses it in the trash. "Sorry about the mess. I wasn't expecting company."

"It's hardly a mess," I say.

I've seen bachelor pads in far worse condition than a few dirty dishes and an outdated TV, which I suspect he barely watches.

The house looks bigger from the outside than it feels inside. The living room, kitchen, a bathroom, and a small den take up the lower floor, with stairs leading up to a loft.

"What's up there?" I nod toward the stairs.

"That's where I sleep," he says. "I can stay down here tonight on the couch. You can have the bed. Come on, I'll show you where to set your stuff."

I follow him up to the dimly lit loft, which has windows just as big as the ones downstairs. A small bathroom is tucked into the corner. The rest of the space holds a bed, a dresser, and a dark mahogany guitar.

"Who taught you to play?" I ask, running my fingers lightly over the strings.

"Take a guess." He chuckles, grabbing the neck of the guitar and sitting on the edge of his bed.

"He was the jack of all trades, huh?" I join him.

"He was good at everything." He smiles, then starts to play a calm bluesy tune.

"Like you," I whisper.

His smile grows, softening the edges of his face. Then he closes his eyes, fingers moving fluidly. I don't think I've ever seen a more beautiful thing—the warm lamplight shadowing his silhouette, the curve of his mouth, the subtle movement of his shoulders as he plays.

"It's been collecting dust downstairs forever," he says without opening his eyes. "But recently, I picked it up again. Been playing a little before bed each night."

I don't interrupt. I just listen, letting the sound wrap around me like a comforting hug. My gaze drifts to his hands —the calloused fingertips pressing the strings, the easy way he shifts between chords.

A minute passes. The song begins to slow and when he strums the last chord, the sound echos in the air.

Without thinking, I rest my hand gently on his bicep. My heart races, the energy shifting into something… *different.*

"Leo," I say, my voice low, my eyes tracing the shape of his mouth.

"Hmm?" His eyes open, locking on mine.

"You're…" I pause, catching my bottom lip between my teeth. "Incredible."

32

Leo

OUR LIPS MEET.

Instinctively, my free hand finds the back of her neck. Her hair is soft, her lips smooth and full.

Without breaking from her mouth, I set my guitar gently on the floor beside my bed. My other arm hooks around her waist, pulling her closer to me.

Her tongue finds mine. It's sweet and warm, tasting of pure honey.

I want to pull her deeper onto me; I need her closer. My hands move to her waist and I grip her body and lift her. Her weight settles over me as her legs wrap around the grooves of my hips. Her arms drape around my neck as she straddles me. Her chest presses fully to mine, only thin layers of fabric keeping my skin from breathing hers.

Fabric I'm fighting the urge to shred apart.

Her kiss intensifies, lips still fused to mine, neither of us caring about oxygen. If suffocating feels like this, I'll take it, again and again, if only with her.

I find the marks on her arms, the ones that are from an unwelcome touch, and I press my lips to each one, erasing that memory and replacing it with this one. Her breath catches as my hands find her curves, guiding the slow circles of her hips against me.

Fuck.

If it feels this good now, I can't imagine what it would feel like to be inside of her. I'm already hard, pressing against the seam of my jeans. I know she feels it, too, her hips rocking slower.

She pulls her lips from mine and her ocean-blue eyes lock on me. She bites her bottom lip, then moves her hands from the back of my neck to the hem of her shirt, pulling it slowly over her head. Her red, silky bra hugs her breasts, the fabric pulled tight as they push against it. Holding eye contact, she reaches her arms behind her back and unclasps her bra, and they spill free.

I press a kiss to each swell. Full and soft, her creamy skin makes my mouth water and some primal part of me comes alive.

Hold it. Do not scare her with it. Make it sweet.

She must feel it, too.

Check her eyes. There it is. A 'yes.'

Her hands slide under my shirt, gliding up my stomach to my chest. Without looking away, she tugs it off me, and tosses it across the room.

Her gaze sweeps over my body the same way mine devours hers, slow and unashamed. Then, her lips return to mine, this time with her bare bust pressed against me.

Skin to skin.

Flesh to flesh.

One perfectly created soul against a messy broken one.

I close my eyes, and let the moment sink deep into me. I've never craved a woman like this before. Never *needed* anyone this way.

Her hips slow, then they halt. She slides off of my lap and

stands. For a moment, I think it's over. That I'll take the couch and spend all night thinking of her lips, her scent... All of *her*.

But she doesn't intend for it to end here. Instead, she slides down her perfectly fitted leggings, revealing long, bare legs. Her maroon-colored thong follows, pooling on the floor.

She's naked now, confident, comfortable in her own skin, standing right in front of me. I study her, memorizing the softness of her collarbone, the shape of her nipples, the silkiness of her hip crease.

She is beauty in its rawest form.

I breathe deeply and rise, towering over her and shed what remains of my own clothes—jeans, boxers, socks—until we're both bare, nothing between us, but a few small steps.

I move first, simply unable to wait any longer. I pull her body against mine, tasting her again. She moans, and I feel my own growl rumble deep within my chest.

I pick her up, her thighs gripping my hips. One spin, and her back meets the bed, her body still clinging to me. My dick throbs, aching to be inside her.

Her hands tangle in my hair, pulling as our kisses grow more frantic, more *desperate*. Our bodies are flush, making it more of a chore to gather a full breath, but it doesn't matter.

Nothing but this matters.

The soft noises she's making are fueling a savage hunger inside me. Her legs start to fall open, a silent invitation.

"I trust you," she whispers in my ear.

Her words undo me more than any touch could. My throat tightens. She could shatter me with that trust, but instead, she's giving it freely.

I pull away just enough to see her beautiful body. Sweat glides down her chest, down my back. My heart hammers so hard, I'm certain it'll break free if I don't act now.

I let go of her hips, sliding my thumb down her thigh until I reach the heat between her legs. Her breath is heavy as I hover there, savoring her slickness, how intoxicating she looks. She starts to tremble the moment I start to rub her most sensitive spot.

Her head tips back as she lets out a gasp, and I don't think I've seen something more enticing in my life. Her body starts to make subtle movements syncing with my thumb.

A plea escapes her lips as she pulls my hips closer to her, legs falling completely open. Her lazy eyes, full of pleasure, find mine.

"I need you inside me," she whimpers, so soft that I can barely hear it.

I exhale, feeling like I'm about to lose control if I don't grant her wish. I take my thumb away from her core and place it inside my mouth, sliding it against my tongue, tasting her sex, before I bury every inch of my length inside her.

A soft yelp escapes her throat. Her eyes glaze with even more pleasure, breath quickening as her nails scrape my back, clawing me closer, pulling me deeper.

She moans again, a sound so sweet it nearly undoes me. A sound that tells me she needs this just as bad as I do. I glide slowly, making sure every thrust fills her completely. I try to savor the look of her flawless face as she begins to lose control beneath me.

I pick up my pace, her sounds falling into rhythm with my movements. I drive harder as I close the distance between her face and mine, plunging my tongue in her mouth. She welcomes it and kisses me back, sucks my tongue then catches my lower lip between her teeth. I taste my blood almost immediately but it doesn't bother me.

I *welcome* it.

Her panting deepens. "Leo," she gasps between thrusts.

My name on her lips... It's *angelic* and the growl I've been holding back finally escapes. I grip her hips, fingers sinking into her sides, watching her breasts spring with every plunge. Her eyes stay locked to mine—those beautiful cerulean eyes.

Her pleasure is mine, and I'll take nothing until she has it all.

I sink deeper and stronger until she grips my biceps and arches her body as she comes beneath me. Her face softens through the pleasure, and my own euphoria crashes over me. I release into her, every ounce of pain, worry, and weight spilling away with it.

I collapse against her, but she doesn't let me go. Our chests heave together, skin slick, hearts still racing.

For a moment, I'm numb.

For a moment, I'm *free.*

33

Layla

THE SCARS ON HIS BODY MOVE WITH EACH INHALE AND EXHALE.

He's beside me now, our skin still warm, his hand resting over mine. The air between us carries heat and the scent of sex.

I turn onto my side and trail the tail of his mermaid tattoo inked into his forearm, his skin breaking out in goosebumps. I slide my fingertips into the dark waves of his hair. His eyes fall closed, and his breathing gradually slows until it matches mine. For a few quiet moments, I just look at him—admire the shape of his jaw slightly hidden beneath a beard, and how unfairly long his eyelashes are.

A thought washes over me. Something that brings me both electricity and solace. *I don't want this to end.*

Not just the night.

This.

Him.

Not after pulling him out of his beautiful, hardened shell.

"Do we need to worry about—" he asks quietly, eyes still shut, his voice lower now, softer than I've ever heard it.

He doesn't need to finish. The answer is *no*. I've been on birth control for four years.

"No," I whisper back, still combing my fingers through his hair, "but I would like to clean up."

"Of course," he breathes, finally dragging his eyes open. The warmth of his body leaves mine as he slips off the bed, grabs a T-shirt from his dresser, and turns back to me. "Towels are in the cupboard in the bathroom, you can wear this." He hands me a white shirt with his crew logo stamped on the back.

As I reach for the shirt, he catches my wrist and pulls me to him, pressing a kiss to the back of my hand. He lets go—of me and the shirt—and smirks.

Blush floods my cheeks, and I feel reluctant to leave the moment, but disappear into the bathroom anyway.

It's small but clean. A medium-sized tiled shower rests in the corner. On the counter: one toothbrush, one tube of toothpaste, one spindle of floss. In the shower: one razor, a bottle of shampoo-and-conditioner duo, one bar of soap.

I find a towel and hang it over the shower top, then turn on the water, letting the steam fill the room before I step in. His soap smells like him—sea salt and driftwood. I lather it over my body, and the soapy water runs down my skin. I inhale the aroma, hoping his shirt smells the same.

I take my time, savoring the hot water, replaying the way Leo looked at me while I was beneath him. Like I was the most beautiful thing on this planet. Heat rushes through me all over again at the thought, the soreness in my core pulses, and my knees grow weak.

Nothing could ever compare.

I let the feeling anchor within me before shutting off the shower, drying off, and combing my fingers through wet hair then finally slipping into his shirt that swallows me whole.

He's back on the bed, propped up against the headboard

when I step out of the bathroom, strumming his guitar, now in a pair of boxer shorts. When he glances at me, he smiles, taking one hand away from the strings to pat the space beside him.

I lie next to him; the heat and scent of us remains in the sheets. He plays until my eyes start to feel heavy, the exhaustion of the day and night closing in on me.

I'm half asleep when I feel him shift. He crawls in beside me, pulls the blanket over us, and slides his arm around my waist, drawing me into the crevice of his body.

Clean, warm, and satisfied.

Safe.

I drift to sleep.

When I open my eyes, the first thing I see is the clock on the wall—ten a.m.

Shit. I was supposed to be at work two hours ago. I didn't even think about work after the chaos with Sam yesterday… and then my night with Leo.

God. My night with Leo. Even the soreness I feel is welcome. A reminder of him woven into me.

I shake my head. Clearly, all of this has distracted me from the mundane things, like my job and setting an alarm.

I grab my phone. A text from Sara:

Running late?

Then another:

I'm worried!

A missed call, too. I quickly text her back:

> I'm okay. So sorry. Yesterday was really crazy. I'm actually not home right now but can explain it all later.

I glance at the space beside me. Empty. It's just me, the sunshine pouring through the windows, and the smell of breakfast foods drifting up from downstairs.

Sara replies:

> All good. Dad is here today. Just take the day off!

I won't argue with that.

I set my phone back on the nightstand and stretch. Despite the bright morning outside, the loft holds a bit of a morning chill. I spot a red checkered flannel tossed over the top of Leo's dresser.

That'll work.

I put it on, splash water on my face, fluff my hair, and make my way downstairs. As I descend, I spot a stack of pancakes, scrambled eggs, a bowl of berries, and shirtless Leo in sweatpants.

"Good morning," I say, surprised at how scratchy my voice sounds.

"Good morning." He grins, eyeing me briefly before returning to the pan he's washing. "How did you sleep?"

"Like a baby," I reply, coming up behind him and letting my fingers drift down the line of his spine. His muscles shift beneath my touch, goosebumps forming.

I stand there, taking in the faint scent of soap on his skin and the coffee brewing on the counter.

He stays quiet, letting me linger until he glances back at me over my shoulder. "I slept like a baby, too."

Reluctantly, I step away and take a seat at the small breakfast table. He wipes his hands on a dish towel and brings me a steaming mug of coffee with a splash of milk.

"Wasn't sure how you take it, so I figured a little milk was safe." He sets it down in front of me. "Glad you found something to keep you warm, the mornings can be a little chilly here. Not the best insulation."

He turns back to the kitchen, plating more pancakes and eggs.

"*You* don't look chilly," I tease, taking a sip of my coffee and letting my eyes roam over him.

He chuckles. "I'm used to it. I actually like the cool mornings, helps me wake up."

Not surprised.

Leo sets a plate in front of me and places the bowl of berries in the middle of the table.

"I'm impressed. This looks amazing," I say, popping a blueberry into my mouth.

"Thanks. I tried."

"Well, you did good."

"You can't say that yet. You haven't tried it." His grin is pure teasing.

I slide my fork into a pancake, cut a bite, and drizzle just enough syrup over the warm, fluffy piece. The first bite is perfect—soft, buttery, sweet. I take my time chewing, letting him see my approval.

"It's perfect," I tell him, already going in for another bite.

"Good."

We eat in comfortable silence—well, more like devouring. I think we both built up an appetite last night.

"So, I missed work today," I giggle, popping another berry into my mouth.

"Oh shit, should we get going?"

"No. Sara said to take the day."

The corner of his lips tug into the same curve I saw last night.

"Does that mean we're hanging out today?"

I nod, because it's all I want to do. Because the incident with Sam is still fresh, and staying close feels right. Because last night was... *magic.* And I think Leo would agree.

His emerald eyes brighten, his dark hair stirring as a breeze moves through the kitchen window.

"I mean... if you're free?" I ask.

He smiles back. "Oh, I'm free."

I watch his lips move as he talks—something about a hike, something about a great ocean view. But it's hard to focus.

Because he is, without a doubt, absolutely and unmistakably *magnificent.*

34

Leo

AFTER BREAKFAST, WE SPEND THE ENTIRE DAY TOGETHER, AND
to be honest, I can't remember the last time I felt this happy.

As if we were kids again, I raced after Layla toward the
trailhead, nearly getting taken out by a tree branch, both of us
laughing so hard we could barely breathe. She stopped every
few feet on our hike to point out some tiny lizard I never
would've noticed, smiling and saying how "cute" it was. She
told me that animals inspired her sketching hobby. And apparently, the girl knows her birds. Like, can name them on sight.
Says her grandpa taught her, which is random as hell, but also
kind of impressive.

Kind of *cute*, as she would say.

I promised a view at the end of the trail, and I think I
delivered. I believe her exact words were: "I've never seen
something so stunning."

I was thinking the same thing, *but I wasn't looking at the ocean.*

We packed sandwiches and found a stretch of beach
where the footprints were just ours. Not one other soul in
sight. We shared a blanket and as we ate, she told me about
her childhood in Los Angeles, spending weekends with her

family and friends. She told me more about her parents, how they met in college and claimed it was love at first sight.

Something she doesn't believe in.

She talked about her camping trips out here in Morro Bay. How, when she decided she wanted to get out of L.A., this was *exactly* where she wanted to be.

She expressed that she feels welcomed by the locals—Sara and Dan at the coffee shop for bringing her in and providing a job and friendship. Izzy with her impromptu shopping spree. Austin with his endless rambling. Nate with his good hugs.

And, well… *Me.*

I wish I could embrace the moment as fully as she is, but as the day zips by, the worry eats at me. Layla has to go back to work tomorrow—back to her routine, back home, back to her responsibilities—and I can't stop thinking that Sam will show up again to take care of unfinished business, something I haven't even told the guys about yet.

They are going to lose their minds, and I don't need that right now. Not with Layla now looking at me, smiling like always, her face freckling even more in the sun.

"Today has been really nice," she says, grinning wide from ear to ear.

"It has," I agree.

She looks back toward the ocean, closes her eyes, and welcomes the afternoon breeze. I hover in the space between keeping quiet and saying what's been sitting heavy on my mind for the last half hour.

"Can we talk about yesterday?" I finally ask, ripping the band-aid off before I lose my nerve.

She opens one eye, aims it at me, and grins. "Which part?"

I can't help but chuckle. I also can't help but feel like a fuckhead for letting this Sam issue infest my mind when there was *so* much more to yesterday.

A *fucking amazing* night. One that I keep replaying over in my head.

"It's not your fault," she says, closing her eyes again. "You may be somehow connected to Sam, but you didn't ask him to go after me."

He came after her. *He came after her because of me.*

"He's after me. He can't get to me, so he's going after the people I care about," I say, even though she's heard this all before.

"He's trying to get a rise out of you." She pauses, opens both of her eyes and shifts her body toward me. "And it's working."

There's a moment of silence before I admit, "Yeah, it is."

"Look, I don't know what his plans were when he came to my apartment, if he even planned to take it further," she says and for a split second, fear flashes in her eyes before she covers it by sliding her hand over mine. "But it didn't happen."

Because I showed up on time. Who knows what would've happened if I hadn't.

"I'm not scared of him, Leo."

She's not scared.

"The guys and I have an overnight trip coming up, but I'll make sure you aren't alone while I'm away," I say. "Sam won't be laying a hand on you ever again." Even as the words leave my mouth, I know I can't control Sam.

But God, I want to.

She looks at me, but decides not to respond. She has to be holding onto some fear and worry about this. A person can't be assaulted by some asshole and not have an opinion about it. She *has* to be holding some of it in.

Holding it in for me… and I think her silence proves that.

"Will you stay again?" I ask, changing the topic.

"Yeah." She smiles. "But I don't think I can miss work again tomorrow."

"Deal."

She stands, brushing the back of her calves where sand clings, her denim shorts speckled with it, too. She looks down at me, and for a fleeting second, I think the heaviness of our talk might send us back to my place for the night, but instead, she looks at me and winks. "I'll race ya."

"Race me where?" I ask, but before I know it, she's sprinting toward the water, stripping her clothes off on the way.

A trail of clothing leads to her bare skin hitting the waves; her hair is golden in the sunlight, and her laugh mixes with yelps about how cold the water is. She shouts something about feeling alive before diving under. I crack up watching her splash around like a child. She drops into the waves, rolling with them, and every time she re-emerges, the sun hits her just right, water dripping off her like diamonds.

She makes it look so easy—shaking off the shadows and chasing joy. Maybe that's why I can't look away, because in her, I see peace.

I let myself enjoy the view for another moment before kicking off my own clothes and running in after her. The water is a shock and so is she.

I feel wild... I *feel alive*.

35

Layla

I WALK INTO WORK THE NEXT MORNING, MY BODY WARM, embraced by Leo's flannel that I stole.

At this point, I've collected both his hoodie and his flannel —and I have no intention of giving either back. That's just what girls do, right?

"Finally! You're here, I need all the tea," Sara squeals as I walk in.

"Okay, let me get situated." I smile, then notice Dan behind the counter. "Hi, Dan. I'm really sorry about yesterday."

"Don't worry about it, shit happens," He says. "We don't run too tight of a ship around here."

Dan's bald head shines underneath the overhead lighting, his long, silver goatee moving as he talks then proceeds to his usual happy humming.

"You think you could stay a couple of hours longer today?" he asks, balancing two trays of pastries, "I need to head up North for a few hours, I don't want to leave Sara alone."

"No problem!"

Besides, I need to keep my mind occupied. Two nights with Leo leaves a girl with her heart racing—and no, not because we had sex last night, but because we didn't. Instead, he made spaghetti, put on an old movie, and we passed out on the couch. It was the kind of tranquil evening that we both needed.

"So, are you going to spill?" Sara asks once Dan leaves.

"I am, after coffee."

"Oh my *God*, you're torturing me!" she says, grabbing two cups of coffee and messily throwing in creamer and sugar into each one.

"Here." She slides one over to me, a few drops of liquid jumping out. "Now talk, woman!"

"Okay, okay!" I say and take a big gulp.

She stares at me, soaking in every word as I explain what happened with Sam after my shopping trip with Izzy. Her brows raise and her lips press tight, like she wants to interrupt in shock but doesn't. Letting her know the details about Sam didn't come as a surprise; apparently, he's harassed Dan before, asking to use the shop as a place to meet "clients." Offered to cut him in on the deal just like he did with Nate. Of course, Dan declined and had to get a little aggressive with Sam before he moved on.

Sara shakes her head, cursing Sam's name under her breath. Her hand finds mine, giving a reassuring squeeze.

"Please don't mention this to anyone else, okay? I'd rather it just stay between us for now," I say.

She nods. "Of course."

The tone of the conversation shifts when I share details of my first night with Leo. I leave out the more intimate parts, but I can't help telling her about the way he plays the guitar— how beautiful it sounds, something she already knows from his past at local events. I tell her how present and strong he feels, how comforting, and how he makes great breakfast foods.

A cheesy grin spreads across her face. "You're *glowing*," she teases, and I can't even argue.

Some locals pop in throughout the day, making small talk and grabbing their coffees, teas, and treats before heading back to their routines. One tourist couple comes in asking where they can eat to get the best view of Morro Rock. They're touring in the off-season, which makes Sara wonder if the busy season will start earlier this year. We make a note to order more coffee beans soon.

The rest of the day kind of lulls on, Sara and I now on our third cup of coffee, and it's already three in the afternoon. We laugh, joking about how jittery we'll be by closing time.

Her phone buzzes, and her cheeks flush red.

"Oh my God! Will just texted me!" she squeals, hopping off the barstool.

I laugh, nearly spilling my drink. "Friggin' finally. Took him long enough."

She starts pacing, chewing her lip. "What do I even say?"

"Maybe… hello?"

She groans and spins in a circle, clutching her phone. "He asked me to go to the movies!"

"He's not wasting time." I grin, feeling accomplished. "Just call me Cupid."

She drops back onto the stool, staring at her phone then typing a response, deleting it, then typing again. Her nerves are so obvious, it's kind of cute. She deserves this.

My own phone buzzes on the counter, stealing my attention as Sara battles her text. An "I love you" from my parents. I smile at the message, feeling warm. I've got to have them out here soon. I miss them.

And I think they just might approve of Mr. Anderson.

36

Leo

I'VE BEEN TOSSING THE IDEA AROUND IN MY HEAD ALL morning.

After dropping Layla off at work, I couldn't shake the nervous feeling in my gut. Being *with* her is easier. Safer. Nothing can touch her when she's with me. But I've only got two more days before I'm out on a three-night trip with the boys—and in those two days, I need to make sure shit isn't going to hit the fan with Sam while I'm gone.

I have yet to tell anyone what happened between Sam and Layla. I will, just not yet. First, I need to handle it my own way before the guys declare war.

That's why I decide to head down a road I didn't think I'd ever drive down again. Ashford Lane, where Sam used to live.

I've asked around town today if anyone's seen him. I got mostly "No," but one of the ladies at the market mentioned he's staying in his dad's old place. I wouldn't be surprised if his dad just handed the house over to him.

High or not. Dealing or not dealing. Victor Murphy *always* bails out Sam. That's why getting law enforcement involved is complicated.

LEO

Ashford Lane hasn't changed. The roads are still uneven, asphalt cracked and faded, weeds pushing up through every break. The houses sit too close together, some with overgrown yards swallowing old rusted boats and broken furniture.

I slow as I pass the third house on the right. The porch paint peels and plastic blinds hang crooked in the windows. It's quiet out here, and not the good kind.

I park in front of the old white house. The wood is splitting, but still holding. Cigarette butts and old beer bottles litter the porch. Part of me wishes it would just collapse already, bury its memories so I wouldn't ever have to come back here.

Goosebumps crawl up my arms despite the sweatshirt I have on. This place gives me the chills. Always has. Probably because this is where I found Joey the first time he overdosed. Slumped over in a busted lawn chair out back, skin the color of ash, lips blue, bubbling at the mouth. I thought he was dead. I still remember the smell of stale beer mixed with something sickly sweet, and the feeling of thinking my best friend was gone.

I let my engine idle for a minute, watching the front door, wondering if Sam knows I'm here. I think about driving off, but I can't. I *can't* just let it go. He's trying to send a message, and I'm trying to send my own.

So I turn off my truck and get out.

The boards on the porch creak under my steps. The smell of smoke gets stronger as I get closer to the house. Just as I'm about to bang on the front door, it opens, and I'm greeted by no one other than the asshole himself.

His initial reaction is surprise, maybe even a little fear before he squares his shoulders.

"Leo. Can't say it's a pleasure to see you." He tries to smirk, but the swelling and bruising along his cheekbone make it more of a wince. He smells like damp clothes and body odor.

"I could say the same."

He snickers. "You're at *my* house, buddy."

I take a deep breath, trying to contain the anger that has already started pulsing through my veins. I hate his face. I hate his voice. I hate everything about him.

"I think you know why I'm here," I say, my fists starting to clench at the memory of his hands on Layla.

He leans against the doorframe. "Maybe I don't."

"You don't belong here anymore, Sam," I say. "You know what you did. You know the damage you left behind and the people you've ruined."

"I've '*ruined*' a lot of people," he says, throwing up air quotes as he reveals his yellowing teeth. "You'll have to be more specific."

I step forward, closing the space between us. "I'm not going to stand by and watch you start over here. Not again. You want to deal your shit, you find another place. You stay away from Layla. You stay the hell away from everyone."

"Right, *Layla*." He draws out her name. "Sweet thing. Real pretty when she's scared."

My vision tunnels. My blood spikes.

Before I know it, I've got him by the throat and slammed against the wall, rattling the loose board behind him. The impact shakes dust from the eaves above us. He starts choking, his hands clawing at my forearm.

I press harder against his windpipe. "Say something like that again. Say one more thing about her. I fucking *dare* you."

He tries to speak, but I press harder. I can feel his pulse pounding against my arm. "You think you're untouchable? You think just 'cause your daddy bailed you out your whole life, it makes you bulletproof? You're not. I'm not scared of you, Sam."

I let him go, shoving him back because I don't trust myself

not to go too far. He stumbles, coughing, one hand clutching his throat.

He looks up, the wound on his cheek now oozing. "She's just some fucking girl, Leo."

The way he spits it, like she's nothing, makes my vision blur red. "No," I snap, stepping back in close so he can *feel* every word. "She's *my* girl."

And just like that, he knows. The claim is made. One more hand on her, and it's war. A war I wouldn't back down from.

"Sell your poison somewhere else. I don't give a damn where you rot. But if you so much as breathe in her direction again, I will end you. You understand me?"

He stays quiet this time.

I start to head back toward my truck, pulse still racing but glance back once more before leaving.

"She's not afraid of you, by the way," I add. "She's afraid of what *I'll* do to you if you push again."

I don't break eye contact until I climb into the truck and slam the door shut. The engine roars, drowning out the sound of my own heartbeat.

He stands there, still holding his throat, fear clear in his eyes, as he watches me drive away.

37

Layla

Truth is, the afternoon weather here feels like therapy.

A little bit of sea breeze, a whole lot of quiet. It clears my head and makes me look forward to my walks home from work.

It's the little things, you know? The fresh air, a bird's song, a sweet treat in the morning or a cozy meal at night. Those are the moments we have to hold onto if we want to stay sane in this world. Otherwise, what's the point?

If not for love, then at least for all the small joys life has to offer. Like coffee, comfy sweaters, and... men who drive a truck that just happen to be parked in front of your building as you round the corner.

Leo.

He's sitting on the bottom step, elbows on his knees, hoodie sleeves pushed up.

Waiting for me.

"Hey you, how long have you been here?" I ask as I near him, placing my hands on my hips.

"Not long," he says, standing. The soft smile of his melts my marrow, so does the warm hug he pulls me in for.

I open my mouth to say something sweet, maybe something about how I missed him, but the trail of blood drops on the stairs take my attention. Dried now, but still very evident.

Oh.

I haven't been back here since Sam's "visit." Since Leo beat the hell out of him.

He notices my gaze and follows it. "Shit," he mutters. "I didn't even see that. Let me clean it up."

His voice is gentle, apologetic, despite my repeated attempts to tell him to stop apologizing, and one thing I've learned about Leo is that he needs reassurance. Whether or not he asks for it.

I grab his arm before he turns. "Hey," I say softly. "Thank you… for everything."

The wind around us starts to wind down. That now familiar flutter in my heart surfaces as his fern-painted eyes lift to mine, seemingly stopping time. I don't drop his arm and he doesn't step away.

"You don't have to thank me," he says, his voice rougher now. "I'd do it a thousand times over."

I swallow, my heart surging with his proximity.

"I know you would," I whisper.

He steps closer, and I feel the heat of him before he even touches me. "I didn't know someone could make me feel this *much*," he murmurs, eyes dropping to my mouth.

The space between us disappears. He kisses me like he's starved, my lips the only thing that can feed him. There's no hesitation—just hands on my waist, my back, my face, like he needs every inch of my skin.

And I let him.

He lifts me, his arms holding me from beneath, carrying me up the stairs so effortlessly. My lower back hits the wall outside my door. His mouth doesn't leave mine as he reaches behind me, fumbling for the handle.

I slide my hand into the purse hanging from my inner elbow, fishing out the keys while my lips stay locked on his. I press them into his hand, and somehow he manages to unlock the door as we stumble inside—a mess of tongues, breath, and hands—before it slams shut behind us.

He spins us so I'm pressed against the wall again, still clutched in his grasp. His large hands cup my bottom as he pulls away and looks at me with starved lust. His eyes darken, his chest heaves, his body presses flush to mine, and I can't remember how to breathe.

All I know is that I never want him to stop touching me.

His eyes roam over me, memorizing every bit. My own eyes begging him to take me right here and now.

"Tell me to stop," he groans, his voice so deep.

My lungs go still. "*Don't.*"

The second the word leaves my mouth, his lips are on mine again—hard, hungry, completely unrestrained.

I melt.

Melt into the kiss, into him, into the way his hands are suddenly gripping my waist, then my thighs. He lifts me higher, like I weigh nothing, and I tighten my legs around his hips as he grinds into me, kissing me like we're the last people on earth. Like this is our last day on earth.

"*Leo*—" I gasp his name, barely more than a whisper. My head drops back against the wall, and I feel him everywhere.

"I've got you," he breathes against my throat, dragging his mouth across my skin. "I've always got you."

God.

The way he says it… like a promise, a vow.

My fingers dive into his thick hair, pulling. I tug at his hoodie, desperate for his skin. He helps, ripping it off over his head with one hand while the other stays locked around me, holding me up against the wall.

Before I know it, my shirt's gone, my bra, too. I don't even remember him taking them off. All I know is I'm suddenly bare-chested and crushed against him, his mouth still roaming everywhere. My collarbone, the swell of my breast, the edge of my jaw.

He's slow about it, but there's nothing gentle in the way he's breathing. Nothing restrained about the way his fingers hook into the waistband of my pants and yanks them down.

I help him, kicking my pants off one leg at a time as the other stays latched on him, my body desperately aching for his —shaking, spun up from his touch, his voice, the way he's looking at me like he's slipping out of control.

Hastily, we unbutton his jeans, sliding them down as he keeps me up. His boxers fall quickly after.

He drops to his knees, still gripping me, and slides my panties off one leg, balancing us. He drinks me in with his gaze, following his palms skimming up my thighs and clutches my waist.

Here we are again.

Naked.

Again.

My center quivers, waiting for him. So close to his erection, so obviously pulsing with intent.

He slowly stands us back up, his eyes locked onto mine. I feel him—hard, ready, pressing against my lower belly.

"Please," I breathe. "*Leo.*"

He doesn't make me ask twice and the second that he's inside me, I forget everything else.

I cling to him, forehead pressed to his. The stretch is deep, I'm almost too full because *damn*... He's a fucking man.

He glides in and out of me, slow and purposeful, savoring

each motion. I moan into his mouth and he swallows the sound.

"You feel—*fuck*—Layla…" he gasps. "You're going to make me lose it."

"Then lose it," I pant. "Leo, please."

That breaks him.

He pins my wrists above my head with one hand, the other gripping my ass to keep me right where he needs me, and fucks me like the world is ending.

Impaled on him, shaking, soaked in sweat and sex. Pleasurably painful.

"Don't stop," I moan.

He doesn't. He can't.

He growls, sweat trickling down his forehead, sucking my lips in for a kiss.

Every thrust punches the air from my lungs and the moans from my throat, and then I'm *falling*. Clenching around him so hard, I see stars behind my eyes, my sounds muffled against his mouth as I unravel in his arms.

My whole body trembles, tightening around him as the pressure builds in my core. And when I come, it's like falling with no fear of the crash landing.

He follows with a groan, burying his face in my neck as he pulses inside me, clutching me tightly like I might disappear into thin air.

But I'm not going anywhere.

Not now.

Not after all of this.

38

Leo

Her warm breath is uneven against my neck. We're still up against the wall, her legs wrapped around me, my arms locked around her.

I shift just enough to set her feet on the ground. She's loose-limbed, and her legs tremble, so I keep my hold on her, pressing a kiss to her temple, then another to her shoulder as she lets me guide us backward toward the bedroom.

I've held a lot of things in my life. Dirty old nets, ropes, knives sticky with fish guts... The residue of grief. But I've never held something like her. So soft, so precious, so uniquely herself.

She lays down and I fall into the soft sheets beside her, our skin still hot and slick with sweat. Neither of us says anything. Words seem so trivial during a moment like this.

I slide an arm under her neck, take a deep breath, and stare at the ceiling, allowing my heart time to slow down its beat. She nuzzles into me, her shaky exhales warming my collarbone as her fingers trace lazy lines across my chest. With my other arm, I hook her closer, hand resting beneath the curve of her thigh.

"You good?" she murmurs, half-asleep.

"Yeah," I whisper. "I'm good."

And I *am*. The truth is... I've never felt this good and this fucking terrified at the same time.

———

I snuck out of bed early to finally clean up the blood drops on the stairs. I found a cleaner and an old rag under the kitchen sink. It was an easy job, since the blood was still fresh enough that it hadn't completely seeped into the material of the stairs. A little bit of chemicals and some elbow grease got the job done.

I hope it won't come to this again. I hope Sam will take me seriously and leave all of us alone. It makes me wary of leaving on my work trip, I'll be out of reach and not able to step in if a situation calls for it. But I've got my people here— Nate, Izzy—they'll have her back when I can't.

I'll make sure of it.

I decided not to tell Layla about my visit with Sam yesterday. She deserves a couple of days of peace, a chance to settle back in. If the message I gave him was clear—and I think it was—he'll keep his distance.

I'll loop Nate in on what happened between Layla and Sam, but I'll hold off telling the boys until we're out at sea, where they can't react on impulse. For now, the best thing I can do is keep it on the down low and try to keep things peaceful. The less attention I give this, the better I'll feel while I'm away.

She'll be up soon, getting ready for work. Ready to take on the day with a big, bright smile.

A smile that's forever branded into my mind.

Back inside, I hear the shower running, the vapor carrying a strong floral scent, her voice humming to a song I don't recognize. I peek inside, the shower screen is covered in steam and splattered soap, just enough to blur her body into a soft outline.

"Layla?" I say semi quietly, trying not to startle her.

"*Leo*," she says, then goes back to humming.

"I'll take you to work when you're ready."

She slides open the shower door just enough to reveal her beautiful, freckled cheeks. "Sounds great." She smiles, then slides it closed.

An impulsive thought passes through me. I don't think she'd mind if she found me ripping that door open and pulling her hot, wet, soapy body against mine. Not after she called my name in pleasure just some hours ago.

The urge grips me hard, but I rein it back and decide to save it for a rainy day.

⸻

She's ready within twenty minutes, hair damp, no makeup, just an oversized T-shirt, a long cardigan, and boots.

Minimal effort but the *most* beautiful.

She grabs a banana out of the fruit bowl on the counter and opens the front door. "Shall we?"

I grin, nod, and we walk down to my truck.

"So, you up for a barbecue re-do tonight? Nate's place again. No Sam… *Obviously*," I ask, hoping she'll say yes.

"What's the occasion?" She fumbles with her bag while buckling her seatbelt.

"We usually do a family dinner the night before an overnight run."

"Right, I forgot about the overnight."

"More like three nights. We're starting the season with a deep-sea haul. It's kind of a good luck thing."

"Good luck?"

"Yeah. When my dad ran his crew, he'd take them out for a couple nights at the start of every season. And every time he did, they had a successful one."

"That's kind of sweet."

"Sweet?" I chuckle. "I wouldn't call it that. It's actually pretty dirty, the sleep is terrible, and when Hank's on kitchen duty, the food sucks."

She giggles. "Well, how about I make you something really good when you get back? To erase the memory of Hank's cooking."

"That sounds really great, actually." I hesitate before adding, "And... Can we keep the thing with Sam between us for now? I'll tell the guys when the time's right."

"I did tell Sara," she admits, "but she promised to keep it to herself. She won't say anything."

I nod. "Alright. Thank you. It's your business to tell, I know that. I just don't want it weighing on everyone while we're gone."

Her hand brushes mine. "I get it and I agree."

I pull up to The Busy Bean. "So... I'll pick you up tonight?"

"I'll be ready."

39

Layla

NATE'S PLACE IS LIVELIER TONIGHT—LESS TENSION AND MORE laughter.

The crew is all here, including Sara and Will. She's been glowing since their movie date, which she talked about nonstop all day at work. I suggested that she bring him tonight, and apparently, she agreed with the idea.

She looks happy, laughing with him underneath the glow of string lights. I like this look on her.

Leo's at the grill with Rowdy and Nate, his shoulders relaxed in a way I haven't seen much of. Around us, food, voices and music weave together like a feast meant to nourish more than just our bodies.

"I'm packing the good stuff this time," Hank brags, carrying a tray of corn out to the grill. "*Real* food. None of that slop."

"Yeah, yeah," Leo says, smirking as he grabs the tongs. "I'll believe it when I taste it."

"Slop?" Austin pipes up. "I'll try anything once."

"You say that now," Rowdy grumbles. "Wait till you've had Hank's 'midnight surprise stew.'"

Hank rolls his eyes. "Ungrateful bastards."

"You know we're just messing with you," Leo says, flipping a piece of chicken. "Honestly, anything warm is welcome out on the water."

I settle into an Adirondack chair near the fire pit, sipping a cold beer and enjoying the crackling flames. Izzy leans in next to me, nudging my arm.

"How's it going with you two?" she asks not so subtlety, drawing looks from Sara and Will.

I glance over at Leo. His back is to me, hoodie sleeves pushed up, backwards hat on, focused on the food. The sweetness of his smile when Nate says something makes my stomach do tiny flips.

"It's going well," I say honestly. "Really well."

Izzy grins. "Yeah. We've *all* noticed."

Sara leans forward. "Is this love?"

Will coughs into his drink, blushing beside her.

I laugh, shaking my head. "It's very new, okay? I've just gotten through that thick exterior. Let's not toss the 'L' word around just yet."

"Sure, whatever you say." Izzy snorts. "Just know that love knows no time."

I know it's true. I'm just grateful to be here, with him, with all of them. We're quiet for a second, all of us watching the guys move around the grill like some sweet little brotherhood.

They're loud and messy.

Loyal.

And in a way that grows each day… They feel like mine, too.

"Let's keep busy while they're gone," Izzy suggests. "We'll need distractions. Drinks at Taboo tomorrow night? French fries? Girls' night?"

I nod automatically, but her words remind me of what's coming.

The ocean. The trip. Three nights. I swallow, feeling the uneasiness dwell in my chest.

"Hey," Izzy says softly, catching it. "They'll be okay. Leo's the best captain out there. They're a tight crew and they've done this a hundred times."

She means well and she's probably right.

Then the tension breaks almost instantly when Izzy cracks a joke that makes Sara snort-laugh. Will chimes in, then Austin, and suddenly everyone's laughing. The music plays from the speaker in the window, and there's a drift that smells like smoke mixed with salt.

Leo walks over with a plate piled high—grilled corn, barbecue chicken, and a fat scoop of potato salad. It all looks delicious, more of the classic barbecue spread this time.

I guess they needed a break from fish.

"You haven't eaten," he says, setting it in my lap with a wink. "Here, a little bit of everything."

"Thank you." I grin, then reach up and tug him down by the front of his hoodie and kiss him.

Not a wild, passionate kiss. Just something sweet and warm, right in front of everyone.

He smiles into it, leaning over me, the shadow of his broad body engulfing mine. His lips linger over mine for a moment, a strand of saliva connecting us. He licks his lips, smiles, and pulls away heading back to the grill.

I catch Izzy eyeing me, her expression sincere. She doesn't say anything, but she nods, like she's a proud mother or something.

I feel it, too.

The pride.

Because of all the men on Earth, somehow I have fallen into the arms of Leo Anderson.

The ride back to my place is peaceful.

The windows are cracked, letting in the cool ocean drift, and Leo's hand rests on the gearshift between us, brushing mine every time he shifts.

He pulls up to the curb in front of my apartment and throws the truck into park. "I'll be back before you know it," he says, glancing over at me, "I'd ask to stay tonight but I gotta pack and it's going to be a really early morning."

I nod, fingers fiddling with the frayed edge of my sweat-shirt. "Three nights, that's nothing."

He gives me a small smile. "You'll be too busy to miss me."

"Right," I say, trying to match the casual tone.

I reach for the door handle, hesitate, then turn toward him. "Just... try not to forget about me while you're out there."

It comes out like a joke. *Mostly.*

"Not a chance in hell." He opens his door. "I'll walk you up."

He gets out and opens the passenger door for me, like always, and I climb out, his hand resting at the small of my back. He walks me to the top of the stairs, stopping just short of the door. I lean against it, turning to face him. He rocks back on his heels, hands in his pockets.

"Try not to get swallowed by a whale or something," I say.

He chuckles. "No promises."

There's a second of silence, words hanging around me that could be said if we were braver. He steps closer, then reaches out, taking my hips into his large hands and pulls me in.

"I'm really glad you came tonight."

"Yeah," I whisper. "Me too."

He leans in and presses a kiss to my cheek and when he pulls back, he rests his forehead against mine for the briefest moment. Then he steps away, backing down the stairs, his eyes on me the whole time.

"Goodnight, Layla."

"Goodnight, Leo."

I stay there, hand on the doorknob, watching him walk to the truck. Once he's inside, he doesn't look over. There's no need to.

Because I know he'll come back.

40

Leo

THE OCEAN ALWAYS GREETS YOU THE SAME WAY.

Cold and wide.

Wild and indifferent.

It doesn't care who you are or what you left behind on land. It just sways and swells and carries you out like it has for centuries.

Mother Earth shares her beauty with those who don't deserve it. And most days, I like that about her. I *belong* to her, even though she's haunted. Out here, everything slows down. The noise in my head gets quieter. The pressure on my chest eases.

Today feels different.

The sky is gray, like it always is in the morning. It's familiar, it's comfortable but my mind isn't on the weather, or the tide, or the first drop of the nets.

It's thinking about a lit porch, and a girl standing on it.

Layla.

Saying goodbye like it's no big deal. Very unaware of the space she's taken up in me already.

Or maybe she is aware, and is just being careful with it.

Protecting herself despite the trust she shows to me. I wouldn't blame her. I'm sure everyone around town has expressed that I don't have a great track record with letting people too close.

But she's different. She slipped in without permission.

The deck creaks beneath my boots as I step out of the wheelhouse. Salt clings to the air, and the cold bites through my jacket. We're a few hours into the open water now, the shoreline non-existent through the haze.

Rowdy is already at the stern, coiling a line. Hank's fiddling with the coffee pot that never brews fast enough, and Austin's gazing out into the ocean.

"See how the clouds part just slightly over the eastern swell?" he says, one hand dramatically extended toward the horizon. "That's what the old sailors used to call a 'blessing break.' It's rare, you know."

This kid, high on life. It's actually kind of nice.

"You're full of shit," Hank mutters, pulling two half-burnt toasts off a pan.

Austin just grins. "That *toast* looks like shit."

I shake my head and move toward the edge of the boat, scanning the water.

"Captain's quiet today. You're usually the most animated on the first day of a long trip," Rowdy grumbles as he walks past me, nudging my shoulder. "Thinking about the haul or thinking about the girl?"

I give him a sideways look. "Since when do you care?"

"I don't." He smirks. "Just nice to see you finally brooding over something besides the fucking fish."

Austin appears with two mugs, handing me one. "He's thinking about her," he loudly whispers to Rowdy. "Look at him. Eyes on the waves, but heart back onshore."

"Keep talking and you're going overboard," I threaten, but I take the coffee.

Austin raises his mug in salute and walks off. I take a sip, staring out at the water again.

We've got a full crew, a long trip ahead, a good forecast and the kind of early morning that usually puts me at ease.

But I don't feel settled. I don't feel the usual relief.

"Alright, what's eating at you?" Hank asks, leaning on the rail beside me.

I hesitate, but it's best the boys stay in the loop and now seems to be a good time. "Sam showed up at Layla's place the other day. Uninvited, obviously."

Rowdy's head snaps up from the line he's working. "What?"

"Yeah," I say, jaw tightening at the memory. "Grabbed her arm, wouldn't let go. I got there in time, but—" I shake my head and my anxiety starts to swell. "Sam's gotta go, man."

Austin's expression hardens. "You confront him?"

"Damn right, I did." I meet their eyes. "Made it real clear that if he ever pulled that shit again, he'd regret it."

Hank gives a low whistle. "Think it stuck?"

"I think so," I say. "He looked like he got the message. But I don't think this is over yet."

Rowdy murmurs something under his breath that sounds like, *"Should've thrown him in the bay."* He drops the line he's coiling and raises his voice slightly. "Hopefully there isn't a next time, but if there is, you better fuckin' tell me. I'll fuckin' finish it." He pauses. "He tried that bullshit with Izzy."

"Trust me," I say, taking another sip of coffee, "I thought about it."

"Thought about it?" Rowdy snaps. "Guy puts his hands on a woman, that's all the thinking I need." He shakes his head and lights a cigarette.

This is exactly why I held off. Last time Sam messed with Izzy, I had to drag Rowdy off him for the same reasons I had to hold myself back.

"The opportunity will present itself, son," Hank says, patting my back and shooting Rowdy a look. "His time will come, and when it does, we'll handle it clean. Not like a bunch of hotheaded idiots looking to make trouble worse. Don't let it get you all screwy in your head."

I hear him, I trust him and I believe him.

He's right, I should focus on the trip, let the work eat up the hours. Most of the time, this is where I'm meant to be—where the language makes sense. But this time, it doesn't, the meaning somehow lost in translation.

For the first time, I don't want to be out here as much as I want to be *back* there.

41

Layla

My morning jog was very much needed today.

I've been tangled up with Leo for the last week, making it hard to stay on my routine. Though, I wouldn't complain if Leo *was* my morning routine.

It's misty, like usual. Chilly, like usual. The ocean is calm as I run past it.

Good. Hopefully, it's calm out there, too.

I stop to catch my breath, staring out over the water, knowing there's no chance I'll see Leo or the guys. They left hours ago, already far from here—out there, beyond the veil.

Izzy said she'd meet Sara and me at Taboo around seven tonight, and before I know it, the day slips away and evening comes quickly. Work was busy enough to keep my mind occupied, the hours slipping past. Sara talked—a lot—about her budding relationship with Will. Which, she admitted, she has me to thank for.

Back home, I pull on baggy ripped jeans and a cropped yellow sweater. My hair falls loose, curling from the humidity.

Izzy picks me up in a hot-pink, skin-tight mini dress. Her

hair is straight, like it usually is, but tonight it's extra shiny, and she's gone heavy on the perfume.

"Um, am I underdressed?" I ask, meeting her at her car.

She looks hot, and I look... *not.*

"Ha—no, silly. I just like the attention." She winks, patting the front seat. "Sara is meeting us there."

I'm surprised to see Nate lying sideways in the back seat as I slide in the front.

"Laylaaaaaa, what's up girl!" he slurs, obviously a bit drunk already.

"Nate is crashing girls' night." Izzy laughs. "And obviously, he decided to have a few drinks beforehand."

I don't mind Nate joining. In fact, I appreciate his presence. He's kind of like the big brother I never had.

"Hey, buddy." I giggle, patting his head.

"Layla, I miss Leo, too. We're in this together." He leans close to me, his hot breath reeking of beer.

I just laugh. "Yes, we are."

Taboo is crowded tonight—maybe a couple dozen more people than last time. Sara arrives shortly after we find a table, looking bright and happy.

"Hey!" I greet her with a hug.

She spots Nate, who's ordering us a round of beers. "Nate is one of the girls tonight?"

"Look, I couldn't leave him unattended," Izzy notes, rolling her eyes. "He misses them as much as we do. In fact, I think even more so."

Before I have a minute to soak in the reminder that I do, in fact, miss Leo very much already, Kyle is standing in front of the table with a tray of shots.

"First round of tequila is on me!" he announces, flashing me a wink.

Nate, back with his beers, cheers with happiness. "Yeah!"

Izzy and Nate clink glasses and throw the tequila back. I

look toward Sara, shrug, and toss one back with her. The pungent liquid hits my throat a little too hard and makes me cough.

"Lightweight, huh?" Kyle smirks, teasing me.

I force a laugh, pretending he doesn't make my skin crawl. Between the way his eyes hover and the fact that he defended Sam that night at Nate's, I know better than to trust him.

"May I sit?" he asks, eyeing the empty spot next to me and Sara.

Reluctantly, I scoot over even though every instinct tells me not to. "Sure."

He eyes the table—Nate, Izzy, and Sara now deep in debate about whether Dockfront or Flynn's is the better restaurant. Nate is obviously biased toward his own, and Sara's obviously biased toward Flynn's as Will works there.

"So, Leo's gone for a few nights, huh?" Kyle asks in a low voice.

"Yep, you know. The ocean calls and all that." I try to sound casual, but Leo's absence gnaws at me.

He smirks. "I'm sure it's not easy for a girl to date a guy like him. Busy for most of the year, girls practically throwing themselves at him during tourist season."

"I'm not afraid of a little competition," I say with a shrug, taking a swig of beer.

"You know, sometimes these overnights turn into more. Plus, it's dangerous out there." He pauses and looks at me. "Not exactly the kind of stability a girl like *you* deserves."

The tone starts to shift from uncomfortable to even *more* uncomfortable, and if Leo were here, he'd probably have Kyle in a headlock.

"What are you saying?" I ask, feeling defensive.

"I'm saying it might be smart to ditch him before he ditches you. Leo isn't exactly the settle-down kind of guy. You know, he's not your only option in Morro Bay." He pauses and turns one of the shot glasses upside down, letting some liquid trickle out of it. "He's got big-time daddy issues, too."

Alright, *this* is done.

"I don't see how this is any of your business, *Kyle*," I respond, raising my voice.

"Hey, I'm just looking out for the new girl," he says, standing up. "Not trying to cause unnecessary drama."

He puts his hands up in defeat and walks away, back behind the bar. Now I don't feel like drinking anymore.

"What the fuck was that about?" Izzy asks.

"I don't know, but I don't like it." I eye Kyle as he tends to patrons. "What's his story anyway?"

"He's been here as long as our families have," Nate slurs. "He's the fuckboy in town. Kind of a loner."

"That makes sense because I'm pretty sure he just hit on me," I say, glancing at the bar, watching him fill a glass with beer.

"Wait, isn't he like in your group?" Sara asks.

"Not really, not consistently. More like when he's bored, he'll come around. Leo doesn't trust him. I get a weird vibe, too," Nate notes.

"Maybe he's just being a typical guy, wanting a chance to play with the new shiny toy in town," Izzy says.

"Ew, gross," I scoff, pushing my beer away and catching a glimpse of the back door opening.

My stomach drops.

Sam Murphy just walked in.

He's got that same smug look as he scans the room. He's with Charlie—the girl who so nonchalantly invited him to Nate's that night—and both of their eyes land on me.

And when they do he smirks.

Not a word. Not a nod. Just a slow, creepy smile that makes me want to bolt for the door.

"What's wrong?" Izzy asks, noticing my gaze.

I tilt my chin discreetly toward the door. "Sam. He's here."

Her eyes narrow as she twists in her chair. "What the hell is *he* doing here? I'm pretty sure everyone in town has told him to back off at this point."

Maybe everyone except Kyle.

"You okay?" Sara leans over and whispers.

I don't respond. Because something else catches my attention.

Kyle's next to him now, chatting quietly with Sam and Charlie. Charlie's arms are crossed, eyes moving around the room, looking uncomfortable. The place is loud enough that no one seems to notice Kyle leaning in as Sam slips behind the bar. Kyle pulls something from his back pocket, passing it to Sam behind the counter.

It's hard to see exactly what it is from here but it's quick, it's subtle, and it looks like cash.

I stare, trying to make sure I'm not seeing things, but Sam tucks the money into his coat and gives Charlie a nod and they disappear back through the door they came in from.

I'm instantly very grateful to be in a crowded place with friends.

Kyle lingers, slowly wiping down the counter even though no one was sitting there, trying to look busy. Then, he walks off like nothing happened.

Izzy sees my face. "Okay, seriously, what the fuck?"

"I think I just watched a deal go down," I whisper. "Between Kyle and Sam."

Her eyes widen. "You sure?"

Nate and Sara also turn their focus on me. "I think so," I say. "It felt off. Charlie is definitely somehow involved, too."

The unease in my stomach twists, his smirk playing in my mind.

"This place feels gross now," Nate says. "And Leo would kill us if we had you anywhere near Sam. Let's go."

Fine by me.

42

Leo

THE SEA IS RESTING TONIGHT.

The stars shine clear above us, the crescent moon hangs low. We're anchored past the cloud bank, the motor silent, the boat swaying beneath us. Hank sings a sea shanty: *"Heave her high, and let the tide take me home."*

Rowdy shuffles the deck of cards. He's chewing on a toothpick, cigarette tucked behind his ear, and for once, not talking shit. That's how I know he's losing.

"Hank, your deal," he grunts, tossing the pack across the crate-turned-card-table we've set up on the deck. The night's still enough that the cards don't fly away, just the occasional light gust. We're circled around it, perched on overturned buckets with our beers, beanies, and coats—bellies full thanks to Hank, who actually made a decent fish chowder.

"Damn right it's my deal," Hank says, cracking his knuckles, getting ready to kick our asses in another round of poker. "Y'all are about to lose more than your dignity."

Austin groans. "Every time he says that, I end up paying for tacos for a week."

"That's 'cause you suck," Rowdy mumbles now with a

mouthful of sunflower seeds. "And you got no poker face. You flinch every time you get a pair."

"You're just mad 'cause I got a catch before you did today," Austin fires back. "With your 'lucky lure' and everything."

I lean back in my chair, beer in hand, soaking it all in.

I've spent the last few years like a man underwater.

Grieving.

Numb.

Carrying too much of my old man's memory and trying not to let it sink me.

I wonder what Layla's doing right now. Izzy probably dragged her out, or maybe she's cozied up with Sara watching a movie. I hope she's safe, I hope she's happy.

I hope she's missing me.

"Earth to Leo." Rowdy snaps his fingers in front of my face. "You folding or what?"

I glance at my hand. It's a shit hand. I toss it down. "I'm out."

"Surprise, surprise," Hank grumbles.

Rowdy narrows his eyes at me, like he can read my mind. "You good?"

"Yeah," I say honestly. "I am."

"Uh-oh," Austin whistles. "Look out, boys. He's going soft again."

"Shut up," I mutter, though a grin pulls at my mouth.

"You missing your girl?" Austin teases, nudging me with his elbow.

"Fuck you," I joke.

I do miss her. But I also know this trip is good for me. For all of us. There's something sacred about being out here. No distractions, no bullshit, just the sea and the people who get you best.

"She's good for you," Hank says, out of nowhere. He

doesn't say much, and never anything sentimental, so we all look at him. "What?" He shrugs. "She's got good energy. Lightens you up."

I nod, because there's nothing else to say. He's right—again.

Hank's words make me think of my mom, too. She had always been a good energy, bright and spirited, before my dad passed away. She's been asking less and less about my day to day over the past two years. Probably because I had nothing more to tell her other than "just been working."

A job she wanted me to quit, but knew that would never be an option.

I wonder if bringing Layla to meet her would bring back some of that light. I can already picture them together. Mom, making too much food and giving Layla a tour of her most prized possession—her garden.

The idea doesn't scare me; in fact, it feels kind of right.

43

Layla

Sara's apartment sits just behind The Busy Bean. It's small, cute and cozy. The walls are painted a pale yellow, and the windows are lined with leafy green plants.

Will met us here after Sara called to tell him that the girls' night—*and Nate's*—was disrupted.

"Dad's out tonight, make yourselves at home," Sara says, already in the kitchen grabbing glasses of water for everyone.

Izzy wastes no time. "Okay, so what the hell is happening? Kyle, Sam, and Charlie—are they like working together?"

I shift on the couch, glancing at Nate, who's now parked on the floor with a half empty beer bottle he took from Taboo.

"Did Leo tell you about Sam…" I hesitate. "Showing up at my apartment?"

Leo had asked me to keep it quiet, but he also said he'd loop Nate in before he left. But this will definitely be news to Izzy.

All heads turn to me. Nate nods, slowly.

"No!?" Izzy says wide-eyed.

"That day we saw him at Dockfront," I say, glancing

between them, "he came over after you dropped me off, Izzy. Said he wanted to send Leo a message."

Nate sighs, setting his bottle on the floor. Sara walks over to him, takes the bottle and replaces it with a glass of water.

"Leo got there first," I say quietly.

"Are you serious? Leo didn't kill him?" Izzy eyes go wide.

"He wanted to," I admit. "Look, I don't want any of you getting dragged into this, either. Leo asked me to keep it quiet until he had the chance to talk with the guys about it. But, I guess, it's out there now."

"Well, he's probably telling them on this trip. Making sure they are far enough away so they can't do anything stupid," Izzy says. "Rowdy would have been impulsive."

Sara sets her water down and sits beside me, her expression unreadable. Nate stares hard at the floor before finally speaking. "Sam asked to use my restaurant. Said it was low-key enough to make a perfect drop point. Offered to cut me in. I told him to fuck off."

"What!?" Izzy's head snaps again.

He nods, eyes lazy. "I haven't seen him since, but… I think Kyle's involved. He's been different lately. I've seen them together a few times."

Izzy swears under her breath. "Oh my God."

Nate looks up. "What?"

"I think he was high at your place, Nate. I wasn't sure, but I had a suspicion. Now it feels more solidified. Plus, he mouthed off to Rowdy before he left which is a really fucking stupid thing to do."

Will speaks for the first time from the La-Z-Boy chair he's sitting in. "He's using *and* he's dealing. Kyle's letting Sam use Taboo."

Everyone turns and stares at him.

Izzy's eyes narrow. "And how the hell do *you* know that?"

Will shrugs. "I work in a restaurant. People talk. Plus I see them drive around town sometimes at night when I am closing up at work."

"Jesus," Izzy mutters. "This is a disaster."

"Yeah," Nate mumbles.

"I can keep my eyes open, let you know if I notice anything else. I'm pretty invisible to them, pretty sure they don't even know my name," Will says.

I twist my lips into a smile. "Thanks Will."

"Well, this is enough excitement for one night. I need some sleep." Izzy stands, walks over and pulls me up into a quick hug. "When the guys get back we'll figure this all out."

Izzy nudges Nate. "Need a ride home, lightweight?"

Nate nods, pushing himself off the floor and hugs me, too. "Call me if anything feels off, I promised Leo I'd keep an eye on you."

"Thanks, Nate," I say, giving him a solid squeeze.

He takes my phone from my hand and saves his number in it. "And don't be alone tonight, stay with Sara."

"You got it." I smile at him.

"Love you, cuz," Izzy says to Sara. "Night, Will."

They leave together, and the apartment quiets down. Will lingers near the front door, hands shoved nervously into his pockets. "Should I head out, too?" he asks.

Sara blushes. "If you want to, but you're welcome to stay."

"Okay, sure." He grins, cheeks matching Sara's.

Sara looks at the clock, then at me. "Will and I are probably going to hang out in the living room for a bit. Want to join us?"

I smile, but the way her face lights up at him makes it clear she wants time alone. "Thanks, but I'm pretty tired."

"Okay, take my bed."

"Are you sure?"

"Absolutely."

"Alright then, you two behave," I say with a wink.

Will's cheeks flush again. Sara leans close, whispering in my ear, "It's going to be okay, you know."

"I know. Thank you, Sara. You're a really wonderful friend."

She hugs me tight and then joins Will on the couch.

I slip into her room and collapse onto the unmade bed. Her pillows are fluffy and smell like fresh laundry. I check out the various decorations she has on her walls. Some paintings of abstract art, photos of her and Dan, and one of her mom maybe, who I have yet to learn about.

I scroll through my phone for a while, trying to distract myself, trying to kill time until I can fall asleep. But it's useless. Sleep doesn't come easy—not with Leo pressed into every thought.

With him, there's no such thing as time.

Only the ache of knowing there will never be enough of it.

The last two days have literally dragged by.

There hasn't been another Sam sighting since Taboo, and Sara and I have been inseparable—working extra hours, watching reruns of sitcoms, even grabbing a couple of meals with Will. I've absolutely been the third wheel, and I'm pretty sure they're getting sick of me.

But they're in luck. Leo comes back tonight, and I'm hoping his first stop is me.

Sara and I are up before the sun today, The Busy Bean kitchen warm against the coolness outside, the smell of butter and sugar already filling the space as we bake pastries.

"So, you counting down the minutes?" Sara teases starting a pot of coffee.

"The *seconds*." I laugh.

The bell on the front door chimes. We expect our usual

first customer, but instead, a woman with light brown, shoulder-length hair walks in, carrying a giant bouquet of sunflowers—big, yellow, bright, and beautiful.

"Layla?" she asks, looking right at me.

"That's me," I murmur, still shocked by how large the sunflowers are.

"My name is Wendy, and I was given strict instructions to deliver these to you this morning," she says with a hint of Midwestern accent, handing me the vase. "Leo came in before he left on his trip—said he was worried about not having service to place the order out on the water."

I stand, dumbfounded.

Not because I have never received flowers before, because I have. But *nothing* quite this large, and absolutely nothing this meaningful.

From *someone* this meaningful.

"These are stunning," I breathe, wide-eyed.

"I've known Leo since he was a baby. His mother and I are good friends." Wendy smiles. "He has never once stepped foot in my shop. Until a few days ago, that is."

I look between her and the flowers, still speechless, my heart racing a million miles a second. Because this gesture isn't like the rest. It's not about sex. It's not about protection.

It's… sweet. It's… generous.

A whole new layer of Leo I didn't expect to see.

Wendy chuckles. "I'll get out of your hair. It's nice to meet you, Layla. You're one lucky lady."

"Thank you so much." I smile, waiting until she leaves before opening the card.

See you tonight

-Leo

44

Leo

It's only been three nights, four-ish days, and I feel like a kid about to meet his favorite superhero.

The second we got back to the docks, I was out of there and racing home for a quick shower. I didn't think Layla would appreciate the stench of salt water and fish guts.

Now, as I knock on her door, my stomach bubbles.

I'm not sure if it's nerves or Hank's failed attempt at tuna casserole last night. But half a minute later, it all dissolves when I'm met with the big blue eyes of a beautiful woman. A woman standing there in a satin slip dress with my flannel sliding off one shoulder.

Either I was at sea one day too long, or she is simply the sexiest woman to exist.

I'm going with the latter.

"Hi," she breathes.

"Hi," I say back.

She opens the door wider so I can fit through. The sunflowers I had Wendy deliver sit in the middle of her island counter, brightening the room and matching her energy. The air smells of garlic and rosemary, which makes my mouth water. A pot of pasta simmers on the stove, steam puffing into the air. A pan of red sauce simmers beside it.

She looks at me and grins, her cheeks blushing slightly. "I missed you," she says, her voice still soft, waiting for me to make the move.

"I missed you, too," I say, closing the space between us.

She bites her lower lip, waiting for me to take it from her. *So I do.*

I pull her in, her soft skin and soft fabric clashing with the roughness of mine, and kiss her.

And *damn*, I don't think I'll ever get used to this.

"You are so beautiful," I whisper, still holding her close.

"So are you," she whispers back, planting another sweet kiss on my lips.

We stand there for a moment before she pulls away, taking my hand and guiding me to her couch.

"Dinner's almost ready, just waiting for the garlic bread to finish baking. I want to hear all about your trip," she says, plopping down and patting the space next to her.

I breathe out, letting go of the air I've been sucking in just by watching her move in that tiny dress.

"It smells great." I sit beside her. "The trip was a lot of hard work… and a lot of beer."

"Doesn't sound so bad." She giggles. "Thank you for the beautiful flowers, by the way. I love them."

She glances at them on the counter, her smile growing even bigger.

"Of course, I'm glad you like them. What have you been up to?" I ask, hoping she only has good things to say.

"Well, also a lot of work, a lot of Sara… and a lot of Will, too." She laughs.

"Oh, yeah?"

"Yeah, they have loved each other since high school. Talk about a slow burn."

I chuckle. "That's cool. He seems like a good guy."

"He is," she says, then her tone softens and she tucks a strand of hair behind her ear. "I also went and had some drinks with Sara, Izzy and Nate at Taboo."

"How was that?" I ask, though for some reason my anxiety is already peaking.

"We didn't stay long." She pauses, her fingers tracing the seam of the couch. "Sam showed up."

I freeze, the room tilts for a second, and my pulse starts to pick up. He better not have even looked her way.

"He didn't talk to me or even come near our table. But I think there's something you should know," she quickly adds.

I stay quiet, gritting my teeth, waiting for the bad news to drop.

"He and Kyle are working together," she says, placing her hand on my knee. "Like... dealing or something. Charlie was there, too."

My blood boils. He's just not going to fucking listen.

"Leo," Layla says quietly, squeezing my hand, "we can't let this ruin our night. I just thought you should know before you hear it from someone else."

"Yeah," I say, monotone, because I don't want to freak out in front of her.

"I'm sorry," she says, pulling her hand away like she's afraid she's said too much, like she's the one who ruined the evening.

But it's not her.

It's him. It's *them.*

Sam and Kyle and somehow, in some way, Charlie is in the fucking mix.

I feel that all-too-familiar weight on my chest, the one I've been carrying the last couple of years. That constant fear that something or someone I care about is going to be taken from me.

Again.

And it's not just the fear of harm to Layla. It's Nate. Izzy. My people. My home.

I can feel myself starting to go dark. Starting to plan. Starting to spiral.

He's not going to stop, not unless I make him.

"Leo." Her voice cuts through my thoughts. She reaches for my hand again, wrapping both of hers around it.

"Hey," she says again. "Look at me."

I do.

Her eyes search mine. "You're here. You're safe. I'm safe. We all are. Nothing happened, and we will figure it out. You don't have to carry all of it tonight."

I swallow the lump in my throat. She's right.

I sigh, letting go of just enough tension to feel my own heartbeat again.

"I just…" I shake my head, dragging my fingers through my hair. "It's like… every time things start to feel good, something tries to rip it all away."

"But it didn't," she says gently. "You're back. I'm here. We have this moment and I'm not going anywhere."

That hits me.

Because *fuck*, I have missed her. This grounding part of her, her laugh, her scent, her eyes. I've been thinking about her nonstop for the last four days. I don't want to waste another minute thinking about Sam, or Kyle, or plans.

I just want *her.*

I cup her face, pressing my forehead to hers. "Thank you," I whisper.

She leans into me. I kiss her again, more passionately and when we finally part, her eyes are glassy and her lips slightly swollen.

"I need to get out of town for a couple of days," I say, still holding her. "Get a little change in scenery."

She nods slowly. "Okay."

"Will you come with me?" I ask. "Two days. Let's go to Big Sur."

"Really?"

"Yes." I brush my thumb along her fingers. "My mom lives there now and I could use some time. With you. Somewhere quiet, somewhere I can breathe without looking over my shoulder."

Her lips part, a smile tugging. "Yes. I'll go."

And just like that, the pressure eases again. Not gone, but manageable.

I think that with her... I can manage anything.

45

Layla

THE DRIVE FROM MORRO BAY TO BIG SUR TAKES ABOUT
three hours, and it hugs the cliffs along the Pacific Coast
Highway the whole way.

Leo's got one hand on the wheel, the other resting on the
open window. Wind ruffles his dark hair as the early morning
sun spills gold over the ocean beside us. The fog is light today,
pulled back and revealing the rugged coastline.

"It's beautiful, isn't it?" he says, glancing over with a grin.
He gestures toward the glittering water beside us.

"It's gorgeous," I breathe, taking it all in.

"I've loved being near the water for as long as I can
remember," he says, gaze drifting back to the sea. "Before I
got into fishing, my dad used to take my mom and me out on
the boat almost every weekend."

"That's really sweet," I say, admiring the way his voice
softens with the memory. "Were you ever scared of the ocean?
I had the fear as a kid that a shark would swallow me whole if
I went in past my knees."

He laughs. "No, never scared. Not even after my dad died.

If anything, it made me want to be out there more. The ocean's the only place that's ever made me feel calm."

"Even after everything?"

He nods. "*Especially* after everything."

Right. *He belongs to it.*

"You're close with your mom, huh?"

"Yeah. We talk every week. I try to come up this way once a month if I can swing it." He pauses, then shoots me a quick look. "Is this weird?"

"Is what weird?"

"That you're about to meet her," he says, eyes back on the road. "I didn't exactly plan it, but…"

I sit up a little straighter. I *am* about to meet Mrs. Anderson. The woman who raised Leo. The woman who, based on what others say, has never met any of his past girlfriends—if that's even what they were.

Suddenly my palms are a little sweaty.

"I wasn't thinking much of it before," I admit, "but I think I'm having some anxiety now."

He chuckles, reaching over to squeeze my hand. "Don't. She's going to love you and she's a total softie."

God, I hope he's right.

There's a lot riding on this trip. Not just breaking free from the Sam drama, but this next step we seem to be taking. The unspoken hope that maybe this—whatever this is between us—is real. Is growing.

"Well," I say, wiping my palms on my pink sundress, "I can't wait to meet her."

He glances at me again. "She's going to be just as crazy about you as I am."

We pull up into a driveway that has a plethora of different kinds of flowers lining it. Lavender, rosemary, marigolds and peonies all seemingly placed in an artistic nature. At the end sits a moderately-sized two-story home, tan with white trim and a wraparound porch.

A woman in a long floral jumpsuit bursts from the house. "Leo, my love!"

She runs to him, half his height, stands on her tiptoes, and plants a big sloppy kiss on his forehead. She has dark hair like her son, very long and wavy.

"Hi, Momma," he says, bending down and squeezing her into a hug.

They break free, both wearing big smiles.

"Hi, Mrs. Anderson, it's so nice to m—" I start to say, reaching out my hand but she interrupts me and pulls me into an embrace.

"Layla, honey. Please, call me Norma. It's so nice to meet you!" she says. "I've heard many wonderful things about you."

Oh? The flutter in my stomach returns. Leo smiles at me, somehow looking more boy-ish around his mother and less stoic man-ish.

"Come in, come in, I have lots of food ready," she sings, signaling us to follow her. "My side of the family is Italian, so I hope you are hungry."

Leo winks at me. "Sounds great, Mom."

The house is beautiful, open, well-lit and clean. Pictures litter the walls, mostly of Leo, his mom, and who I think is his father. One in particular stands out to me. Leo with his dad, on the deck of a boat. He's maybe six or seven, has a couple of missing teeth, but looks so happy next to his dad who has a spotted fish hooked to a lure.

"His name was Dean. I remember this day like it was yesterday," Leo says, standing behind me and grazing the picture with his thumb.

I grab his other hand softly. "He was very handsome, like you."

We stand there and admire the other photos scattered about. Leo describes some memories to me as Norma clanks around in the kitchen.

"Kids! Let's eat!" she calls.

The kitchen which doubles as a dining room is just as beautiful as the entryway. Pastel-colored tiles, bright walls, a large circular dining table. A display of fresh sandwiches and salads lie in the middle. Along with potato chips and chocolate chip cookies.

"What do you like to drink sweetie? Tea? Lemonade?" Norma asks.

"Lemonade sounds great," I say, taking a seat at the table.

"Perfect, I just made a fresh batch." She pours us all a glass. "Leo loves it, too, but he likes his extra sweet. Too much sugar for me, so there's some on the table if you want to add more."

I take a sip; the taste is just right, the coolness refreshing.

"It's perfect."

She smiles. "Let's pray."

Leo sits across from me, Norma to my left. She takes my hand, while Leo reaches across and holds my other.

"Lord, we thank You for the gift of this day and for the love we share around this table. Bless this food You have provided, that it may nourish our bodies and strengthen us. May this time together fill our hearts with gratitude, joy, and peace. In Jesus' name, amen."

Leo and Norma exchange a smile as she gently squeezes both our hands before letting them loose.

We spend the afternoon exploring the house and the land around it—the open sky above, redwoods nearby, the ocean faintly audible in the distance. The property is peaceful. Wild in some parts, manicured in others, suiting her perfectly.

She points out her budding garden, full of colorful vegetables and earthy herbs. She shares that she moved here about a year after Dean passed, and said it was too painful to stay in the home they shared. Too many ghosts in the walls.

She tells stories as we walk. Mostly about Leo as a kid. Sunburned and barefoot, catching sandcrabs and insisting he could out-fish his dad by the time he was nine. There's so much love in her voice when she speaks about them—Dean and Leo both. I catch her glancing at her son when she thinks he's not looking, like she's so proud of the man he's become.

Over iced tea and leftover cookies on the back deck, she turns her questions toward me. She asks about my childhood, my parents, the things I loved about growing up. She asks how I found Morro Bay, and why I stayed.

She's beautiful. Just like Leo. Same eyes and the same warmth.

There's something familiar in her laugh, too, that husky chuckle that reminds me of the way Leo sounds when he finally lets himself be happy.

I offered to take us out to dinner, but she waved the idea off—she'd already made lasagna from scratch, with caesar salad and homemade blueberry pie. I was still full from lunch, but I ate every bite because it was impossible not to.

After dinner, I helped her clean up the kitchen. We swapped funny stories while we rinsed dishes and passed utensils, laughter from the three of us filling the time.

And just like Leo promised, she welcomed me with open arms.

46

Leo

"DAMN," I WHISTLE, RUNNING MY HAND ALONG THE SIDE OF the old 1979 VW Vanagon. "Still can't believe this old thing survived the move."

The yellow paint's faded, but she's still standing.

"Just how you left it," Mom says, arms folded. "Though, I'm not sure it'll start anymore."

The sun disappeared hours ago, leaving the sky a deep, dark blue. After dinner, the three of us sit on the porch with a bottle of red that Mom only brings out for special occasions. The really good stuff she hoards unless she has a special guest over.

She likes Layla. I can see it. I can *feel* it.

Mom stretches, yawning. "Alright, kids. It's getting late. I'm heading in. We have another fun day ahead tomorrow." She pauses, turning toward us. "Want me to set up the guest rooms?"

I glance at Layla. She's leaning on the back of the van, moonlight reflecting off of her golden hair. She looks up at me with those beautiful eyes, and I know she's game before I even ask.

"Actually," I say, rubbing the back of my neck, "I think we'll stay out here tonight. If you're up for it?" I ask Layla.

She beams "Sounds adventurous."

Mom smiles knowingly, then turns to Layla. "Honey, today was really lovely."

Layla opens her arms and pulls her in for a hug. "It really was. Thank you for everything. The food, the stories, all of it."

"Goodnight, Mom," I say, pressing a kiss to the top of her head.

"Sweet dreams, my dears!" she calls as she walks slowly up the gravel path, disappearing into the house.

The night settles perfectly, the kind that only belongs to this place—salt and pine mingling in the air. I pull open the van's back door, and it's just as I left it.

"Your mom is so wonderful, Leo," Layla says, stepping up into the van and ducking slightly to look around inside.

I follow her in.

"Yeah," I say, flicking on the little battery lantern I always kept in the corner, surprised it still works. "She really is."

The light glows against the old panel walls. The thin mattress is still covered in the faded flannel blanket I used to sleep on, band stickers peeling along the wood beside it.

It smells musty, but in the best kind of way. In the '*I grew up here*' kind of way.

"Joey and I practically lived in this thing during senior year of high school," I say, remembering when he stole an abused dog from a terrible neighbor and kept it in here until we found it a new home.

"I love that," Layla says, eyes on the old stickers. "How did you acquire such a gem?" She laughs.

"It was my first ride, actually. My dad found it in an old lot and said if I could fix it up, I could have it. So I did. Spent an entire summer working on it."

"You definitely earned it then," she says, sitting down on

the mattress and drawing a heart shape on the fogged-up window.

I sit down beside her, the old material creaking beneath my weight, and take her in. She looks so damn good like this —barefoot, relaxed, her hair loose and wild from the breezy evening.

"This place..." she murmurs, looking around. "It kind of feels like a time capsule."

"Yeah," I agree. "Kind of forgot how many nights I crashed back here. After parties. After fights with my parents. After pretty much... everything."

"Do you miss that version of you?"

I think about it for a minute. "Parts of him, maybe. He was restless, but happy. Didn't really know what he wanted, but at least he was living life."

Her smile is quiet. "He's still in there, you know."

"Yeah, well," I breathe out, "he evolved into someone who can't *stop* feeling. Only now, it's just pain most of the time." I glance at her, surprised that I'm letting myself be this vulnerable. "I've let it take over. Let it define me."

She looks down, fingers tracing the frayed edge of the blanket beneath us.

"I'm sorry," I say quickly. "Didn't mean to—*shit*—I didn't mean to bring the whole mood down."

"Don't apologize, Leo."

She lifts her eyes to mine. So deeply sapphire, so full of understanding.

"Your pain," she says gently, "it's beautiful."

My heart beats everywhere at once. In my throat, in my ribs, down to the ends of my fingertips.

"I know that's what you need," she continues. "Permission to be you. So I'm saying it again. Your pain is *beautiful*. It matters, and it shaped you."

I'm just staring at her now, eyes burning with something I

haven't let myself feel in a long time. She's not afraid. She sees it all and doesn't even flinch.

"I don't want you to fix it. Or change it," she says. "I just want to be next to you through it. So it doesn't have to eat you up alone."

I don't have any words to say. The wind rustles outside, brushing through the trees. She shifts, and we are suddenly closer than I realized. Her breath is warm, laced with the smell of sweet red wine.

"What are you thinking?" she whispers.

"That you can't be real."

Her breath hitches, just a little. I reach for her hand, threading our fingers together. Her skin is smooth against my callouses.

"And that you have no idea what you are doing to me."

Her eyes find mine, her lips part, and I don't wait.

I lean in, close enough to feel her inhale, to witness the rise and fall of her perfect, plump chest. And I kiss her.

It deepens quickly, her hands in my hair, my palm sliding along her bare thigh, her body moving instinctively toward me.

She shifts into my lap naturally, like her body's been craving this, just as mine has.

I don't just want her.

I *need* her.

And I'm thinking I kind of like what it feels like to not be so goddamn broken.

47

Layla

His mouth crashes onto mine.

No, not a crash... A declaration.

A plea.

A fucking storm.

And I want to drown in it.

My hands tangle in his perfect hair, his chest presses tight to mine, my back slides against the worn material of the blanket as he lays me down. Gentle but possessive, like I am his.

Like I've *always* been his, even if we've only just begun to figure it out.

I can feel him... *All* of him.

His body presses between my thighs, spreading me open. I arch up against him, tugging his shirt until it's over his head and tossed somewhere into the abyss. Goosebumps take over the second his skin meets mine.

His name tears from my throat when he grinds on me. I don't care if anyone is nearby, if they can hear my begging, hear his roar.

Let the trees be a witness.

Let the wind *watch.*

"I want you," he groans.

And I answer with a gasp, legs wrapping around his waist like a possessed banshee.

"Then take me."

It becomes chaotic and poetic all at once. His teeth and tongue meet my lips, my neck, my collarbone. He curses under his breath when he finally gets my dress off, shoves his pants down, and rips my thong away. Clothes are thrown in every direction, and I moan as his hands slide up my bare hips, his fingers digging into the flesh of them.

He pauses, panting, sweat already dripping from his forehead, landing in the hollow of my neck.

"Layla," he whispers, "I need to *taste* you."

His words envelope me. I don't need to give him permission. He already owns it.

His eyes lock on mine as he lowers his face between my thighs.

A slow, teasing lick makes me jolt, then his tongue plunges inside of me. His intensity draws a gasp from my core when he sucks me into his mouth, savoring and devouring me in the same breath.

My head tips back, a cry breaking free as I give myself over to him—his tongue flicking, lips sucking, pulling me tighter into the spiral he's creating. Every nerve is awake, every breath a shake that I can't control.

I'm teetering, already so close to breaking apart. The release pulls at me, begging, but I hold it back because I need *more.* I don't just want to come. I want to come with him, wrapped around him, taking all of him when I finally unravel.

"Leo," I gasp, his tongue moving against me like it was made just for my pleasure.

He pauses and looks up, those deep green eyes claiming every piece of me.

"I need you," I say, breathless. "All of you, inside me—*right now.*"

He grins. "I'm yours, Layla. However you want me."

He shifts upward, aligning himself with my opening, and fills me in one perfect thrust. My body arches off the van floor and we move like wildfire. Fast and frantic, breathless and starved. My back slams down again, my legs clamping tighter around his hips. His forehead crashes against mine, our moans colliding until they're one sound.

I've never felt anything like this. Not even close. This isn't just sex... It's so much more.

Every single part of me crumbles beneath him, and he feels it. Like he's in tune with my heartbeat, my breath, the very core of me.

He starts to slow. What was wild and unhinged has transformed into something else entirely.

The rhythm softens, becoming a tide instead of a storm. A calm pull, instead of a crash. His hips roll against mine like the sea smoothing the shore.

His mouth finds mine again. Our lips meet and melt, tongues tangling, the taste of salt and sweat. He sucks my bottom lip gently between his teeth, and I whimper against him, hips rising to meet his with every slow and aching glide.

It's softer, but no less intense.

If anything, this part feels like... love.

He bows his forehead to mine, and when we finally fall over that edge, it feels like *home.*

48

She's lying asleep in my arms.

It's silent, except for her soft breathing, the hoot of an owl and the distant crash of waves through the cracked window. I should be asleep, too. I should be completely wrung out and content.

But my mind refuses to quiet.

I stare at the ceiling of the van, heart still pounding like I just ran ten miles instead of making love to the woman curled against my chest.

Because that's what it was. Not just sex. Not just release.

It was *her*.

Like she knows something I don't. Like she believes in a version of me I've never seen.

Her leg is draped over mine, her naked body pressed to me. I run a hand down the slope of her spine, she shifts slightly but doesn't wake.

Trusting *me*, even in her sleep.

And how? How does someone trust so simply? So easily?

I've spent years building up walls. Holding in the pain.

The grief.

Locking everything down, keeping most people at arm's length.

But somehow, she's here. Like my walls were meant for everyone except her. Like they were invisible, like they simply didn't apply to *Layla Dumont.*

I was the seawall, and she was the sea… crashing into me, over me, *through* me.

I've carried the weight of my father's absence for so long. It's been dragging me down, making me afraid to find peace, because peace itself can feel dangerous.

But tonight, with her rested against me, it doesn't feel so heavy.

The thought creeps in—the sea always takes back what it gives. What if she's no different? What if this slips through my fingers the second I believe in it?

I don't know what any of this means yet. I don't know what tomorrow will bring or the day after.

But there's something that I *do* know.

I'd burn for her.

I'd drown for her.

I'd be remade in whatever tide she pulls me into.

49

Layla

THE HEAT WAKES ME, THE SUN BEAMS THROUGH THE STEAMED windows and shines over Leo and me—tangled legs, messy hair, bare skin.

"Good morning." His deep, scratchy voice is the perfect thing to wake up to.

I wonder how long he's been lying here, letting me sleep, waiting patiently while the sun rises.

"Good morning," I say, sitting up and letting the blanket fall, baring my chest.

His eyes find me instantly. That crooked smirk spreads across his face. The same boyish grin I saw yesterday, the one that makes my stomach flip.

"How'd you sleep?" he asks with a wink.

I like this version of him. Flirty and soft.

"What do you think?" I tease, leaning in to press a kiss to his lips.

He's still smiling when I pull back. "There's a little coffee place a few miles down the road. I usually run down there and grab one for my mom when I'm here."

He sits up beside me, stretching, revealing his toned abs. "I can bring one back for you, too."

"That sounds amazing." I grin, admiring his physique. "I'll go keep Norma company while you're gone."

I glance around, realizing I probably shouldn't greet his mom like this. "Uh… Where's my dress?"

Leo laughs, reaches under himself, and pulls it out. "Found it."

"Cute." I giggle, tugging it on. "My bag's still inside, right?"

"Yep," he says, sliding his jeans on. "You've got time to freshen up if you want. Mom's probably in the garden."

We finish dressing and swing open the back doors of the van. Fresh air rushes in immediately, crisp and tinged with pine and ocean salt. It's cooler than I expected, but not unpleasant. I pause, letting it fill my lungs, letting last night's memories linger inside of me.

Leo hooks an arm around my waist, settling a kiss to the side of my head. "Be right back."

"Drive safe, sailor."

He gives me another quick smile before climbing into his truck as I slip quietly through the front door of the house.

He was right; Norma is in the backyard. I spot her through one of the windows tending to her garden. I head into the bathroom, change into the leggings and sweater I packed, swipe on some deodorant, and give my face a good wash.

After, I join Norma outside. She's humming as she waters her tomatoes.

"Good morning, Norma," I say, only slightly startling her.

"Oh, hi, honey. I thought I heard some commotion."

I blush, not sure if she's referencing the van opening and closing this morning or… last night.

"Leo's out, getting us coffee."

"Oh, perfect. It will be a good time for us to take a walk then." She wipes her hands on her blue jeans, sets her watering can down, and leads the way.

We walk down her street. The houses are perfectly spaced apart, all appearing well taken care of. Birds chirp around us, and beautiful flowers and trees line the porches while the wind lightly rustles through them.

"Dean was a very hardworking man," Norma says as we pass by two squirrels chasing each other in circles. "He loved very deeply. Leo is a lot like him in that way."

"He and I met when I was barely eighteen. I worked at a gas station at the time, and he would come in every day to buy a cheap turkey sandwich. He didn't come from money"—we turn down a road similar to the others—"but he was always so sweet and always said hello to me. Then, one day he bought two sandwiches and asked if I would sit and eat one with him, and I did." She pauses and waves to a neighbor.

Her words settle into me, leaving me quiet and grateful to share this moment with her. To learn more about the depths of the man that they both lost.

"We would eat together a couple of times a week, then it was multiple times a week, and eventually we were inseparable. We got married just a year after meeting and when my Dean died, I didn't think I would make it. I was beyond heartbroken. I wanted to die with him, but I had to take care of Leo. He needed me. A boy losing the dad he loved so incredibly much… It broke him," she says, stopping to take my hand in hers. "I did the best I could, but I was broken, too. Still am. The only thing I find comfort in is that I'm aging and I'm closer to joining the love of my life than I was yesterday. Each day is one step closer."

LEO

She lets go of my hand and we continue to walk.

"It's morbid, I know. But it's the truth. Leo is strong, he's smart, but he's still shattered. We will never heal from that. We never got to say goodbye and we will never recover from our loss." Her eyes start to fill with tears.

I think of when Leo told me about the Harbor Master and Victor Murphy—how their hatred and evilness denied a family the chance to mourn, a chance to recognize their loved one in the most fitting way.

"I found comfort in an odd place, but Leo is still drowning in that grief."

I put an arm over her and pull her into my side as we walk. "He is a wonderful man, Norma. You've done a tremendous job raising him. I can't begin to imagine what you two went through."

She offers me a half-smile. "I'm telling you this because you bring some peace to his world, and for that I am indebted to you."

"No, you're not. I... care about him, Norma."

"Oh, I know you do. I can see it in your eyes." She beams. "He loves you, Layla. I know my son, and I've seen that twinkle in a man's eye before. It's how Dean looked at me when we fell in love."

Love.

A word I've never said to anyone outside of family and friends. A word I've only heard in heated moments. None of them the truth.

"He told me about the first night you two met at that bar. Told me about the new girl in town, how pretty she was, how he thought she wouldn't be stimulated enough to live in a small town. Not someone like her," she says, chuckling now. "And now, here we are."

My cheeks turn rosy, and a smile pulls at my lips as her words sink in. The heaviness of grief moves into something softer, and by the time we're walking back toward the house, the air feels warmer. Some moments are quiet, others filled with easy small talk about neighbors or local events and when she invites me to come back up for the Big Sur Jade Festival, it doesn't feel like just a visit anymore. It feels like an open door.

We aren't gone long, so by the time we get back, Leo's waiting for us inside with two hot cups of coffee. "There are my girls. Where were you two?" he asks, kissing Norma's cheek and then mine. The words catch me off guard a little, but in a good way, a *belonging* way.

Leo passes me my coffee, his fingers brushing against mine, sending that familiar shock I'm growing accustomed to.

"Just getting to know each other, hun," Norma says, winking at me. "Now, who's hungry?"

50

Leo

AFTER BREAKFAST, MOM INSISTED ON TAKING US INTO BIG SUR Village.

The drive was short but scenic. Layla rode up front with Mom, feet on the dash, humming along to the classic rock station that was on the radio.

We spent the late morning wandering through little shops that I could have done without, but they were very excited to check out the small boutiques tucked between coffee houses and cafés. I followed behind while the two of them moved from store to store, laughing, pointing things out to each other, chatting like they'd known each other for years.

I'd never seen Mom like this with anyone before. She left her parents house as a very young adult, claiming they had a complicated relationship. I never pried, but I know it left her cautious with people. So, it was always just her and my dad... and then just her and me.

This is different. This is sisterly.

Layla was in her element, finding handmade pottery and taking deep breaths whenever we passed a store that smelled like lavender or fresh bread. I didn't know she was into art, but she lit up at the sight of an art stand, where they spent a good ten minutes getting giddy over a painting of a naked man.

Which Mom ended up buying.

I bought them lunch at a café on the corner. Layla ordered a cold cut sandwich, Mom went for a giant salad. It was one of those cafés that doubled as a brunch spot, and the two of them took full advantage of the bottomless mimosas. I just sat there with my burger, watching them cheers their drinks every time they took a sip.

I haven't told Mom about the Sam mess, and I don't plan to. Nothing good would come from it—only sleepless nights and more worry than she already carries. Let her have this. Let her smile and laugh with Layla without the shadow of what could be waiting for me back in Morro Bay.

Before we left the last shop, Mom surprised Layla with a gift. A silver chain with a colorful sandglass pendant. Tiny and beautiful, just like her.

"Something to remember today by," Mom said as she handed her the box.

Layla gasped, animated as always. "Are you kidding? This is perfect." She took it out immediately, her entire face lighting up, and clasped it around her neck. "Thank you. Seriously, thank you so much, it's so beautiful."

Mom just smiled and patted her arm. "You're such a delight."

She really is.

⌣

"Today was perfect," Mom says as we walk side by side along the beach.

Layla's a few paces ahead, crouched near the waterline, picking through shells. She holds one up to the light, then tucks it into the pocket of her jacket. Probably for her windowsill back home. Another chipped one follows, and I think about how even broken things can still be worth keeping.

"Yeah," I say quietly, watching her. "I think we all needed this."

"I think so too, honey," Mom replies. "You better not let that girl go. You won't find someone like her ever again."

I chuckle under my breath. "Really? *Never* again?"

She shoots me a look. "I'm serious, Leo. Most people don't take others as they are. They fall for the idea, then try to reshape them into someone else. But that one"—she nods toward Layla, who's pocketing a couple more shells—"she accepts you. All of you. Even the parts you try to hide."

I glance at her, then back at Layla. The wind catches her hair as she turns toward us, cheeks pink from the cool air as she makes her way closer.

I think Mom's right.

Layla sees all the parts of me... The *broken* pieces.

And she stays. She chooses me.

Mom slips her hand through my arm, giving it a squeeze. "Your father would've liked her, too," she says tenderly. "Don't wait too long to tell her how you feel, life can be cruel with its time."

Even if Mom were wrong, even if I wasn't ready to admit what this is... Layla's not someone I'd let go of easily.

She's the type you anchor to when the tide threatens to pull you under.

51

Layla

EVERYTHING ABOUT THE BUSY BEAN MAKES ME HAPPY—THE drip of the coffee pot, the low chatter of morning conversations, the smell of cookies baking. Dan even framed and hung up my sketch of the shop's outside view.

It's only been a little over a week since Big Sur, but it already feels like a lifetime ago. Leo's been busy with work, but he still visits me every evening. And every evening, I get the same rush of butterflies.

I reach for a mug from the clean side of the sink, stack it with the others, and catch a glimpse of the sandglass pendant Norma gave me laying on my chest. I haven't taken it off since she gifted it to me.

Norma was… *magic*.

Warm, funny, quick-witted, kind. She made the whole trip feel like a giant fluffy blanket. And Leo, he was a different version of himself there. He was softer and lighter, her presence meant everything.

"Are you daydreaming or having some kind of stroke?" Sara asks, walking past me with a tray of dirty cups.

"Neither," I say, smiling into the mug I'm drying. "Just thinking."

"Don't hurt yourself," she teases, nudging me with her hip. "Still thinking about the trip?"

"Yes," I admit. "It was so peaceful. His mom is amazing. She made lasagna and blueberry pie from scratch, and I've been craving more ever since," I add, even though Sara has already heard all about the visit.

"Maybe I should give my mom a call," Sara notes, leaning against the counter.

I glance at her. "Has it been a while since you talked?"

She shrugs. "She moved to North Carolina right after I turned eighteen. Said she wanted a change, but really, it was because her aunt got sick. She went to take care of her, and then she just never came back."

There's no bitterness in her tone, just a matter-of-factness that makes me hurt for her. "That must've been hard."

"At first it felt like she was choosing her aunt over me. But they were close, and when she passed so suddenly... I understood. Mom never got to say goodbye. Grief changes people. It rearranges *everything*."

I nod slowly, mulling over her words. "You're right... That must've been really difficult. Kind of reminds me of Leo and Norma and how they didn't get the closure they needed, either."

"What do you mean?" she asks, handing me a clean towel to replace the damp one I've been using.

"They wanted to do some kind of sea memorial, like a paddle out, or a flotilla of some kind down near the docks for Dean. The Harbor Master at the time denied it." I pause, a hint of sadness itching me. "Sam's dad was working with him in some way, and they came up with a reason to say no."

"Oh, wait, I remember that actually. My dad went down there to try to figure out what was going on but came up short. The whole town tried to rally, but they kept saying it was some kind of weird ocean bacteria that was passing through," she scoffs, "it was bullshit."

"It's heartbreaking." I frown.

"Thank God that Harbor Master retired, he was a menace. Always randomly shutting down entry and exit for boats, causing lack of work for the fisherman. A lot of places here rely on those fish, you know?"

She shakes her head, and heads out to the front to wipe down a few tables.

I stay behind, drying and stacking more mugs, but the sadness creeps in anyway. Norma's words resurface—how she expressed she's literally just waiting to die. How she's only here for Leo. The thought twists in my heart, because I can still hear the ache in Leo's voice when he talks about his dad. I hate that they both have to carry that weight.

Maybe Sara's right. Grief does rearrange everything. But maybe it can be rearranged into something better. Something *healing*.

And then it hits me. I know what I need to do.

I grab my phone from the back counter and walk out onto the side patio, away from the noise, away from the people.

I dial.

"Layla, hey girl!" Nate answers, his voice cheerful.

"Hi, Nate," I say. "I need your help with something."

52

Leo

It's Sunday.

We were supposed to work today. But Hank, Rowdy, and Austin all came down with something nasty that knocked them on their asses overnight. Some kind of flu.

Thank God I didn't catch it.

It's been a heavy week. Out before sunrise, back after dark. Pushing the edges of our usual routes, testing new waters. Trying to leave the well-worn spots alone long enough for the fish to rebuild. Give them room to breathe, to repopulate.

It's a cycle. Something you only learn from years of listening to the ocean. Never trying to outsmart it.

You can't outsmart the sea.

The water's been calm lately. A silent permission from her to let us do our work. Minimal wind, no surprises and long hours of endless blue.

With the crew out, I couldn't say no when Layla texted me asking if I could help with a few things around her place. A leaky faucet, a busted doorknob, a couple of lightbulbs. All things I've probably got lying around in my garage.

Besides… I've been missing her.

A lot.

To go from our Big Sur visit to diving headfirst into work has been somewhat of a rollercoaster. Thankfully, Sam's been quiet—no one's seen him—so that's one less thing to worry about.

When I get to her place, she opens the door with a smile. She's holding something draped on a hanger, still wrapped in plastic from the dry cleaners.

"Hey, you," she says, kissing my cheek. "Before we get started, I need to run a quick errand. Will you take me?"

I pull her into a hug, instantly feeling calm. "Of course."

She looks beautiful today. Not just pretty, but like *done up*. A long navy dress that hugs her in all the right places, her hair pinned half-up, some makeup making her eyes look even more ridiculous than usual.

"You look—" I pause, stepping back to take her in. "—really fucking good."

"What do you mean?" She twists her lips into a sassy smile.

I squint at her, reading the nervous energy she suddenly has. "I mean, this is a lot of look for a Sunday. What's the occasion?"

"Nothing," she says too quickly, pushing past me out the front door and down the steps. "I just felt like looking nice."

"Well, you succeeded," I say once we reach my truck, opening the passenger door for her. "Where are we heading?"

"To Nate's," she blurts as she climbs in.

"Nate's?" I raise a brow. "Since when do you need dry-cleaning and a dress to see Nate?"

She turns toward me. Her expression is halfway between a smirk and annoyance. "Look. Just don't ask questions. Just… *drive.*"

I chuckle under my breath. "Okay, then."

Because this is Layla.

And when it comes to her, I'll do whatever she asks.

———

The closer we get to the dock, the less sense anything makes.

The lot's completely full. Cars lined up, people every-where. Not the usual kind of weekend crowd, either. I spot Nate first, standing near the edge of the marina in a nice button-up shirt, grinning the biggest grin. Sara's beside him, holding Will's hand.

"What the hell..." I say under my breath, slowing the truck to a crawl.

That's when I see Rowdy. Then Hank. Austin. All standing out there on my boat. Very much *not* sick. They're laughing and talking, very much alive and well. Izzy's with them, too.

Layla lied.

They *all* lied.

"Layla," I say slowly, glancing over at her. "What is this?"

But she just smiles and reaches into the back seat, pulling the hanger forward. The one she brought out of the house earlier. She slides the plastic off and holds it up. A crisp, white dress shirt.

My *dad's* shirt.

The one my mom has kept for years, unsure why neither one of us could ever bring ourselves to give it away.

She offers it to me gently. "You might want this."

It takes me a second to piece it together—why everyone's here, why they lied, why she's in that dress. And when it clicks, it knocks the wind out of me.

I stare at it for a second before taking it, my throat already forming a lump.

I put it on and button it up and as we walk toward the

dock, I realize just how many people are here. Friends, family, people I haven't seen in years. A few old fishermen I recognize from when I was a kid—friends of my dad's. Even Wendy, the town florist, is standing by a fold-up table, handing fresh white lilies to those passing by.

She hands one to Layla as we approach, then a small closed box to me. Her eyes wet with tears, but she doesn't speak.

And then I see it.

The photo.

A large black-and-white image of my dad, young and smiling, in his captain's hat. It rests on an easel at the entrance to the dock.

Framed... Honored.

This isn't just a gathering. It's a *flotilla*.

Lines of boats stretch out in the water. People already aboard, some holding flowers, others simply standing still, looking toward the sea.

I turn back toward Layla.

She's watching me. Still holding that damn smile, holding in tears herself. Her dress sways in the breeze. Her cheeks flush and her hair dances against her shoulders.

She's never looked more beautiful.

Or more like home.

"What did you do?" I whisper.

Her eyes are glassy now. "I just... listened."

I swallow hard and look out again. On my boat, I see my mom now, standing with Dan. She waves when she sees me, tears falling down her cheeks. Beside her are Hank, Rowdy, Izzy, and Austin, all gathered quietly, waiting for me.

This isn't just a memorial. It's closure... A final goodbye.

For years, I've borne the heaviness of my dad's loss. Quietly and alone. Not wanting to burden others with my feelings.

But Layla took that burden. She *knew*.

And she gave this to *me*.

Without asking. No hesitation. Just love.

Tears sting my eyes, making the view in front of me blur. I wipe them away, looking back at her one more time, trying to figure out how to say everything I'm feeling.

There are no words big enough.

So I reach for her hand, and whisper the only words I can form.

"Thank you."

53

Layla

THE SEA IS PEACEFUL AND STILL.

The air carries a light chill, the sun shines but not too harsh. It's like a gift. Like nature knows what today means and has decided to behave out of respect.

We're about three miles offshore now. The boats around us follow in a line. Spaced out just enough to move together in unity.

Leo's boat leads the way.

The deck is quiet. No music. No noise beyond the sounds of the engines and water lapping against the boat. I watch him from the side, my heart barely carrying everything I feel. I've been holding back all kinds of nerves for the last three days in frantic preparation for this. The amount of community that came together is just so pure, so wholesome.

When I asked Norma for permission, she cried through the phone for nearly two hours. The new Harbor Master gave me no grief. Said he'd be happy to help and even mentioned meeting Dean once when he was lower on the totem pole.

Leo's crew, his friends, his people, the town, all immediately said yes and were more than happy to be included. In fact, those who couldn't get out on the water closed down their shops and businesses in honor of Dean Anderson.

Or maybe just for Leo and Norma themselves.

He's gripping the wheel now, one hand resting on the edge of the helm, his eyes focused on the sea. His father's shirt clings to his back, outlining his muscles, the wind catching the fabric just enough to make it ripple around him.

God, he's beautiful.

Not just in that easy, rugged, manly way—even though, yes—the jawline and broad shoulders don't hurt. But it's different today. His beauty is more humble, more full like he's finally letting himself feel it all.

No shields. Just ache and grace.

He hasn't spoken much since we left the dock. Just a few nods. A few thank yous. A look that said more than I think words ever could.

And I don't need him to say anything. This isn't a moment for words, it's not a moment for me.

This is for *him*. For the man who lost his father too soon and learned how to bury pain so deep, it nearly swallowed him. For the man who kept showing up anyway, who took care of everyone else before he ever thought to take care of himself.

This is for Leo.

This is for Norma.

She's sitting on the bench behind him, tears of mascara still streaming down her face as she holds a framed photo of Dean in her lap. Austin's beside her, quiet for once. Dan, Sara and Will are near the edge. Rowdy, Hank, and Izzy stand near the bow, silently chatting.

Leo finally turns to me. "I think we're far enough," he says.

He anchors, then walks over to the edge, reaches into a small wooden box Wendy handed to him earlier and pulls out a single white lily. He glances at his mom, holding his arms open for her to join.

Together, they step forward.

Norma kisses the photo one last time, then sets it carefully at the base of the helm. She places her hand over Leo's as he holds the flower, and then, together, they drop it into the sea.

We all watch as it floats. So delicately, so bright in contrast to dark water.

One by one, the others follow. The surface of the ocean becomes a soft white scatter.

Leo watches in silence, hands resting on the edge of the boat, head bowed. And then, just before I reach for him, to hold him as he says his final goodbye, he turns and pulls me into his arms.

He offers no words. Just *him*, wrapping himself around me. I hold him close, I hold him tight.

He draws back just enough to look at me. His eyes are red, but not broken. For the first time, he looks *whole*.

And just like that, the last wall around him finally falls.

54

Leo

It's been a few days since the flotilla, and I can still see the lilies drifting over the water every time I close my eyes.

It feels strange… carrying that goodbye around for years without knowing how weighty it really was until I got to let it go. It still sits with me, of course. Just because I got to say a proper farewell doesn't mean the loss of my dad doesn't still exist.

It's a different feeling now. I still ache, but I feel more at peace with it. The sharp grip it once had on me has dulled. I'll forever see him everywhere, but now with more clarity. Instead of only finding him in my pain, I see him in my memories— our time at sea, or at home with Mom. His laugh on the boat, the way he spent hours teaching me to tie a proper bowline knot, the smell of his jacket after long days on the water.

He's no longer just the absence I've carried. He's part of the horizon in me, always guiding and reminding me of where I come from and who I want to be.

I feel lighter. Even though the waters are getting choppier.

A storm is moving in within the week, so we are hustling

trying to get some work done beforehand. We should have a few solid days before it gets here.

"Burgers for dinner at Nates!" Austin announces, securing the bait buckets.

"I'll meet you guys there," I say, tying off the boat when my phone buzzes in my back pocket.

Surprisingly, it's a text from Charlie.

I haven't heard from her in a while. I reached out a couple of times, just to check in, but she never responded. After that, I let it go. Part of me didn't want to keep pushing, not when I'm still unsure about how deep her connection with Sam— and apparently Kyle—runs. And honestly, I think reaching out again would've just stirred up anger I've been trying to keep at bay.

> Can we talk? Just us.

It's odd, it's unexpected but something tells me I should hear what she has to say.

> Sure. Behind Dockfront in 20?

She doesn't reply, just shows up fifteen minutes later and immediately starts pacing by the back entrance of the restaurant when I arrive.

"Hey," I say, walking toward her. "Everything okay?"

She looks up, tugging at her long sleeves. Her pupils are blown, her skin dull, she looks much thinner. She looks *high*.

Not good.

"I shouldn't be saying anything," she whispers, her hands shaking. "But I can't keep my mouth shut if someone's going to get hurt."

My stomach starts to churn. "Is this about Sam?"

She looks around us, her eyes darting a million miles a second, then gives a quick nod.

"He's planning something. A big deal with some guy from San Francisco. Said he needs to help move some *product*, and he's been scoping out the docks."

I feel that familiar unease trickle into my body.

"He said you've been a problem, Leo. That people respect you too much, and that's bad for business." She hesitates, picking at her chin. "I think he's making the move... *tonight.*"

"Why are you telling me this now?" My fingers dig into my palms.

"Because I didn't sign up for this shit," she snaps. "I thought I was helping someone make a few side deals, getting a free high... Not whatever *this* is. He's paranoid and so fucking unstable right now. And I'm afraid if you get in his way—"

She doesn't finish the sentence.

I run my fingers through my hair, breathe and try not to lose my composure right now.

"I appreciate the warning," I say through clenched teeth. "But you need to stay the hell away from him, Charlie. Get out of town for a while, put distance between yourself and Sam."

Her eyes stretch. "Just... Just be careful, okay?"

She backs away fast, almost stumbling as she turns. The truth hits me hard—something *has* to be done.

⁓

The guys are already at Nate's when I show up. Each of them scarfing down burgers and already two beers in.

"Hi," I say, walking in and heading straight for the ice chest. I grab a beer, crack it open, and take a big swig. "We've got a problem."

Rowdy looks up mid-bite, grease on his fingers. "That doesn't sound good."

They listen as I explain what Charlie told me. About Sam's deal with some guy from San Francisco tonight and that he's intending on using the docks to meet him.

Nobody speaks for a moment. The only noise the scrape of Nate's spatula against the grill.

Hank is the first to talk. "That fucker is trying to use *our* harbor?"

I nod. "He knows the coastline well enough. If he drags our names or licenses into it, that could wreck us. It's not just *our* boats, it's the whole town that relies on this water."

Austin wipes his face with his sleeve. "San Francisco means bigger players. That's not a worm like Sam, Cap. That's people with guns and money."

Nate finally sets the spatula down. "And if they think we're standing in the way—" He stops at that.

I join them at the table. "We need to watch, *quietly*. Keep eyes on the docks, on Sam. No confrontation unless he, or they, confront us first. If this is as big as Charlie made it sound, I want something we can take to the Harbor Master or even the state officials if we have to."

"Man, I've been waiting for this asshole to slip up." Rowdy grins.

"This *has* to stay clean," I say, slightly raising my voice. "If someone bigger is involved, we need to be smart. This isn't just local bullshit anymore."

"You sure you can trust Charlie?" Hank asks the obvious.

"No, but what am I supposed to do? Ignore it?"

He shakes his head no. We've played this game before, but never on this level and definitely not with something that might reach beyond Morro Bay.

"She used to be one of us, guys. I know she was never as

238

close as we are but… she's fallen down the same hole Joey did. We can't discredit her, or give up on her."

I pause; the memory of the nights we watched Joey fade start to creep in. "When this is over, she's going to need our help."

The table goes quiet and they nod in unison.

"Then we have to get to the docks before Sam does," Nate says.

"We'll stay on the boat tonight," I lay it out. "Take turns making a loop every couple hours."

"You got it," Hank says, downing the rest of his beer.

"Yeah, we're in," Rowdy adds, Austin nodding in agreement.

"I'll hang out at Dockfront, and keep an eye out," Nate says.

I sigh and take another swig of beer. "Good." Turning to Rowdy, I add, "Let's keep the girls out of this one. It's best if both Layla and Izzy don't know."

Rowdy dips his chin. "Agreed."

I wolf down a burger, then run home to grab some overnight gear before making my way back to the boat. It's not the first night I've slept out there, and it sure won't be the last.

―――

The moon is shining bright by the time I'm back at the dock. The guys are already on the boat with the lights out. Speaking quietly amongst each other inside the galley. I feel the tension start spreading through me, the anxiety brewing in my core. Sam himself is easy. He's a scrawny little shit that I could take with one swift move with my elbow. I've done it before and I'd do it again.

But this bigger fish, this person from San Francisco is what scares me. It's bigger than our small town. New people, probably smarter people taking advantage of an idiot like Sam to use a location that would be tougher to sniff out.

It doesn't hurt that Sam's dad, though retired now, still has some strings he can pull within law enforcement.

It's just too much to ignore.

Plus, this is Layla's home now, too, and she makes me feel like this life, this town, this fight, is worth *everything*.

55

Layla

MY APARTMENT SMELLS LIKE LAVENDER.

I've had a candle burning for the past hour, trying to mask the musky dampness. It comes out strong when the air gets more humid.

Dan said a storm was rolling in soon, said it's going to be one of those slow-moving ones that creep up on you.

I haven't heard from Leo all day. Which is fine. I know he's busy. Out on the water, prepping for the storm, maybe untangling some rope.

But, I miss him and it kind of makes me feel achey and blue.

Sara's out with Will. Izzy's probably sleeping off her hangover from a bachelorette party she went to last night. So, it's just me and my thoughts.

I curl up on the couch, blanket around my legs, phone in hand, scrolling mindlessly until I see a video that kind of reminds me of my mom. I should call her. I've been distant. Wrapped up in this town, my new life, happily tangled in the world of Leo.

It rings twice before she answers. "Layla!" she says. "Hi, sweetie!"

"Hi, Momma, how are you?"

"It's so good to hear from you!"

I tuck my chin into the soft blanket. "I'm sorry I've been so distant."

"Oh, honey," she sighs. "Thank you for saying that, but you're out there exploring life, we understand."

"I miss you guys."

"We miss you, too. A lot. Your dad was just saying yesterday it's been too long since we've seen our girl."

"Put me on speaker?"

She does, and a second later, I hear him. "Hey, baby."

"Hi, Dad."

"How's it going out there? Living life to the fullest?"

"I am," I say, and mean it. "I'm *really* good actually."

There's a pause, and then Mom says, "You met someone, didn't you?"

I laugh, pulling the blanket tighter around me. "How did you know?"

"I'm your mother, Layla, I sensed it the second I picked up the phone."

"Well, his name's Leo. He's a local fisherman here. Was a man of very few words at first…" I trail off, smiling to myself. "But I was able to squeeze more out of him."

"Ohhh," Mom breathes. "One of *those*."

"Is he good to you?" Dad asks.

"The best," I say. "He makes me feel… safe."

A memory rises to the surface. I was seven the first time I woke up from a nightmare and couldn't fall back asleep. There was a storm pounding against the windows, which was an odd thing to experience in Los Angeles. I remember the thunder cracking so loud, it made the walls shake. I snuck into my parents bedroom with a stuffed rabbit in one hand.

My dad didn't tell me to go back to my bed. He just scooted over, lifted the blanket, and patted the mattress. I climbed in between him and mom. She pulled me close and whispered *"You're safe, we've got you."*

And I believed her. Even as rain slammed against the windows and thunder boomed throughout the house, I believed her.

That same feeling. That sureness that I was held, protected, and secure floods through me as I think about Leo.

"I've fallen for him," I say quietly into the phone.

There's a long stretch of silence before Dad clears his throat and says, "Well, if he makes you feel safe, then it's a good sign. Still, I'd like to look him in the eye myself. Just for a father's peace of mind."

I wouldn't want it any other way.

"Will you come visit soon?" I ask.

"Absolutely," Mom says. "We'll figure it out this week. Maybe next month? We need to meet this man ASAP."

"Yeah," I say, smiling. Feeling excited. "I'd love that."

We talk a little longer, about a visit date, about the storm coming, about what I've been sketching lately and when I hang up, the silence in the apartment feels a little less lonely. It feels more like excitement to merge my old life with my new. Knowing they will fall in love with Leo just as easily as I did.

56

Leo

Rowdy shakes me awake.

I blink up at him, groggy. "What?"

"It's Sam," he says quietly. "He's here."

I sit up quickly and swing my legs over the edge of the bunk. The cabin is dim, lit only by the battery-powered lantern we've been using to avoid drawing attention.

I peek at the clock on the wall—2:07 a.m.

"A boat just pulled up," Rowdy whispers. "Sam got on it. And someone else, I think it's Kyle."

I hurry over to the narrow circular window, pushing the curtain back just a touch. "It's too fucking dark," I murmur. "I need a better angle."

"Hank's tucked behind one of the old charter boats. He was able to get closer, he's filming," Rowdy says. "They didn't see him."

Good. Smart.

Austin starts to move in the corner bunk, and he sits up. "What's going on?"

"Stay here," I whisper. "Eyes open."

Rowdy and I slip off the boat, trying to keep the noise of

our boots against the wood from drawing attention. The sea is too quiet and too still.

Eerie.

We post up between the stacked lobster traps and bait bins, tucking ourselves behind the low wall that leads to the next slip. Between the dim light of a dock lamp and the glow of the moon, there's just enough visibility to see what's happening.

I see them now.

A small vessel, unmarked. Tied quick and sloppy to the dock. Sam is hunched near the bow, talking quietly. Kyle stands beside him, hands tucked in the front pocket of his hoodie, wearing a backpack. There's two other guys, one of them tall with an expensive looking jacket. He's leaning on the rail while the other guy does the talking.

San Francisco.

Kyle looks around the dock before handing over the backpack. The shorter man of the two zips it open, peeks inside then zips it back up before giving an approving nod.

A random gust of wind picks up, my pulse spikes and Rowdy freezes beside me as a loose crate tips, crashing into the water. Sam snaps his head toward our side of the dock. We stay hidden in the shadows, holding our breath until his focus shifts back to the men on the boat.

Hank, crouched about ten feet from Rowdy and me behind a row of barrels, lifts his phone a little higher.

Sam still doesn't see us. They're too busy looking over their backs toward the road, making sure no one is coming.

I spot a faint light in one of the windows at Dockfront. Must be Nate with his phone, hopefully getting more pictures and videos from another angle.

I think we've got them.

I nod toward Rowdy; he smirks. We don't take lightly to

people treating our home like it's expendable. Like it's just some stop on the way to somewhere dirty.

Not here. Not our town.

Kyle says something to Sam and they hop off the boat, they untie it and not even a minute later, it's already pulling away. Sam lingers for a minute, sending a glance in all directions, watching his back, believing he just won.

He still doesn't see us.

But we saw everything.

———

The next morning, we're standing in the Harbor Master's office, all five of us lined up waiting to put this shit to an end.

Harbor Master Reeves shuts the door behind him and pulls his reading glasses down from his head. "Jesus," he hushes, watching the video play. "This is a bit shocking."

"We've got timestamps," Hank says. "Photos, too, from Dockfront."

I nod in response. "We didn't confront. Just documented it, we kept it clean."

"I got a call last week from one of the business owners on Main," Reeves says, looking at me. "Said they saw Murphy lurking around down there one night. I tried to find him, I wanted to bring him in for some questioning but the guy's been slippery. He's kind of hard to track down."

He scrolls through the footage again. Pauses on the moment Kyle hands over the duffel bag.

"This…" He taps the screen. "This might be enough. I'll be forwarding everything to the coast enforcement office. If they want to pull in local PD or state narcotics, that'll be their call. But now we've got a case."

We're all silent. Small smiles forming on each of our faces.

"You men did good," Reeves says. "This could've gone

real bad if you didn't play it smart. Appreciate that you didn't try to be heroes."

"We just want our fuckin' harbor back," Rowdy says.

"Yeah," I agree. "Before it becomes something we don't recognize."

Reeves presses his lips together and nods. "We'll handle it from here."

We leave the office quietly, stepping out into the early morning fog, the heavy air carrying the familiar odor of the salty sea.

"Now what?" Austin asks, rubbing the back of his neck.

"Now?" Rowdy repeats, lighting a cigarette. "I'm going home, eating a fat bowl of cereal, fucking my girl, and sleeping 'til tomorrow."

"God bless," Austin whispers.

Hank's already halfway to his truck, Rowdy not far behind. "Get some rest, men," Hank calls over his shoulder. "Y'all look like shit."

"Back to work in the morning!" I call back.

Rowdy just waves without turning around.

I turn to Austin. "Seriously. Rest up. We've got maybe two days left to prep before that storm hits."

"You got it, boss." He nods, pulling his hoodie up. "What about you?"

I glance out toward the harbor. The masts of the boats are barely visible in the thick haze. "Don't worry about me. I've got something I need to take care of."

He smiles smugly, reading between the lines. "Give her my best."

I laugh quietly. "Go home, man."

I head home, and once I'm out of the shower and ready to take the best nap of my life, I pull my phone from my pocket and scroll to a name.

The only one I want to see tonight.

Layla.

57

Layla

"Late! I *know*! I know!" Sara announces as she barrels through the backdoor of The Busy Bean. Her sweater hanging off one shoulder, ponytail a mess, and cheeks flushed.

The shop smells like cinnamon this morning. I'm behind the counter in a cozy matching sweat set and already halfway through my second cup of coffee. Izzy's here, too, seated at one of the tables.

"Jeez, why so flustered?" I ask Sara.

"No reason."

"Oh my God," Izzy chimes in, sipping on a cup of hot tea. "You had *sex.*"

Sara's cheeks redden even more. "Don't judge me." She throws a napkin at her. "Wait—how do you know that?"

"Because Rowdy came home about an hour before I came here. He did me right on the kitchen counter." She laughs. "I know an after-sex face when I see one."

Will pops in from the same door Sara barreled through just moments ago. His already red-hued face is even rosier than usual.

Izzy tilts her head to the side. "Well *hello*, Will."

He clears his throat. "Morning, ladies."

Izzy and I laugh together, my attention only to be drawn from them to my phone when it buzzes. A text from Leo:

> Meet me tonight? The docks around 7. Dress warm.

My heart jumps. My whole *body* does.

———

The sun is nearly set when I make my way toward the docks. The air is cool, feeling grateful that Leo told me to dress warm. I'm wearing the jeans I wore the night we first officially met at Taboo, paired with a soft long sleeve and a fleece-lined Softshell jacket.

Leo's already here, leaning against the railing, legs crossed at the ankle, arms folded as he watches me walk toward him. His beige canvas coat looks to be keeping him warm, his hair messy from the wind.

As I get closer, that beautiful crooked grin starts to spread across his face. He pulls me in by the hips and kisses me.

"I've been thinking about you all fucking day," he murmurs into my mouth. "Couldn't get you out of my head." His thumb brushes my jaw. "You ready to hit the water?"

His words give me goosebumps as I look up at him. "With you?" I smile. "*Always.*"

He takes my hand, leading me to a boat I haven't seen before. Much smaller than his fishing boat. Sleek and weathered, with the name *Norma* painted in gold along the side.

"I haven't seen this one," I say.

"It was my dad's," Leo says, helping me aboard. "His personal boat. I keep it tucked away."

I squeeze his hand as he guides me to the small interior cabin. It's cozy, with a mini fridge, narrow counter, and a simple couch along the wall. Two slim doors sit toward the back. One, a bathroom, maybe a bed behind the other.

It smells faintly of lemon and wood.

"This is nice," I note, turning to him.

He watches me, his eyes creased with that sweet smile. "Glad you think so."

"Romantic, even," I tease.

"I've spent many trips here." He grins. "All good memories."

"And counting."

He holds his hand out again. "Come on. Let's get out on the water."

The boat vibrates beneath us as we move away from the dock, the lights of town fading behind us. Morro Rock disappears in the distance. The stars start to trickle more clear in the sky the further we go.

"How far are we going?" I ask loudly over the gale.

"Not far," he calls back. "Just enough."

We fall quiet, and I lean back against the seat, letting the wind rush over my face. The chill bites my skin, but it feels good. Leo's at the helm, looking all captain like. His hair dancing, his mermaid tattoo peeking out from beneath his sleeve.

God. I will never get over how breathtakingly beautiful he is.

Eventually, the boat slows, rocking gently in the open water. Lights from shore are now just distant specks.

"This look like a good place to drop anchor?" he asks, tossing it overboard without waiting for my answer.

"Perfect," I say.

He stands beside me, brushing his hair behind his ears. "So."

"So?"

He smiles. "Wanna fish?"

"Like… actually fish?"

He laughs and hands me a pole from the deck storage locker. "You know how to cast it?"

"I think so," I lie.

Leo steps behind me, his hands guiding mine, and I can't help but remember the first time he was this close. Back then, he was just the brooding local who taught me how to surf… before I knew how much more he would become.

His chest presses against my back, his voice basically a whisper in my ear. "Hold down this button, and when you throw the line out, let it go. Just like that."

We move together, casting it out.

We fish like that for a while. Talk about nothing and every-thing while snacking on popcorn and pickles. A snack he packed just for me but appears to be enjoying as much as I am. He tells me about the scar on his chest and how a night of drinking and fishing turned into an unfortunate collision with Rowdy's lure.

I laugh so hard that my stomach hurts and he just watches me like it's his favorite sight in the world.

We didn't catch anything, but that's okay. The company and the music from Leo's guitar brought more excitement than any catch could. He strummed and sang a song his dad sang to him when he was young, a lullaby for the sea. His voice was low and raw, and when he looked at me mid-verse, it felt like the song was maybe meant for me, too.

Once the wind started to pick up more and the air became much cooler, so we decided to move inside the galley.

"Thanks for coming out," he says, making me some hot tea on the tiny stove, "I know fishing isn't exactly every girl's dream date."

"If only you knew," I say softly. "*You're* kind of a dream, Leo."

He tilts his head. "Is that so?"

"I'd sit on a smelly boat with you for weeks if it meant nights like this."

He doesn't joke or deflect. He just holds his eyes on me, memorizing the moment, knowing how fleeting perfect nights can be.

58

Leo

HER VELVETY SKIN IS WARM AGAINST MINE.

The boat begins to rock harder, maybe the storm's moving in quicker than I thought. The bed is too small, my legs hang off the edge, but I couldn't care less. Not with her curled against me—her hand on my frame, her cheek rested on my shoulder.

All I can do is stare at her.

She's naked. Her skin glows in the dusky overhead light, her hair damp, but soft and fragrant near my nose. She's a vision, and I'm already addicted.

I run my hand along the dip of her waist, committing her curve to memory, even though I know there's no chance in hell I could ever forget it. Though, sometimes I do fear that if I blink, she'll disappear. That I'll wake up from whatever perfect dream this is.

She tilts her chin up, catching my eyes. "What?" she whispers.

"Just looking," I say, brushing her hair back. "Don't think I've ever seen anything prettier."

She smiles, her freckled cheeks rosy.

I let my hand trail down her arm. "You remember the first night we met?" I ask.

"Of course I do, it wasn't that long ago."

"I remember seeing you walk in, thinking *who the hell looks that good walking into a dirty old bar?*"

She laughs.

"Then Joey showed and I lost my temper"—I cringe a little at the memory—"but you weren't scared. Just came over and helped me pick up the broken pieces."

She props herself up on her elbow. "There was never anything to be scared of," she says softly. "All I saw was someone hurting." She pauses and bites her bottom lip. "Most of the time, fear just wears the mask of anger."

Her words wrap around me as I hear the first drops of rain tapping against the cabin roof, a reminder that we should probably head back soon. But I don't feel the push to leave just yet; there's one more thing I need to do. One more thing I need to say.

It's actually kind of terrifying how much I belong to her.

How much I *love* her.

I shift my body just enough to cup her face, to guide her jaw toward mine.

She stills.

"I love you, Layla."

Her gaze locks onto mine, looking caught off guard at first, then softening almost immediately. Her fingers trace along the side of my neck. Her eyes saying it all, like she's been waiting for me to finally let her all the way in.

"I know." She smiles, bringing her lips close to mine. "I—"

She's interrupted by a thump from outside. I freeze, pulling back to listen.

"What was that?" she asks, lifting her head higher.

"Stay here," I say.

"Leo—"

"It's probably nothing. But I want to check."

I hop off the bed and stand, reaching for my jeans. No shirt. No shoes.

Layla sits up, pulling the sheet to cover herself. Her eyes follow me as I move toward the cabin door that leads up to the deck.

"I'll be right back," I say.

"Be careful."

"I will." I glance back with a quick smile.

I step outside and the air hits me; it's cold and dark, and the boat starts to rock even more with the intensifying waves. I scan the black water around us—*shit*. The storm *is* hitting early.

The boat heaves against the growing swell, my bare feet slipping on the slick floor as I move forward to make sure everything is still in place. We need to get out of here. As I turn to head back down, a dark shadow in the water catches my attention.

A small, unlit boat.

Then I catch another shape in the corner of my eye—a person, quickly climbing aboard. For a split second, the moon-light reveals the side of his face.

Sam.

That motherfucker.

I grip the edge of the boat, my pulse surging, every muscle tensing as I try to gather my thoughts and plan my move. He hasn't seen me yet, he's on the opposite end. Then, I notice that he's not alone as another figure climbs in behind him.

I creep toward the cabin slowly, trying to maintain my balance and stay out of sight.

Layla's voice floats from below as the lights switch on. "Leo?"

Shit.

"Stay inside!" I yell. "Don't come out!"

Sam and the person with him snap their heads in my direction, spotting me instantly. He steps forward, but it's the other one who meets my eyes. *Charlie.* Tears and mascara streak down her cheeks, her lips tremble as she mouths, '*I'm sorry.*'

My stomach turns to stone.

Sam snarls, taking an unbalanced step toward me.

"You *ruined* my life," he spits. "Had to stick your nose in where it didn't belong. Could've walked away, but you had to play fucking hero."

The rain falls harder as I search the deck for any rope, tool, anything I can use but everything is stowed away. Nothing but the howl of the storm, salt spray now stinging my eyes.

"That deal was going to change everything. I was gonna be *rich*," he growls, stepping closer. "But you just had to go and snitch on me. Now they won't touch me and my trail's hot, I'm screwed and it's *your* fault."

He's too close now, so I step back, trying to keep distance between us. The storm has rolled in faster than any forecast could've warned, and the boat lurches violently beneath my feet as the sea churns harder around us.

"Now I'm gonna ruin *yours*," Sam spews, eyes flicking toward the cabin. Toward Layla, who's now standing at the top of the cabin stairs, barefoot in my T-shirt, wide-eyed, looking afraid.

Panic explodes in my chest.

"Leo..." she tries to call, but her voice seems to be caught in her throat.

No.

Charlie moves and stumbles, slipping on the wet deck; she hits the floor hard. Sam turns his head just for a second.

It's all I need.

I lunge, planting myself between him and Layla. My arm

flies out to shield her, but Sam's already charging forward like a wild animal.

"Go!" I shout, my hands gripping her shoulders as I guide her back. She stumbles against the doorway, but catches herself.

I turn back toward Sam, but before I can see his direction clear, his weight slams into me, driving me hard against the side of the boat. My feet slip beneath me, the slickness of the deck offering no grip, and suddenly, he has the upper hand. His eyes, full of hate, lock on mine as he takes one vicious breath and shoves with everything he has.

Before I can even grasp what's happening, the deck vanishes beneath me.

I catch one last glimpse of Layla. Her beautiful face twisted in raw terror.

It burns into me.

And then I fall.

59

Layla

CHARLIE'S SOBBING.

Sam's hunched over, clutching his arm like it's about to detach from his body. His face is contorted and he's yelping in pain. But all I hear is water.

Pouring rain.

Howling wind.

My breath comes in gasps as I run to the rail. My hands slam onto the cold wet metal, my soaked hair plastered to my face, my eyes scanning the dark water.

Nothing.

Nothing but waves and rage and the taste of salt on my tongue. A mix of tears and sea.

"Leo!" I scream. My voice tears through the wind, but it's immediately swallowed by the storm.

No.

No, no, no.

"This can't—" I choke, barely able to draw in air. "Help!" I cry out again, louder now, my throat burning. "Somebody, please! *Help!*"

But no one will come. No one can even hear me. We're too far from shore, too far from help.

And Leo is gone.

My knees hit the deck and I don't care that Sam and the traitor, Charlie, are somewhere behind me, in the abyss.

The panic is animalistic. Wild. A wail builds in my chest and rips from my body.

I shake.

I tremble.

My lungs are confused, every breath feels *wrong.* Every second that he's out there feels like it's pulling me further from myself. From the world... From any chance that this is just a nightmare I can wake up from.

Because, it's *not.*

The water crashes against the boat, stronger now. Almost like it's furious. Like the sea herself is hysterical, like she's shattered, too.

And somewhere, in the chaos, I feel it.

He's not coming up.

"Leo!" I scream again, raw and broken. I call out, again and again until my voice cracks into nothing.

My entire body trembles now, from both the bitter cold and the crushing realization. I grip the railing, fingers white, knuckles aching, pulling myself from the hard floor. Eyes locked on the darkness where he vanished.

He was *just* here.

We kissed. We made love. He told me he *loved* me. Held me like I was his entire world.

He finally gave me his entire heart.

And now the ocean has it.

Charlie stumbles toward me, her face soaked from tears and rain water. "I didn't know," she sobs. "Layla, I didn't—"

I turn to her, rage boiling in my soul. "Don't you *fucking* say my name!"

Her mouth opens, then closes and she backs away.

"You brought Leo into this," I seethe. "You let Sam walk onto this boat, knowing what was going to happen."

She shakes her head, eyes wide. "It wasn't supposed to go this far."

I don't care. I can't. Hate scorches through my veins.

Sam groans again in the background, crumpled over and swearing, still holding his arm.

Let it hurt.

Let it fucking scorch.

I glance back at the water. The fury inside of me pauses and a sudden calmness overcomes me. Then, I feel… nothing.

Just a cold, hollow pit forming in my chest, engulfing me.

No heartbeat. No breath. No subconscious contest. Just a silent decision.

I lean over the edge once more. One more search, just one more slither of hope that maybe, m*aybe* he'll burst through the surface, coughing and swearing and *alive.*

But the sea gives me nothing.

He's gone and something breaks inside me.

I can't hold myself up any longer. So, I clutch the side of the boat and do the only thing that makes sense at this moment.

The only thing that feels *right.*

I climb onto the edge.

"Layla, no!" Charlie screams behind me, but I don't listen to her.

I jump.

The cold hits like knives. Saltwater rushes into my nose and mouth, shocking my body, stealing what little breath I had left.

I don't fight it.

I *want* it.

I need to feel what he felt. I need to be where he is.

The current grabs me instantly, thrashing me from side to side, but I don't care.

The darkness surrounds me.

I open my eyes, searching through the black, hoping... praying... even hallucinating would be better than this emptiness.

My lungs burn and my organs scream.

But I *stay*.

His voice echoes in my head.

"I love you."

I love you, too, Leo. I love you so much it's... *killing* me.

The pain grows louder than the world. My chest heaves, tight with pressure, but I don't kick. I don't swim.

In fact, I think that I... I sink.

If this is the only way I can be close to him again, then let it be.

The ocean wraps around me.

A tomb.

Memories flicker in my mind. His laugh, the way he tucked my hair behind my ear, how he looked at me like I was magic.

I close my eyes again and I see him, smiling, reaching for me.

Please, I think. *Please just let me go to him.*

My limbs go heavy. My thoughts begin to drift and the panic fully softens into peace.

And I give in. I let myself love him fully and completely, even if that is the last thing I ever do.

But then...

A hand.

It's grabbing my arm.

I thrash, instinct taking over, confusion spiraling. *No!* I try to scream, but it's just bubbles and muffled sounds.

I don't want to go!

But the hand is pulling harder now. An arm reaches around my waist and drags me up.

Up.

And then… darkness.

Everything disappears.

60

Layla

I HAVE THIS NIGHTMARE THAT I'M DROWNING.

A dark, vast ocean surrounds me. My skin prickles with goosebumps, my lungs fill with salt water until not even the faintest scream can escape me. I don't feel alone though. In fact, I feel like I belong here and someone is in the abyss with me.

The seaweed wraps around my ankles like shackles and pulls me deeper, and I think I can hear the sound of a siren's song. It's hard to tell if it really is a creature of the sea, or if it's something inside of me.

Either way, it calls.

So, deeper the kelp pulls and louder the siren sings, the world around me starts to fade into a dark oblivion—

But I wake up.

The room is too quiet, and the air smells faintly of coffee and rain, the slapping of the drops against the window the only sound. My body is stiff and cold beneath heavy blankets that I don't recognize, and my mind is sluggish as I try to wake.

I realize that it's not my bed that I'm in. It's a couch and it dips beneath me as I start to move my aching body.

Then, I feel *it* almost the second my eyes fully open. The cold and complete emptiness within me.

I shift my head slowly to the side. Sara, Izzy, Rowdy, Hank, Austin and Nate—they're all here. Plus an older gentleman that is a stranger to me.

They all sit in silence, their shoulders hunched, their clothes stained with tears and snot. Their eyes are red-rimmed, their expressions blank.

Ghosts.

Shells.

My voice cracks when I speak, my throat sore. "*Leo?*"

Sara, sitting by my feet, closes her eyes, and gently reaches for my hands. She grabs one and holds it tightly, folding it in both of hers. "You'll be okay," she whispers.

But her grip trembles, and her voice is spread too thin. She doesn't believe it. None of them do. I can feel it in the silence and the way no one will look me in the eyes.

"Where am I?" I manage to ask.

"At our place, Lay," Izzy says softly, shifting down to sit on the floor beside the couch. She rubs my arm lightly. "You were in and out of consciousness, and the emergency rooms were slammed with storm injuries, so we brought you here instead." She nods toward the stranger in the room. "My neighbor used to be a nurse practitioner—I called him, and he came over to make sure you were okay."

I glance at the short, bald man. Normally, I'd thank him, but I can't. All I can manage is a weak nod.

"Who pulled me out?" I ask, the memory rushing back through me. "Wait..." I pause, remembering the hands pulling me from the water, too small to be a man's hands. "*Charlie.*"

They exchange glances. Izzy nods. "She called us on the way in. We met you at the docks."

"She was there, she——" I start to say.

"We know," Izzy interrupts, sparing me of the memory. "She told us everything."

Rowdy sits on the lazy boy across from me, staring at the floor, his foot tapping on the carpet, over and over and over again. He looks angry, lips pressed so tightly together they could bleed.

Hank sits by the window, his large frame bent forward, arms resting on his knees. His shoulders shake as he wipes at his face, wiping away evidence of his own heartache. I can see how hard he's fighting. Trying not to think of what he—*we*—lost.

Silence falls over the room, and that's when I know.

He's really gone.

My chest caves in on itself. The air leaves my lungs in one screeching exhale.

No.

I close my eyes again, wishing I hadn't woken up at all.

Rowdy stands and makes his way toward me, hesitating for a brief moment. Then, he leans down and presses a soft kiss to the top of my head. "I'm sorry," he murmurs. "We should've protected him. We should've protected *both* of you."

My breath comes out in hitches.

Hank stands next. His boots drag heavily across the carpeted floor, but his hand is surprisingly gentle as it cups my ankle through the blanket. "He loved you, Layla," he says. "He'd talk about you even when he wasn't. Smiled like a fucking idiot every time your name came up." His voice catches, and he has to turn away quickly, staring hard out the rain-slick window.

"You made him happy," Austin says, swallowing back a sound. "Which was something he had clearly lost."

I start to cry again, silent tears slip down my temples and leak onto the fabric of the couch.

"We're gonna stay with you," Rowdy says quietly. "Through all of it. You're one of us now, okay? We're not going anywhere."

These men. So tough, so weathered, so resilient are unraveling right here beside me. Unraveling *with* me... and still, somehow, trying to hold me together.

They lost their brother.

And I lost the only man I've ever truly loved.

———

Nate takes me home once Izzy's neighbor said I should be okay, as long as I stay hydrated and get some rest.

The second we roll up to my place, my mom spots us, running from my dad's parked car before Nate's car has even stopped.

"Sweetheart," she chokes, rushing to my side as I step out. She wraps her arms around me, holding on like I might disappear into thin air. "Sara called and we got here as fast as we could."

I cling to her, burying my face in her shoulder, breathing in the familiar scent of her perfume. My dad comes up behind her, grabbing my hand with both of his and pressing his lips to my knuckles.

"You're okay, Layla," he says quietly, though his voice wavers. "You're okay."

But I'm not.

"I'm so sorry." My mom's face crumbles. She brushes my damp hair from my face, tucking it behind my ear like she used to when I was little. "It's going to be a long road, hon, but we're here for you. We'll take you back home, and we'll get through this together."

Shivers ripple through my body.

"I won't leave," I sob. "Don't take me back to L.A. I'm *not* going."

Her tears still drop and she looks at my dad before saying, "We just want you safe."

"We can help you heal," he adds, his thumb rubbing over my knuckles.

"I don't want to heal," I cry. "I want *him.*"

Before they can say anything more, Nate appears from around the car, offering them a broken smile. "I think she needs some rest, let's get out of the rain."

Nate guides me up the stairs. My parents follow, still hovering, still worried, but they keep a few paces behind, torn between wanting to be next to me and knowing I need this moment with Nate.

"How did this happen?" I ask him as we reach the top of the stairs.

Nate wipes a tear. "Sam followed you in his boat. He must've waited until it was dark and thought you'd both fallen asleep."

I stiffen, listening, trying not to scream as he takes my keys and jiggles them in the door, unlocking it.

"Charlie was with him," he says, voice full of exhaustion, full of his own heartbreak. "She thought… She thought she could calm Sam down, that maybe if she was there, she could stop whatever he was planning."

"But she couldn't," I whisper.

Nate slowly nods. "She said Sam lost it. Yelling about Leo ruining everything and then—" he swallows hard. "Then he snapped. Charlie said it happened so fast. Then you jumped in after him."

I close my eyes, remembering the feeling of the cold swallowing me. The silence and the darkness. "She pulled me out."

"She did," Nate says, tears now streaming down his face.

"She tied herself to a rope, jumped in after you, caught you before you were pulled too far. Somehow she hauled you both back in. She said it was the drugs and pure adrenaline—twisted as that sounds, it's what gave her the physical strength." He pauses. "She couldn't find Leo... and Sam left her behind. She brought you back to the harbor and called us right away."

"And Leo..." My voice breaks.

"The coast guard has been out there all last night and all morning," he says. "Boats, helicopters, divers. They're still searching, but—"

I bury my face in my hands.

"And Sam?" I manage to utter. "Is he... just *free*? Is he going to get away with this?"

"No," he says, guiding me to my room, my legs heavy. "They found him at home a couple of hours ago, almost dead from an overdose. He's in custody now. This time, there's no getting out. His dad can't cover for him, not for this." He squeezes my arm. "They have Charlie's statement and the footage we got—" He stops mid-sentence.

Footage? What the hell is he talking about? "What footage?" I snap.

He exhales through his nose. "We caught Sam and Kyle making a deal, we turned everything into the Harbor Master."

"That's what Sam was yelling about..." I trail off. My chest should be burning with anger, with betrayal at being kept in the dark, but I'm too hollow for it. The fury never comes, just the ache. Because it doesn't matter.

Nothing brings him back.

"You aren't alone, Layla," he says softly, his eyes wet. "You *won't* be alone, this is something we all get through together."

"I don't think I can do it," I cry. "Could *you*?"

He sits down next to me on my bed, and pulls my shoulder under his arm. "I don't know if I can, either... but we can try.

We'll do it *with* him. Everything he gave us... He isn't gone, not completely."

It's meant to be comforting, but it only makes me cry harder.

Because I didn't just lose a man I loved.

I lost my safe place.

I lost my *home*.

61

My skin is pale, dark circles ring my eyes, and my lips are cracked and chapped from crying.

I don't recognize myself in the mirror.

I haven't showered. The salt still clings to my skin, and part of me wants to keep it there, like it might be the last trace of him. Part of me wants to wash it all away.

I pull on Leo's flannel, the one I've been holding onto, and wrap myself in what's left of him.

Norma is on her way. Nate was the one who called her. He said she asked where I was, and when he told her, she barely spoke. Just whispered "I'm coming" and hung up.

The thought of seeing her without Leo curls my stomach. She's already lost so much, and now she has to face it all over again. I don't know if I'm strong enough to see her break—or if I'm strong enough not to.

I watch the rain litter the street through my living room window. When her car pulls up to the curb, I meet her outside, my sobs breaking loose again at the sight of her.

She steps out slowly, her hands gripping the door to keep her steady. Our bloodshot eyes meet across the short distance, and she crumbles. We collapse into each other, holding tightly and squeezing like we're both trying to hold the other one up.

She tries to speak, but her voice breaks on the first word.

"I know," I say before she can try again. "*I know.*"

We cry together on the wet sidewalk until my mom hurries out, wrapping both of us in her arms. She doesn't say anything; there's nothing to say. She just holds us and helps us up to my apartment.

Inside, everything feels so wrong. Like the world has stopped and forgotten how to start again. The silence is thick, broken only by small sounds that feel offensive in their normalcy. Like the tea kettle's whistle and the whir of the fridge.

My mom moves through the kitchen, pouring each of us a hot tea. My dad and Nate sit at the island, silent, staring at nothing. Norma and I sit curled together on the couch, her hand still gripping mine.

Rowdy's at home with Izzy. He needed a minute of quiet, a chance to let his anger out freely. He promised they'd be back before nightfall, reminding me that we need each other —and he's right. Now more than ever, we do.

We're tied together like a net. Frayed in all places, strained at every knot… somehow still holding.

Nate said that Hank and Austin are at Taboo. Drinking themselves into a stupor because it's the only thing that dulls the grief.

No one has seen Kyle. He must have taken off once Sam was arrested.

Fucking coward.

I don't even have space in my chest for anger, but the thought of their names brings it bubbling to the surface anyway.

"I don't understand," Norma whispers, her voice so fragile

it nearly disappears. Her hands cover her face. "How could this happen? How did we lose him?"

I lean into her side, gently wrapping my arm around her shoulder.

"I don't know," I say, because that's all I have.

She weeps quietly, and I cry with her.

The tea my mom hands me goes untouched. It smells too good, too *alive*. I can't hold something so warm, something that should be comforting when everything inside me feels so cold.

I'm not ready to pretend life is normal. I don't think I ever will be.

The day inches forward. Dreadfully slow.

By late afternoon, the smell of roasted vegetables and herbs starts to fill the apartment. My parents are cooking to distract themselves. To provide nutrition for the rest of us who probably won't even eat a speck of it.

The sound of a knife hits the cutting board, the sizzle of garlic in the pan. It feels so *wrong*, like noise where there shouldn't be any.

Nate is asleep on the recliner, and even in his slumber you can see the ache in his heart.

"I need to get out of here," I whisper to Norma. "Do you want to walk to the beach with me?"

She doesn't hesitate, she stands and takes my hand in hers and we leave without a word.

The air outside is humid, now a lighter drizzle. A break in the storm that is predicted to last for days. Our bare feet crunch against the damp sand, the sea wind tangling our hair, the horizon bruised in gray.

"I understand why you jumped," Norma says softly, her voice shaking. "Into the water, I mean."

I glance at her, and her eyes are wet again. She's looking out toward the waterline, where the waves are still rough.

"I would've done the same," she continues. "When Dean died... I thought about it. I wanted to follow him, just for a second. Just to know where he went, just to know he wasn't alone."

Tears prick my eyes, and I bite down on my lip.

"But I had Leo. And Leo had me. So I stayed." She swallows. "Now, I don't know what to do. I'm not a mother without a son. I don't know who I am now."

"You still are," I whisper.

She looks at me, unbelieving. "Dean still exists out there." She smiles small. "In the water. In the wind. In everything he ever loved."

We sit down in the sand, side by side, our hands still clasped between us, the cold seeping through my sweatpants.

"I know Leo will, too," she continues, "it just feels different."

"What do you mean?"

Tears start to fall again. "I mean when Dean died, I *felt* him die. Like he passed right through me. I didn't *feel* Leo die."

Her words hang heavy, just like the clouds around us. We watch the waves, foaming and endless, and I want to believe her. Because even in the grief and heartbreak and absence of him... I feel him.

I feel him everywhere.

62

Layla

IT'S BEEN THREE DAYS SINCE LEO WAS RIPPED FROM US.

The not-so-funny thing about love is that there's no warning of what happens when it's torn away.

There's no theatrical explosion, or burst of light from the sky. It's cold, and there's an unbearable silence in every thought and in every single breath.

I managed to shower this morning. It took everything in me to climb out of bed, out of the same clothes that I've been in for days.

Mom offered to wash my flannel. *Leo's flannel.* The one that still has his scent clinging to it.

I ignored her and just left it draped over the back of a chair, but when I came out of the shower, it was gone. I found her in front of the washing machine, holding it over ready to toss it in with the load she was about to run.

I lost it. Sank to the ground with panic. My forehead pressed to the floor, sobbing.

Screeching.

"I'm sorry," she kept repeating through her own tears. "I didn't know, sweetie. I didn't know."

She hadn't started the cycle. Hadn't closed the lid, hadn't even dropped in detergent. She pulled it out the second she saw the look on my face. How could she have known? It's just a piece of clothing to everyone else. But to me—

It's the last piece of him I have left.

Eventually, I pull it back on. It hangs even looser now. Or maybe I'm starting to wither away from days without food. Nothing but sips of water here and there.

I slip into jeans. Brush my hair. Not because I want to, but because I need something to do that feels normal. I press my fingers to the necklace Norma gave me, the one from that perfect day with her.

With him.

I had a dream last night. The sun was bright, the music was loud. He was dancing, shirtless, smiling at me like we had just made love for the first time. His laugh wrapped around each of my limbs... A vocal hug. He spun me in his arms, kissed me under the sky. I was safe.

He was alive.

Then I woke up and remembered... everything.

Mom tried to bring me breakfast. I declined again.

"You haven't eaten in days," she said, setting the plate near my bed anyway.

Three days.

He's been gone for three days.

Norma's gone home for now. She sends short texts, a quick proof of life. I worry about her having nothing to live for now. At least in her mind. I promised her I'd drive up to see her the second I was able to think more clearly.

If that day will even come.

Everyone's been in and out the last couple of days. My sister called, too, told me she'd be on the first flight from New York if I needed her.

Sara stops by in between her shifts; she's working more to

cover my absence, but also to keep her mind busy. Dan joins, bringing fresh cookies that only Dad ends up eating.

The guys have been coming and going, too. To hug me, to cry into my shoulder while I cry into theirs. Hank and Rowdy stayed all day yesterday, talking endlessly about Leo. At first, shedding tears, but once they were all dried out, they tried to relive better memories.

"Hell," Hank shared, *"one time Leo got his damn boot stuck in a bait bucket. We're mid-haul, he's reeling in this monster, and the dumbass can't get free. So there he is, one foot sliding all over the deck, the other clanging around in a bucket, chasing that fish across the boat".*

He and Rowdy laughed, until the realization hit them again. Then the cycle of tears started all over.

When they aren't here, they're drinking every waking minute. Izzy's been trying to hold them together. Trying to hold all of us together.

What an impossible task.

"Okay," Mom says. "Get up."

Her voice snaps me out of my reverie as she sits on the edge of my bed. "I'm trying to be gentle, Layla, but I'm sincerely worried about you."

I roll away. The blankets bunch around my waist. I feel like I'm floating in a body that no longer belongs to me.

"The rain let up. The farmer's market is open," she continues, rubbing my back. "Let's walk around. We'll stop by Dockfront. I'm sure Nate will be there."

I ignore her.

"Layla," Mom repeats, her voice breaking through.

"Fine." I sigh.

I don't want the fresh air. I don't want food. But I *do* want Nate. Someone who loved Leo almost like I did, someone who really understands this ache. The thought of seeing him is the only thing that gets me moving.

Fifteen minutes later, we're walking. The air is humid, light sprinkles falling from the sky. Still gray. Still dreary.

The town is quiet.

We pass the docks, my heart aching at the mere sight of it. The planks are slick with rain, and the smell of bait sticks to the air. Bouquets of flowers, mason jars with candles, and single lilies lie clustered in small piles near the ropes that tie Leo's fishing boat to the dock. A few handwritten notes are tucked beneath stones so the wind doesn't steal them away—ink bleeding from the drizzle. A fisherman's cap rests on one piling, weighted by a large shell.

It feels like the whole town has left pieces of themselves here, a vigil for someone who belonged to all of us.

I pause when I see a child's drawing, colors blurred from the rain but still clear enough to make out a stick figure with a fishing pole. My chest caves in, the air knocked right out of me. I turn away, my belly clenching, unable to bear it.

My mom squeezes my hand, guiding me forward until the harbor is behind us.

The market is sparse. A few booths are set up with some homemade candles, baskets of vegetables and jars of honey. A man plays a slow song on his guitar under a tree near the corner.

It sounds like Leo.

Not his song, but the feeling of him.

Soulful and full of waves.

I don't speak. Mom doesn't push, she just walks beside me and holds my hand, for comfort—or maybe protection.

⌒

Eventually, we reach Dockfront.

Nate greets me with an embrace. Our arms linger around

one another, holding each other much longer than any normal hug. My sobs soak his chest while his fall into my hair.

"Come sit," he says, voice scratchy. "I just made tomato soup."

I nod as he leads us to a corner table. Locals watch with pitiful eyes as I slink across the floor, their own tears brimming, too.

The rain returns; it starts slow but quickly changes to a downpour. Thunder rips in the distance.

Mother Earth is mourning with us.

Nate brings two bowls of soup to Mom and me and joins us at the table. The warmth should be comforting. But it's not.

The TV above the bar flickers, static warping the screen. Another storm warning scrolls across the bottom.

I force two spoonfuls down my throat. Mom eats slowly, every so often glancing at me, but stays quiet. I'm sure she's content that I'm out of the house and had at least a tiny bit of substance.

The TV screen stutters, pauses, flicks back on. The audio is muffled, almost annoyingly. I wish someone would just shut the damn thing off. I try to tune it out. But then I hear it.

Something that shouldn't be real.

"...*found alive off the coast of Avila Beach*..."

My spoon clatters into the bowl.

I look up to the screen and freeze.

The words scroll slowly, stuck for a moment, frozen.

UNIDENTIFIED MAN FOUND ALIVE NEAR AVILA BEACH.

My heart stops.

No.

No, it's a mistake. A cruel mistake.

I look at Nate. His eyes are wide, his mouth slightly open, hands still trembling.

Mom gasps beside me. "Layla…"

I push myself out of my seat. My elbow catches the bowl, sliding it to the floor, shattering next to my feet. Tomato soup covers my shoes in the mix.

I move closer to the TV, not sure if I'm even breathing. But my heart is working, pounding so hard it hurts.

The screen resumes, showing a shot of the rescue team. Men pulling in a man on a large piece of driftwood, a glimpse of tangled dark hair.

"Could be anyone," Nate whispers, now standing next to me. "It could—"

"It's him."

I don't even question it.

"It's him."

I stumble for the door.

"Layla, wait!" Mom calls out.

I'm already gone, sprinting through the pouring rain. The storm lashes against me, soaking my clothes entirely, but I don't care. I burst through the front door of my apartment, breathless and wild-eyed, startling my Dad who is watching the same news station.

The words are still stuck on the bottom of the screen. *Man found alive.*

"Layla, what's going on?"

I ignore him, grab my car keys and almost tumble face first back down the stairs to my car.

Please, God.

Let it be him.

Let me get there before this dream fades again.

63

Layla

THE RAIN IS A BLUR ACROSS MY WINDSHIELD, MY WIPERS working overtime. I don't even know where I'm going exactly, just that the man was taken to a hospital in San Luis Obispo. I call Nate, my hands shaking so bad I can barely hit his name.

"Which hospital?" I ask before he can say hello.

"Sierra Vista," he says, breathless. "I'm on my way."

"I'll see you there."

I hang up, enter the hospital name into my GPS and floor the gas. The roads are slick, and the sky roars above me. I can't stop thinking about that image... Dark hair soaked, face not even visible, but my soul... My soul *screamed.*

It's him.

It has to be.

Because if it's not... I won't survive this a second time.

I park crookedly and barely turn off the engine before I'm sprinting toward the doors. I slip once on the wet pavement, nearly falling because my heart is faster than my feet. But I don't stop running.

The hospital is in chaos when I get closer. Media vans

parked in the lot, people with video cameras and microphones in the faces of staff members trying to turn them away.

I hear one of them say something about not having much information at this time, that they are trying to stabilize the man. They suspect that he *could* be the fisherman from Morro Bay that has been presumed dead for days.

I bolt through the crowd and into the front doors. "I need to see him!" I shout at anybody and everybody.

The nurse behind the desk looks up, startled. "Ma'am—"

"Please!" I hurry to her, slam my hands on the counter, my voice breaking. "The man who was found off the coast. I need to see him. I *have* to."

She looks down at her screen, then toward a security guard by the door, then back at me, reading my face.

Pain.

Desperation.

Need.

Love.

Her voice softens. "Are you family?"

"I'm—" I choke. "He's *mine*."

She watches me for a moment, glances at my trembling hands. Then she nods and gestures for someone behind the doors. "Wait here."

I wait for the minutes that feel like hours before another nurse appears. "Follow me."

I do.

I can't tell if my legs are moving or if the floor's carrying me. I count the doors we pass. One. Two. Three—

She stops.

"Just in here," she says gently.

Then she steps aside, and I see the man. Curled in the hospital bed. Tubes taped to him. His skin sunburnt, lips cracked, beard unkept.

It's him.

My Leo.

Alive.

I don't feel the floor beneath me, or the wetness of my clothes. I don't hear anything despite the constant beeping of the machines he's connected to. I just move to him, slowly. Afraid that if I move too fast, he will disappear. Still uncertain if this is real, or just another dream.

My knees buckle when I reach the bed, I lightly graze his arm with my finger. *He's real.* I fall to my knees, clutching the edge of the hospital bed, and press my forehead to his arm.

"Leo…" I whisper. "Leo, *please.*"

"Honey, he's in rough shape," the nurse says, "I don't know if he's going to be awake any time soon. We started the liquids, and we're trying to bring up his body temperature slowly."

She offers me a small, sympathetic smile. "Would you mind giving me his full name? We need to set up a file for him, and until now, we haven't had any information. I just want to make sure he's taken care of properly."

Her voice softens even more as she adds, "There's a waiting room down the hall that's a little more comfortable than this, if you—"

"I'm not leaving," I say, interrupting her.

She looks at me, understanding in her eyes. "At least let me get you some dry clothes."

"Thank you," I whisper, "and his name is Leo Anderson."

She smiles and steps out.

"Leo," I whisper again, gently sliding my hand into his.

I stay at his side, watching his chest move with his shallow, uneven breaths. His skin looks unfamiliar. Too ashen and too raw. I hate that I can't tell if he's in pain or just gone some-where deep inside himself to survive.

Fear fills my throat: what if this is the last time I ever see him like this, alive? What if he slips away before I get the words out that I should have said sooner?

I bow my head, pressing his knuckles to my lips. "Please, come back to me." The words spill out of me like a prayer.

There's nothing but the sound of rain against the window and the hollow ache in my chest.

———

I stay beside him, listening to his heart beat as he drifts between stillness and tiny movements. He murmurs something in his sleep, too broken to make out, just fragments of dreams, but I run my fingers through his hair, whispering, "I'm here." Even though I don't know if he can hear me.

The storm outside has settled, still drizzling, but no longer pouring. A soft knock at the door pulls my attention away from Leo.

"Holy shit," Nate breathes, his voice cracking as he steps in slowly. "He's really here."

"He is," I cry and greet him with an embrace.

"Took them forever to let me in," he says, not able to take his eyes away from Leo. He steps closer and manages a broken smile. "Damn, he looks like shit."

"I think it's the best he's ever looked." I laugh softly. "Do you think he knows how loved he is?"

Nate shakes his head. "He's gonna know. Between you and me, and all of us he'll never forget it." He looks at me. "Nice outfit by the way."

The nurse brought me a dry pair of teal sweatpants and a T-shirt, both two sizes too big, but I don't care. I'm warm, and *he's* alive.

Nate steps closer, resting a hand on Leo's foot under the blanket, needing to touch him to believe it's true. "You've got the whole town a blubbering mess." Nate chokes on a laugh that turns into a sob. "You broke our goddamn hearts."

I see it on his face—relief, though still a heavy presence of fear. I recognize it because it's exactly how I feel. Maybe anyone would in this moment.

Suddenly, Norma flashes through my mind. "Oh my God, I need to call Norma!"

I turn to find my phone but Nate stops me. "You stay here. I'll call her right now. I just needed to make sure it was actually him first." He lets go of Leo's foot and steps toward the door, but glances back one more time before stepping out. "It's really fucking good to see you, buddy."

My eyes stay glued to Leo. The man I fell for moved through the world like solid waves—invincible, armored. Seeing him now, fragile and hooked to machines, is unsettling.

My phone lights up with texts from my parents and Sara. *Love you,* one reads. *Call when you can.* And I will.

The moment he wakes up, I'll be screaming from rooftops.

Nate returns shortly. "She's on her way," he says, sinking into the corner chair. "I called the guys, too. They went ballistic. They're on their way as well."

"Good," I whisper. "He needs them."

Nate nods, and we just sit there together, waiting.

Waiting for Norma, the guys, Izzy.

Waiting for the doctors to come in and give us another update.

Waiting for him to wake up and finally put our hearts at ease.

64

Layla

THE LAST TWENTY-FOUR HOURS HAVE BEEN AN EMOTIONAL rollercoaster. Some moments I feel hopeful, others feel very heavy.

Norma arrived, eyes rimmed in tears and bloodshot from days without sleep. At first, she swore he couldn't be real. She thought exhaustion had finally caught up with her and this was a hallucination. Then she reached out and touched him, felt the warmth, and collapsed to her knees, thanking God.

Though, she kept saying she wouldn't believe it until he opened his eyes.

One of the familiar nurses offered Norma a cot in the break room, assuring her it would be quiet and that staff would alert her immediately if he woke.

Hank, Rowdy, Austin, and Izzy are here, too—in the waiting room now. We've been rotating; the hospital only allows three visitors in the room at a time.

They came back one by one, faces streaked with tears but also… smiles.

Now, it's just Leo and me, and the silence around us. Norma is resting in the break room; Nate, Izzy, and the rest of

LEO

the guys have gone to find us some proper food. Something warm and more filling than what the hospital has to offer.

Some of his normal color has returned to his cheeks, and his temperature has normalized. I keep talking to him, knowing that he's still somewhere in there.

"Leo," I whisper, running a thumb across his cheek. "I'm so glad you're here."

I move my hand to his.

"I just wish you could hear me. I wish you'd wake up and tell me that it's all going to be okay."

The rain outside starts to pick up again, tapping harder on the windows.

"The moment our eyes met, I understood what love was." A small smile lifts at my mouth. I look up at the ceiling as my eyes start to leak. "By the scale of time, we're new."

A tear falls.

"But my soul says otherwise. It says that maybe this—*us*—can't be measured in real time."

Another tear.

"My soul's tied to yours and there's just too much left. Too many memories and mistakes to make." I drift my gaze back to him. "We need you. We *all* need you."

I press my forehead to his shoulder.

"Please just wake up, Leo." I sniffle. "Wake up for me, and I'll owe you everything."

An eerie stillness takes over the room, as if time itself has stopped. The silence grows heavier, and I wonder what any of this means. Why are we given love only to lose it? Why do we feel everything and then become numb in the same lifetime? In the same *moment*?

Why do the good times end too soon while the bad ones linger forever?

Why... *Why* did this happen to him? My tears fall more freely, and I feel the ache ignite in my chest all over again.

"Why?" I sob, the word ripped out of me and hurled at the emptiness, a demand for an answer from God, or the sea or anyone or *anything* that will listen.

My cry startles even me as it bounces off the bare white walls but it's… movement that grabs my attention.

Leo's eyelids start to flutter, and for a second, I think I'm imagining it—that my mind has finally broken from wanting him too much.

Then, the faintest shift. His hand twitches against mine, and he lets out a low grunt.

His lips part. "Layla?" His voice is hoarse.

Oh my God.

"Hi," I cry. "I'm here."

His hand tries to reach; it's so weak, but he still manages to lift it and brushes it against my cheek.

"Are you real?" he whispers.

"I'm real."

He tries to move, but winces.

"No, no—don't move," I say quickly, smoothing his hair back, cradling his face.

Tears drip from his long lashes, my thumb wipes them away.

"I heard you," he says. "In the water. I thought… I thought it was heaven."

I cry harder.

"I thought I died," he adds. "But all I could see was your face."

I crawl into the bed, careful not to tangle with any of the tubes and lay my head on his chest. "You're not allowed to die," I whisper. "You're not allowed to leave me. Ever again."

I kiss his cheek. His eyebrow. His chin. His mouth.

"I love you," I breathe. "God, Leo. I love you."

His eyes close again, but his smile remains. "I know," he whispers. "That's what kept me alive."

I lift my head to get a better look at him. "How did you...?"

The word *survive* lodges in my throat, too heavy to say out loud. He still looks fragile—skin blotchy, lips cracked, his body fighting exhaustion. There are more tests, more unknowns ahead. But I can't let my mind go there. Not now. Not when he's right beside me, breathing.

Leo exhales slowly. "I... I don't know. Everything after I hit the water is... pieces." His voice cracks, and he swallows before going on. "The waves... They pulled me under so fast. The water was so rough, yanking me in all kinds of directions." He pauses, eyes half-shut. "I swam... as much as I could. Treaded water until my legs went numb."

He looks at me, his green eyes dulled but still just as gorgeous. "Then after that, I just... held on."

I sniffle. "To what?"

He swallows slowly.

"To you."

65

Leo

EVERYTHING HURTS.

My lips are split, my skin feels tight, sunburned, raw and it stings. I taste something metal and bitter in my mouth, and my muscles throb and ache.

Even just breathing is somehow painful.

But, I'm not in the water anymore, and it takes a minute to register that I'm in a hospital.

That I'm alive.

The memories have been coming back in fragments.

Layla, lying next to me in bed on the boat, glowing like a Goddess. The fight with Sam, quick and confusing. Then, being shoved overboard.

I remember hitting the water hard. Getting the wind knocked out of me before I even surfaced, and once I did, the boat had already disappeared. Nothing around to grab onto, no one to call out to.

Just cold, black, endless water surrounding me.

I swam, unsure if I was even going in the direction of land. A current appeared out of nowhere, pulling me even further into the sea, or closer to land. I couldn't know. But it did bring in a large piece of driftwood. Just big enough to hold most of my body out of the water.

I latched on and didn't let go. I counted waves, birds, anything to keep from counting the hours.

It rained nearly the entire time. I tried to open my mouth and drink as much of it as I could, but it was never enough to feel satiated, to be hydrated. But it was enough to keep me breathing. Enough to keep my organs from shutting down.

I don't remember the last day. Just that the clarity in my mind started to fade. I hallucinated. Clouds turned into faces. *Her face.* Seagulls started speaking in human voices. *Her voice...* calling my name.

I thought it was death, playing dirty. I thought all that was left was one final swell to finally take me out.

But somewhere in between feeling certain that death was close and hanging onto the hope of a miracle, I was pulled in.

Hands.

Shouting.

A glimmer of sunlight.

The roar of a boat engine.

A crew from harbor patrol. I heard them shouting that they spotted something floating.

Me.

When they poured water in my mouth and covered me in blankets, they said I was hypothermic. They said my core temp had plummeted, and my pulse was almost unreadable. I was severely dehydrated, sunburnt, and they suspected that there was no way that I wasn't in acute renal distress.

They rushed me to the hospital and started fluids. Monitored my kidney function, checked for organ damage and somehow pumped warmth back into my veins. I remember the sting of IV needles, nurses' voices pulling me back when all I wanted was to sink into sleep.

Now I'm here.

In a room, in a bed.

And she's beside me.

Layla.

My body aches when I try to move, and I wince at the pain.

"You okay?" she breathes.

I try to smile. "I am now."

Before either of us can say more, there's a knock on the door. Mom steps through it slowly. Eyes in disbelief.

"Mom," I whisper.

She bursts into tears seconds later. "Oh my God," she says, rushing to my side.

"My baby. My sweet boy." She throws her arms around me as carefully as she can and starts to sob into my shoulder. Her hands can't seem to stay still. She's touching my face, my arms, my chest like she has to prove I'm solid—that I am real.

I do my best to hug her back, even though every muscle protests.

Her tears soak into my hospital gown. "The second I heard what happened…" She pulls back, looking at me. "Leo, it was torture."

Layla watches us, smiling, new tears forming in her eyes. She eases herself off the bed and meets my mom on the other side. She wraps her into a hug and lets my mom cry into her hair.

"I'll give you guys a minute," Layla says softly. Squeezing my mom's hand one more time before she steps out of the room.

"I can't believe this," Mom cries, "I just simply can't believe this."

I pat the spot next to me on the bed. "Come sit."

She does, and rests her hand on my head. "Leo, there is a God, and he loves us, my son."

I smile and whisper, "Yeah, I guess so."

We sit in silence for a few moments; mom cries as she holds me. Her voice trembles. She wipes her cheeks and sniffles. "I get why she jumped."

What?

"Who?"

She looks at me, like she's scared to say it out loud. "Layla, honey," she says, brushing my hair back. "She was just going to die with you. Everyone thought she was out of her mind, but... I understood."

I stare at her, and my heart shakes loose.

She smiles through her tears and leans forward to kiss my forehead, just like she did when I was a kid. "I'm so thankful that you're here, and I can't wait to bring you home."

Home.

I'm not there yet, not physically. But I will be. And when I get there, I know exactly what I want to do with the time I've been given.

Mom tells me the whole town paused when I was gone. That for three days, Morro Bay didn't breathe. That my boys —Nate, Hank, Austin and Rowdy—had lost their minds and tried to find peace at the bottom of a liquor bottle. She tells me that people brought flowers to the marina, lit candles near the docks, bent their heads and prayed.

They *mourned* me, and I don't know how to hold that.

Layla and now Nate slip back in. "Oh, man," Nate says, coming to my side and taking my hand. "Boy, are you a sight for sore eyes."

"Nate," I mutter, "so are you."

"The boys are out there," Nate says, wiping a tear and jerking his thumb toward the waiting room, "and they're getting antsy. The staff won't let them back yet, but they're making their presence known."

"Rowdy said—and I quote—'Tell him I'll break the next

guy's nose if they try to shove past me. So he better hurry up and get better.'"

I start to laugh, but stop when the pain shoots through my ribs.

"Hank kept it simpler," Nate continues. "He said, 'Good. He's not at the bottom of the sea, and that's all that matters.'"

"And Austin," Layla adds with a giggle, "just kept saying you owe him about a hundred breakfast burritos for putting him through this."

The sound of her laugh hovers, light against the heaviness that I'm sure these days have held. I manage a smile. "I can't wait to see them."

As the quiet settles again, Mom reaches for Layla's hand. They step closer together and stand at the foot of my bed. These two beautiful women, looking at me, eyes full of love and fear and all of the human feelings. We stay like this for a while, just looking at each other, crying.

And I think… I think that we have *all* the power to heal the broken things. If the ocean didn't take me, then maybe grief won't, either. Maybe love—this messy, furious, relentless thing… really *can* hold us together.

TWO WEEKS LATER

The air smells like the ocean. Like salt and kelp, just how I like it. That's why I chose this house in the first place. Close enough to the water, far enough from the townies.

I lean back in the old wooden chair on my porch. After two weeks of people and helping hands, I just need a minute to hear the sea again. My abdomen still aches when I breathe too deep, but it's welcomed, a reminder that I'm alive.

Alive.

That word means something different now. Survival isn't enough anymore. I owe it to myself to actually start living.

Layla hasn't left my side once in the last two weeks. I have Charlie to thank for that. For pulling her out of the water when she got the crazy idea to jump in after me. Thank God, Charlie was there... I wrote her a letter at the rehab she checked herself into. Layla did, too. Charlie has a good heart, she just got wrapped up in the mess. A mess that's too easy to get wrapped up into, and I am forever grateful for the choice she made that night.

And Sam... Well, he's no longer a dark shadow here. He's locked away, for good this time and that relief is monumental.

There's laughter and commotion inside the house. Hank grunts at someone else for drinking the last beer. Austin, probably. The front door creaks open. Layla steps out, holding two mugs of something warm. Her cheeks are blushed, hair pulled into a soft braid over her shoulder. She hands me one of the mugs, sits beside me on the other chair, and tucks her knees up.

"Chamomile," she says. "Norma insisted."

I glance at the window behind us. Sure enough, Mom's watching through it, but quickly disappears back in the kitchen once she sees me spot her.

"Chamomile," I repeat. "Did you sneak any rum in it at least?"

She looks around to make sure no one is listening. "Just a splash." She winks.

We sit in silence for a minute. Just the two of us, wrapped in the cool air and the sounds of a full home.

Layla lightly nudges me with her elbow. "I think they're ready for you."

"Who?"

She nods toward the house. "All of them."

As if on cue, the door bursts open and Nate shouts, "You done being a moody pirate yet, or what? We're starving!"

Laughter trails behind him. Austin talking up a storm in Hank's ear. Izzy rolling her eyes at Rowdy, bickering about something.

Sara, Dan, and Will are already seated at the long fold-up table Mom managed to squeeze into the kitchen. Layla's parents—Scott and Andrea—whom I've only known for a week, are just as wonderful as she is. They move alongside Mom, setting the table and carrying out dishes piled high with hot, colorful food.

"Oh, and we have one more guest," Layla says, just as a truck pulls up.

I watch the driver cut the engine, too far to spot their face. Dark boots hit the ground as the door swings open. The truck door blocks my view—then when it slams shut, I see who it is.

Joey.

He looks healthier. Stronger. He grins at me, and I feel like a missing piece of myself has been found. He jogs toward the porch and even though I can stand on my own, Layla helps me up. I don't need the assistance, but I like the excuse to let her hold me.

The second Joey's close enough, he grabs my shoulders and pulls me into him. Pain throbs through my ribs, but the relief of holding my best friend—my brother—trumps the ache.

"It's good to see you, man," he says into my shoulder.

"It's really good to see you, too, brother." I smile, pulling back just enough to look him in his sober eyes.

He slings one arm around my back, Layla takes my hand on the other side, and together we walk into the house. The second we do, the room quiets, but only for a brief moment, before everyone excitedly greets Joey and then gets settled for dinner.

We eat.

We talk.

And eventually, the sun sets as Layla laughs and shines next to me, smelling floral and looking stunning.

My family.

Some not by blood but in every other way that matters the most.

66

Layla

THE SKY IS A SOFT GRAY-BLUE TODAY, CLUTTERED CLOUDS IN some spots, sunny in others.

Leo asked if we could visit the dock. Just the two of us. No noise, no people hovering, never getting enough of him.

Just him and me.

And the sea, of course.

He moves slowly, still a little stiff. His steps aren't as steady as usual, and his skin is still healing, but he's more beautiful than ever.

I reach for his hand, threading my fingers through his. He grips back, thumb tracing my knuckles. We walk down the old wooden pathway toward his boat.

"I would come down here every time I missed him," he says quietly. "It felt like the only place I could still hear him. The sea made him feel close."

I lean my head on his shoulder for a few steps. "And now it's the place I almost lost you."

We stop walking, turning to face the water. The tide rolls in, gently. As if it wasn't tearing our worlds apart just a few weeks ago.

He turns to look at me, the softness in his eyes, the strength in his jaw. He's always been both anchor and sail.

His free hand reaches up, brushing hair from my face. "I can't believe you jumped in after me."

"How could I not?"

"I would have done the same," he says, his voice just above a whisper.

I know he would have; I don't doubt it for one second.

We continue walking. The harbor stretches in front of us, boats bobbing as we pass by, finally reaching Leo's boat—his father's boat—bobbing along with the others. It's tied at the edge of the dock. Sitting there, just waiting for him.

When we reach it, he lets go of my hand, closes his eyes and runs his fingers over the railing.

He climbs aboard first, then reaches for me. I take his grip, letting him help me up. He walks slowly around the boat, probably remembering the last time we were here.

I thought it would be more haunting, but it's not, really.

We don't go anywhere, just on the stern with our legs dangling over the water.

"Izzy told me once," I say, remembering her words, "that I'd have to share you with the sea."

Leo's head turns toward me, lips twisting into a smile.

"But she was wrong," I go on, staring out beyond the water. "The sea already owned you, Leo. Long before I came along. It raised you and shaped you. It loved you in its own brutal, wild way."

I glance at him.

"So, actually... the sea is sharing you... with *me*."

His eyes shine. He lets out a soft breath, almost a laugh. "That's the most beautiful thing anyone's ever said to me."

He leans in and presses his lips to my temple. A kiss that tells me everything he can't find the words for. I press my hand to his chest, over his beating heart.

"Here we are," I whisper. "Returning you back to it."

He wraps his arms around me from the side, and we sit like that for a long time. The wind picks up gently, tossing my hair across my face. I tuck it behind my ear and smile when I feel his chin rest against the top of my head.

The clouds start to thin. A larger patch of sun slips through, casting light across the water. The sea glitters in front of us. The boat sways gently, and I let myself believe in forever.

Even if it smells like salt and diesel, even if it means he'll be back out there before too long, it's okay now.

Because I believe that she will always return him back to me.

67

LIFE IS STRANGE.

One moment, you're sinking. Next, you're learning how to float again.

And somewhere in between... you fall in love.

I don't know what comes next.

I don't know if the sea will call me back, or what stories the wind still wants to tell.

Somehow, I've been given two soulmates in one lifetime. Maybe it means I'm blessed. Maybe it means I was broken enough to have two angels. I don't know everything, no one does.

But I do know this:

If the universe has tides, she's the moon that pulls mine.

And I'll follow her... wherever this wild, aching life dares to lead.

Because she's in all of it.

The sea. The wind. The stars.

Layla.

She is... *my home.*

Acknowledgments

Oh, *Leo*. My very first book baby. I initially wrote this story in 2019–2020, during a time when I wasn't in the healthiest headspace. Writing has always been my outlet, but this book was my first real realization that *this* is what I love, and what I want to keep doing.

I first published it as a novella and had my friends and family read it. Of course, they were supportive and told me all the things I wanted to hear. But when I reread it after I had grown a bit as a writer, I realized how much better it could be. I saw how much deeper, fuller, and more layered with love and angst it deserved to be.

So here we are. *Leo* has grown from a novella into a full-length novel, and I couldn't have done it without my people.

To everyone who read Leo in its first life—thank you for giving him a second chance.

To my readers: let's be honest, you make this possible. Every DM, every review, every sale, and every kind word inspires and encourages me to keep going. Thank you so much for choosing this book and spending some of your precious time with it.

To my friends and family, I love you. Thank you for supporting me throughout this wild writing adventure.

Raelynn, my sweet baby Rae—thank you for your patience when I'm in full "writing gremlin" mode. I know the ever-growing pile of coffee mugs, the diet Dr. Peppers, the wild hair, and the bags under my eyes aren't the prettiest sight, but you still root for me. *You* inspire me the absolute most.

To my beta readers—Lexi, Bree, Dee, Kerri, and Brianne—thank you for the time you spent reading, critiquing, and providing such valuable feedback. It's hard for a writer to see everything, and your insight made this story so much stronger.

A special acknowledgement to Brianne and her father, Mike (a.k.a. "Cappy Ray"). I never had the pleasure of meeting him, as he left this earth too soon, but I want to take a moment to honor the knowledge of captaining, fishing, and all things sea-related that he passed down to his daughter, and that ultimately found its way into *Leo's* story. May he rest in peace and live on in the hearts of his loved ones.

To Maya (@mysticbookmarketing) and Ashley (Ash Tree Editing), a big, big thank you for your editing services. I love writing stories, but when it comes to grammar and such, I'm a bit of a hot mess. Your work on this book is so valued. I *adore* you both and can't wait to work with you again.

To my cover designers—@booksnmoods (Retail Edition) and @rejenne.com (Author's Edition)—thank you for your time and artistry. I love these covers *so, so* much. They capture the heart of this story beautifully.

To Vanessa and Rhiannon, thank you for being the first eyes on this story and for guiding me in the right direction.

To @wildwoodvirtualassistance, @bookedbycoley, and my street team, thank you for helping me with this release. Promoting a book is no easy task, and I would have been completely overwhelmed without you. I appreciate you all dearly.

Shoutout to my indie author friends. This s*** is hard, but the support within this community is such a beautiful thing.

I hope you enjoyed *Leo* as much as I loved writing it. Morro Bay, California, is one of my favorite places to visit, and it was the perfect backdrop for this love story. If you ever go, stop by Sun-N-Buns Bakery and try the vanilla chai—it's the best.

With all the love,
Rose D. Bentley

About the Author

Rose D. Bentley grew up in the sunny suburbs of Los Angeles, California. She writes moody contemporary love stories inspired by poetry, nature, grief, and the infinite layers of emotions. Her work explores themes of love, healing, loss, and found family. She is the author of *Leo* and *Just Knock Three Times*.

When she's not writing, she's embracing motherhood, thriving (and spiraling) on caffeine, and finding comfort in the cozy things in life.

www.rosedbentley.com

www.ingramcontent.com/pod-product-compliance
Lightning Source LLC
Chambersburg PA
CBHW050014120726
47903CB00006B/1772